Katee Robert learned to tell stories at her grandpa's knee. Her favorites then were the rather epic adventures of The Three Bears, but at age twelve she discovered romance novels and never looked back.

Though she dabbled in writing, life got in the way – as it often does – and she spent a few years traveling, living in both Philadelphia and Germany. In between traveling and raising her two wee ones, she had the crazy idea that she'd like to write a book and try to get published.

Her first novel was an epic fantasy that, God willing, will never see the light of day. From there, she dabbled in YA and horror, before finally finding speculative romance. Because, really, who wouldn't want to write entire books about the smoking-hot relationships between two people?

She now spends her time – when not lost in Far Reach worlds – playing imaginary games with her wee ones, writing, ogling men, and planning for the inevitable zombie apocalypse.

Visit Katee Robert online:

www.kateerobert.com
www.facebook.com/AuthorKateeRobert
www.twitter   robert

Katee Robert learned to tell stories at her grandpa's knee. Her favorites then were the rather epic adventures of The Three Bears, but at age twelve she discovered romance novels and never looked back.

Though she dabbled in writing, life got in the way – as it often does – and she spent a few years travelling, living in both Philadelphia and Germany. In between travelling and raising her two wee ones, she had the crazy idea that she'd like to write a book and try to get published.

Her first novel was an epic fantasy that, God willing, will never see the light of day. From there, she dabbled in YA and horror before finally finding speculative romance. Because really, who wouldn't want to write erotic books about the smoking-hot relationships between two people?

She now spends her time – when not lost in Far Reach worlds – playing imaginary games with her wee ones, writing, eating popcorn and planning for the inevitable zombie apocalypse.

Visit Katee Robert online:

www.kateerobert.com
www.facebook.com/AuthorKateeRobert
www.twitter.com/katee_robert

THE WEDDING PACT

KATEE ROBERT

piatkus

PIATKUS

First published in the US in 2015 by Forever, an imprint of
Grand Central Publishing, a division of Hachette Book Group, Inc.
First published in Great Britain in 2015 by Piatkus

1 3 5 7 9 10 8 6 4 2

A CIP catalogue record for this book
is available from the British Library.

ISBN 978-0-349-40969-6

Printed and bound in Great Britain by
Clays Ltd, St Ives plc

Papers used by Piatkus are from well-managed forests
and other responsible sources.

MIX
Paper from
responsible sources
FSC® C104740

Piatkus
An imprint of
Little, Brown Book Group
Carmelite House
50 Victoria Embankment
London EC4Y 0DZ

An Hachette UK Company
www.hachette.co.uk

www.piatkus.co.uk

To Tiffany Reisz. You said I wrote one of the filthiest sex scenes you'd ever read, and I've never received a higher compliment! This one's all yours.

THE
WEDDING
PACT

ACKNOWLEDGMENTS

I still have to pinch myself sometimes, because this can't possibly be my reality. I am forever grateful to God for allowing me to do something I love beyond all reason—and being able to pay the bills while doing it.

A huge thanks to Leah Hultenschmidt for loving James and Carrigan just as much as I do, and for helping make this book shine. Your comments never fail to make me grin and help me polish the story into something truly epic. Thank you!

Big hugs to the entire Grand Central team. You guys are amazing and have made this a truly phenomenal experience.

Thanks to my agent, Laura Bradford, for always being in my corner. I couldn't have done this without you!

Flowers and candy and drinks of choice to PJ Schnyder, Jessica Lemmon, and Julie Particka for your endless support and for being there every step of the way. Your enthusiasm is contagious and motivating in the extreme!

Thank you to John Nave for always being there to answer my questions about various weapons and police procedures, even though they seem to get weirder and weirder as time goes on. You never blink—or threaten to arrest me—so you're pretty much a rock star.

Thank you, thank you, THANK YOU to my readers. Your response to this series has been overwhelmingly positive and never fails to make my day. I hope you love James and Carrigan just as much as you enjoyed Teague and Callie.

I'm always grateful to my husband, but never more so than while drafting this book. Juggling moving and buying a house and a thousand other little things while writing could have been a nightmare, but you handled it—and me—like a pro. You're the best. Kisses!

CHAPTER ONE

She wasn't here.

James Halloran drank his beer and did his damnedest not to look like he was searching the dance floor below for someone specific. Just like he hadn't shown up here five nights a week for the last four months, even though he was needed elsewhere. With his old man in the slammer and his little brother causing more problems than he fixed, all of James's attention should have been on getting his people back onto stable ground.

Instead, he couldn't get *her* out of his head.

Carrigan O'Malley.

He didn't know what he would say to her if he *did* see her. Apologize? Considering the last time they'd seen each other, he'd kidnapped her, tied her to his bed, and his father had been a few short hours from killing her... Yeah, there wasn't a fucking Hallmark card that covered that.

He scanned the club again, this time telling himself he was looking for potential enemies. The ruling families of the underground might technically be at peace, but that didn't mean he wanted to come face-to-face with one of the O'Malley men. He understood why they wouldn't hesitate to try to take their pound of flesh out of him, but that didn't mean he was going to play whipping boy. They all had their roles to play—Sheridan, O'Malley, and Halloran. He couldn't have changed things, even if he'd wanted to.

When he let himself think about it, though, he regretted the fuck out of Devlin O'Malley's death.

He reached for his beer, only to realize it was empty.

"Want another?" The short bartender didn't look old enough to drink, but she was good enough at her job not to give him shit for showing up, having a single drink, and leaving. Over and over again.

"No, thanks." *She* wasn't coming tonight, just like she hadn't come any night since the one where she'd blown his fucking mind in a supply closet. Before he realized exactly whose ear he'd been spilling filthy words into. Before she said her name and everything changed. Before he made the decision that labeled him just as cold a bastard as his old man.

Carrigan O'Malley. The daughter of the enemy. The one woman he sure as hell needed to keep his hands off.

Her absence made sense. If he had sisters, he would have gotten them the hell out of Dodge before shit hit the fan, and he would have kept them somewhere safe while things played out. The power situation wasn't stable in Boston—not like it had been a year ago—but it was evening out. It *had* to. He was all too aware that

war among the three families was the least of their con-
cerns if some outside threat decided to take advantage
of the power fluctuation. He knew the Sheridans and
O'Malleys—knew how they thought, knew what they
wanted, knew how they'd react to a given threat.

Better the devil he knew than the devil he didn't.

He'd been in talks with Colm Sheridan and his daughter, Callista, about securing peace. She, at least, wasn't
willing to let the past get in the way of the ultimate good.
The reluctant admiration he'd first felt when she turned
herself over to him, admitting that she'd pulled the trigger that ended his older brother's life, had bloomed into
full-fledged respect. Teague was a lucky son of a bitch—
and so was everyone under Sheridan protection. Callista
Sheridan was a force to be reckoned with.

Somehow, James didn't think Carrigan would be as
willing to let the past go. She was prickly and prideful
and had a furious temper—and he knew that after having
been around her for less than three days.

Enough of this shit.

He pushed to his feet and headed for the spiral staircase leading down to the main floor. Since it was a
Tuesday night, the place was far from packed, but there
was still a cluster of dancers sweating and grinding in the
middle of the floor, and plenty of people standing around
the lower bar, waiting for drinks. He scanned their faces
out of habit, not really expecting anything but disappointment.

His gaze landed on familiar green eyes, and he
stopped short. He had to be seeing things. It had happened before—he'd been sure it was her, only to approach and realize he'd been projecting her image on

some other pretty brunette. But then she shook her head, like she was trying to dispel his image, and he *knew*. James took a step toward her, still having no fucking idea what he was going to say.

She turned tail and bolted.

He was giving chase before making a decision to do so. The voice of reason piped up to point out that running her down wasn't going to do a damn thing to reassure her that he wasn't up to no good, but it wasn't like he had another option at this point. She wasn't going to sit there and have a conversation with him.

That didn't stop him from hauling ass through the doors and out into the street. He looked left and then caught sight of her further down the block, making impressive time considering the six-inch spike heels on her feet.

But he had the advantage on open ground.

James poured on more speed, closing the distance between them. She cast a panicked look over her shoulder, and it was almost enough to make him stop. Only the knowledge that he wouldn't get another chance like this again kept him moving. That and something inside him that he was reluctant to name. It felt a whole hell of a lot like the conscience he'd thought was dead and gone.

She was less than six feet in front of him. It was now or never. "For fuck's sake, *stop*."

"Leave me alone."

He put on a burst of speed and hooked an arm around her waist just as they reached the corner, jerking her to a stop. "Hold on for a second."

She drove her elbow into his stomach, and then slammed her heel into his toe. Even through his boots, he felt it. "Get off me." Her struggles increased. "Let go!"

He let go, holding his hands up and gritting his teeth against the throbbing in his foot. "I'm sorry, okay? I just wanted to talk."

"You have a funny way of showing it." She glanced over her shoulder, checking to see if he had other men with him, or maybe looking for an escape route. "Goddamn it, I knew better than to come back here."

"I'm not going to hurt you." *I never would have let them hurt you.* But the words wouldn't come. He might have stood back and let her and Callista Sheridan escape that night, but he could have done more. He'd taken the path that resulted in the least risk to him, and something horrible could have happened to either of them as a result.

She laughed, a low, broken sound. "You know, considering our history, I find that hard to believe."

What could he say? She was right. In her position, he would have done more violence than an elbow to the stomach. Hell, he would have drawn a gun and put an end to the threat once and for all. But things with them were different. She damn well knew that he didn't want her hurt, abduction or no. "No one laid a hand on you."

"No, you just threw me in a trunk, and then tied me to a bed and—" She shook her head, drawing his attention to her mass of dark hair. "I don't know why I'm still standing here. Stay the hell away from me."

This was it. She would walk away, and it was entirely likely that he'd never see her again. He'd never see his album again. The last link he had to his mother. It was a stupid sentiment, but he'd never been able to fully pack away the old photo album. To know it had been in her possession for the last four months...It left him feeling edgy and strangely vulnerable. He couldn't tell any-one that she'd taken it without admitting what it meant to him, and that was handing a loaded gun to the O'Malleys. No fucking way was he going there.

That's the reason you're here, dipshit. You're not fawning over some woman, no matter how hot she is. She took something from you and you want it back. "Where is it?"

She stopped, but she didn't turn back. "Where is what?"

"Don't play dumb, lovely. It doesn't suit you." He took a step closer, close enough to see the way her shoul-ders tightened, as if she could sense his proximity. "That album wasn't yours to take."

She gave him an icy look over her shoulder. "Even if I did take something—which I didn't—I wouldn't have kept it."

She was bluffing. She had to be. He made himself hold perfectly still, all too aware that one wrong move would send her fleeing into the night. "Liar."

"Whatever you have to tell yourself to sleep at night."

It struck him that maybe she *had* gotten rid of the al-bum. She had no reason to keep it. It was nothing to her—less than nothing. He strove to keep his thoughts off his face, but from the curiosity flaring in her green eyes, he did a piss-poor job of it. "I'll make you a deal."

"That's rich. You have nothing I want."

Maybe not, but he wasn't above playing dirty. Not in this. Not in anything anymore. James closed the dis-tance between them in a single step and grasped her chin tightly enough that she couldn't pull away. "Give back what you stole, and you'll never have to see me again."

"And if I don't?"

"Well, lovely, then I'm going to have to take that as a sign that you still want me as much as you did four months ago. Which means you want to see me again—and again, and again."

Her eyes went wide. "Are you seriously offering *not* to stalk me if I give back this thing I supposedly stole? What kind of deal is that? It's bullshit."

She wasn't afraid anymore, which was a goddamn relief. Instead there was a spark of anger vibrating through her body, and she was eyeing him like she wouldn't mind taking a chunk out of his hide. He preferred this Carrigan to the frightened one. As long as she was focusing on where she wanted to hurt him, she wasn't thinking about the threat he potentially posed. "I said you and I have unfinished business, and I damn well meant it."

"Wrong." She snorted. "Finished business is the only kind we have—ancient history. For the last time, get your big paws off me."

He released her for the second time. "I'm not bluffing."

"Neither am I." She turned around and walked away.

This time he let her go. He had no goddamn right to threaten her, but the thought of never seeing the album again—it sure as fuck wasn't the thought of never seeing *her* again—made him twitchy. It wasn't a threat he'd have made six months ago, but he wasn't the same man he'd been then. He'd given up trying to be better than the rest of the Hallorans. That same violence and aggression that ran through their blood ran through his, too.

No matter how much he hated it.

Things had gotten out of control after his older brother's death four months ago. Even now, knowing what he did about the monster Brendan was, his absence was still a weight in James's stomach. He didn't choose his family, and half the time he didn't like them, but they were all he had. The Halloran empire in Southie. All the death and unforgivable shit, and for what? A few square miles of land in the part of Boston no one else wanted?

He waited until he saw Carrigan climb into the back of a cab before he turned and headed for his car. He wasn't quite thirty yet, and he was so goddamn *tired*. It never ended. The power games, and the unforgivable acts, and the compromises on what he used to think of as his honor. There was nothing left of it anymore, and hell if that didn't send a pang of loss through him.

Not for the first time, he wondered what his mother would think of the men her beloved sons had turned into. He couldn't shake the belief that he was failing her. But she was dead and gone some fifteen years, and his old man was very much among the living. The only link James had to her was the album Carrigan had taken—a shrine to the man he might have been in different circumstances.

That man was dead and gone as surely as his mother was. In reality, he'd never stood a chance. His course in life was set the second he came into this world as a Halloran, and any chance he had to choose a different path had gone up in smoke with Brendan's death.

Now it all fell to James. The responsibility of keeping the Halloran name from disappearing the same way other enemies of the Sheridans had. People still talked about what Colm Sheridan did to the MacNamaras, though the details were sketchy now, thirty years later. All anyone knew was that it was horrific enough that no one had challenged him since.

James couldn't let that happen to his people. And they were his, whether he wanted the responsibility or not. The only other option was walking away and letting his idiot of a younger brother take over, which was as good as signing the death warrant of everyone who depended on the Hallorans to keep shit in check in their territory.

Besides, where would he go? This was his life.

His options were sink or swim—and if he sank, he'd take a hell of a lot of people with him. So he got up every day, and he swam, even though some of the shit he was required to do turned his stomach and made him lose sleep. He did it because there was no other option.

He slid into the driver's seat of his cherry red '70 Chevelle and sighed. His life would be a whole lot less complicated if he could let the specter of his night with Carrigan O'Malley go. She hated his ass, and for good reason. Spending more time chasing her was courting more problems than he had resources to deal with. Life was too tenuous right now to throw something like this into the middle of it—the whole thing could erupt like a bonfire at the first spark of trouble.

* * *

Carrigan huddled in the back of the cab, trying not to shake. James motherfucking Halloran. She should have known better than to risk going back to the same club he'd taken her from, but it had been a test. Avoiding that location meant she was afraid. Carrigan had learned a long time ago that every time she refused to face her fear, it got more powerful. A fear left unchecked took away her control.

And control was one thing she didn't have nearly enough of as it was.

Why the hell was he there? In the months and months of her frequenting that club, she'd never once seen him there. And she *would* have seen him. James was the kind of man who stood out, even in a crowd. He exuded danger that even the most oblivious idiot could pick up on—every time she'd seen him, even in the most crowded room, he had a good six inches of empty space around him. People might not realize why they gave him wide berth, but *she* did. Because he was the kind of man who did very bad things without hesitation. A predator.

The fact that he was big and blond and gorgeous in a rough kind of way was only the icing on the cake if a woman was into that kind of thing. She'd been exactly that kind of woman the last time they'd met, and she'd like to say she'd learned from her past mistakes. James Halloran was a man she needed to avoid like the goddamn plague.

She'd bet what little freedom she had left that he'd never been there at the same time she was. As tempting as it was to chalk it up to a coincidence, it was too damn much to believe he'd been there tonight by chance. Which meant he'd been looking for *her*.

She shivered. Taking the album was a mistake. She'd known the second she opened it and saw its contents that he wouldn't rest until he had it back in his possession.

If she had half a brain in her head, she'd send the thing back to him and good riddance. Even as the thought crossed her mind, she shook her head. As questionable as it was, she wasn't ready to give up that pawn—especially since it was important enough for him to seek her out.

He said he'd been thinking about that night.

He lied.

He *had* to have lied. The sex obviously didn't mean shit to him since he'd thrown her in a trunk less than ten minutes afterward. Not to mention that every remaining member of his shrinking family had been all too happy to threaten to kill her—and worse. They would have done it. She wasn't naive enough to think they wouldn't have.

Hell, her own father did worse than that to people who crossed him. There was no reason to believe James would have suddenly developed a conscience and played white knight to her damsel in distress. Yes, he'd stepped aside and let her and Callie go when they were sneaking out. He might have let them escape, but that didn't mean he wouldn't have stood by and watched her tortured and killed if his father commanded it. Her body burned at the memory of how he'd kissed her, of the look in his eyes when he'd growled that they had unfinished business.

Stop it.

Which was why it was so incredibly unforgivable that her brain kept circling back to him in the intervening months. She could claim Stockholm syndrome until she was blue in the face, but it wasn't the truth.

The cab pulled up in front of her family's home, saving her from following that train of thought any further down the rabbit hole. James Halloran was the enemy, and she'd be every bit the stupid bimbo her father thought she was if she forgot that.

Carrigan paid the driver and climbed out of the cab.

She made it all of three steps when she realized what she'd done—she'd come home wearing her clubbing clothes when she was supposed to have been at church, praying for her father's immortal soul. *Goddamn it*.

"Rough night?"

She startled, nearly tipping over her heels, and spun to face the male voice. It took all of a second to recognize who it belonged to. "Cillian? What the hell are you doing lurking out here?" The middle child of seven—and third boy—Cillian had lived as much a charmed life as possible under their circumstances. He'd always been kind of an idiot, but he'd never had to face the same things she and her sisters had. Or even that Teague and Aiden had. There had been no one requiring him to grow up, and so he'd happily played at being a Lost Boy.

Until Devlin died.

It seemed like so much of their lives centered on that one tragedy. Things had been a certain way. Before Victor Halloran lost his mind and declared war. Before things escalated to the point of no return. Before a bullet from a Halloran man snuffed out the life of the best and brightest of their family. Now life was divided into Before Devlin and After Devlin. She rubbed a hand over her chest, wondering how much time it would take to dull the edge of pain that thinking about him brought.

As Cillian moved closer, the toll the last few months had taken on him was written all over his face. Even in the shadows, his eyes were haunted. He glanced at the intimidating front door to the town house, the trees lining the street making the darkness feel more absolute despite the lights peppered between them. "I wasn't ready to go in."

To face their reality.

Was there anyone in their family who didn't want to run as far and fast as they could to get away from the hell they lived in? Carrigan didn't think so. Six months ago, she would have put Cillian on that short list. Maybe even Devlin, too. Now? Now Devlin was gone and everything was different.

Devlin was the one who had still maintained an aura of innocence despite everything. The one who might have escaped the net their father was so intent on tangling them in. The net called *family*. She almost laughed. Who was she kidding? No one escaped. Not Devlin. Not Cillian. Sure as hell not her.

And what would you do if you did *escape?*

There was no point in thinking about it. This was her reality, and she had to make the best of it that she could. Carrigan looped her arm through his. "I'm not ready, either. Want to go for a walk?"

He glanced down the street. The same direction he'd been coming from—the direction of the pub where her brothers had all been walking back from the night everything went to hell. "It's not safe."

She could argue that it was as safe as it ever was, that they were supposed to be back to peacetime relations with the Hallorans, and that Teague marrying the heir to the Sheridans had made sure that they'd be fine on that end as well. But the memory of James waiting for her in that club was still too fresh. It wasn't safe. It might never be safe again. "The Commons?" It was cold enough that she was already starting to shiver, the faint wind cutting through the thin fabric of her dress.

He hesitated, and she thought he might refuse. "You still have that Taser that Aiden gave you?"

"I don't leave the house without it anymore." It wouldn't have made a difference that night when James threw her in the trunk because she hadn't had her purse, but she didn't go anywhere without it now. What had started as almost a joke was now a reassurance that she had a way to defend herself.

"Good." Cillian shrugged out of his coat and draped it over her shoulders. "You know, it *is* December. There's even snow on the ground."

"I didn't want to have to check a coat." She clutched the fabric more firmly around her. He was hardly underdressed in a three-piece suit, but it wouldn't be long before he started to feel the cold.

They made their way down the block, her heels clicking in the darkness. With the snow covering the grass and decorating the trees, it looked like something out of a fairy tale. Like if she just walked a little farther, she might find a stray streetlamp that would signify she'd stepped into a different world.

Except that kind of thing only happened in storybooks.

She slipped her arm through her brother's. There was so much to say, and nothing at all. What could she say that would make anything okay? It wasn't okay.

"I thought you were at Our Lady of Victories."

It wasn't really a question, but she answered anyway. "Sometimes I need a break." A break that no church could give her, despite what her father believed. She'd tried when she was still in high school. They attended every single Sunday morning Mass, and she'd thought that maybe the salvation she was looking for could be found inside those four walls. So she'd spent hours on end there, praying with every ounce of will her sixteen-year-old heart could muster up. Praying for someone to save her.

Silence had been her only reply.

So she'd gone looking for salvation in other places.

In all the years since, the closest she'd come to salvation was what she felt that night in James's arms.

CHAPTER TWO

James cruised through Boston, letting his mind wander even as his route did. Finally, a few hours before dawn, he had to admit that he was stalling. It was time to go back to the house. At some point in the past, it might have actually been a sanctuary, but it'd been a long time since he thought of the house where his old man had reigned like that. In reality it was more like a prison... but less cheery. With a curse, he turned on the next street and started for Southie.

Everything was so fucking complicated since he took over. The initial transition hadn't been tough—not when the feds swooped in and took his old man away. Unforgivable as it was, James wasn't sorry to see him go. Victor Halloran would have killed Carrigan and put them in a position where none of them would walk away alive. Hell, he'd *planned* on it. Going out in a blaze of glory and all that shit.

He hadn't asked anyone else if that's what *they* wanted. He hadn't given a fuck.

So, yeah, James wasn't exactly crying a river that his old man was locked up for the rest of his days. The part he wasn't thrilled with was being thrust into a position of leadership that he'd never wanted.

It was all so wrong. Brendan was the heir—the one who'd been trained for this shit, the one who the mantle of responsibility was supposed to fall on, the one who'd step up and take over. But Brendan was dead and, in the quiet moments when James was actually alone, he couldn't help but think it was a blessing in disguise. Because, in pretty much every way that counted, Brendan was worse than their old man. Worse by a long shot.

So James did the best he could, and some days he actually fooled his ass into believing it would be enough. Today wasn't one of those days, not when he still had Carrigan's look of fear tattooed across his brain. Fear he fucking deserved.

Goddamn it, what had he been thinking, going back to that club over and over again? That she'd eventually show up and throw herself into his arms for a repeat of the first time? He knew damn well that some things couldn't be taken back—and with good reason.

But a stupid, idiotic part of him had dared to hope otherwise.

He shook his head and pulled into the garage, lifting his hand in greeting to Michael. The man nodded in response, but he didn't relax, which was enough to kick James's instincts into high gear. Something was wrong. He shut off the Chevelle and climbed out. "What's up?"

"Trouble, boss."

There weren't any of his men he'd trust beyond a shadow of a doubt, not with Brendan's specter hanging over them, and his little brother, Ricky, thinking he was hot shit now. Too many of his men didn't like the slow and steady way James preferred to do business. They thought that he should have taken up the banner of war that his old man had dropped, and run with it. Those damn fools only saw the potential profit of war—not the cost.

Even if James was as bloodthirsty as they wanted him to be, he knew how to look around him and see that the odds weren't in the Hallorans' favor. The marriage of Teague O'Malley and Callista Sheridan had allied their two families into a powerful position. Too powerful to fuck with and think he'd come out on top. But these idiots weren't thinking like that. They didn't care that the other two families combined had superior numbers and firepower.

And they sure as fuck hadn't stopped to think about how convenient it was that the feds had shown up right in time to save the day. Someone on the other side was a rat, and a rat high enough up the ladder that the feds felt invested enough to interfere.

It could be Carrigan.

He brushed the thought away and focused on Michael. "Tell me."

The man shifted. He was always doing that, as if he had run naked through some poison oak or was jonesing for a hit of something. It didn't help that he looked a whole hell of a lot like a weasel with his narrow face and beady dark eyes. For all that, he was as trustworthy as they come, and he'd never played James false. Yet.

Michael looked away. "It's Ricky."

Of course it was. *Fuck*. He'd gone and mishandled shit back when they were on the verge of war, and ever since then his kid brother seemed determined to be the biggest pain in the ass known to man. Every time James turned around, he was fucking something up or pulling some stunt that put people in the hospital.

Or the morgue.

"What's he done now?"

Michael shifted again, making him want to shake the answers out of the man. "He and some boys went out joyriding."

It wasn't the worst they could have done until...He stopped to think that the last time his brother and his *boys* went out joyriding, one of the O'Malleys ended up dead. *Fuck again.* How hard was it to understand James's order not to do anything to agitate the issue between their family and either of the others who ruled in Boston?

Apparently too goddamn hard. "How long ago?"

"Couple hours."

Cold settled in his chest, and for once, he actually welcomed it. Cold meant he didn't have to feel, didn't have to think about how fucked up his life had gotten. Didn't have to dread what came next. He just did what was necessary. "And no one thought to pick up a fucking phone and inform me of this?"

Michael flinched. "We tried, boss. You weren't answering."

He fished his phone out of his pocket and, sure as fuck, there were three missed calls. God*damn* it. He thumbed through his contacts until he found his brother's number and dialed. It rang through, the generic answering service setting James's teeth on edge. He ground out, "Get your ass home right goddamn now, Ricky."

This was what his life had come to—calling his brother like some sort of fucking parent whose teenager was out of control. His brother was twenty-seven years old. He should be past stunts like this. He *was* past stunts like this.

James spun on Michael. "Who'd he take with him?"

"Robert and Joe."

Worse and worse. Those two were more likely to pump Ricky up than keep him from getting into trouble. Shit was going down, and James had been too busy feeling sorry for himself to cut it off before it started. He cursed long and hard.

He had two choices. He could go try to track down his idiot brother and hope he found him before something happened that no one could take back. But that would make him look weak as fuck, and his men would file it away. Even if they didn't do a damn thing about it now, it would come back to bite him in the ass when he could least afford it.

Or he could wait here and confront Ricky from a position of power.

"Send him to me in the study when he's back."

"Will do, boss."

He stalked into the house, wanting a shower and ten good hours of sleep. Neither was on the schedule at the moment. He went into the study and dropped into the chair behind the desk. The fireplace sat cold and empty, just like it had every day since his old man was taken away. He'd always hated that fire, hated coming in here, where it was so hot it felt like he was walking into hell itself and meeting with the devil.

Considering his old man, it was a pretty fucking accurate description.

Since he had no idea how long it would be, he got started on some paperwork that he'd been avoiding for far too long. Even illegal businesses needed records, and they had only just now gotten the tally for everything that was lost in the warehouse that the Sheridans destroyed four months ago.

If his old man had kept better books, they wouldn't have had to trace all the shipments back to find out exactly what was missing. They wouldn't have had to hold off three separate business deals until they could figure out if their partners were taking advantage of their lack of knowledge to screw with them. As a result, he'd had to spend far too much time behind this desk.

He fucking hated this desk.

Sometime later, the door opened and Michael came through, dragging Ricky behind him. James's little brother was spitting mad, cursing like a sailor, and obviously drunk. *Great*. Michael didn't say shit, just shoved Ricky into the room and disappeared through the door, shutting it firmly behind him.

Ricky glared at James. "What the fuck?"

"Want to try that again?" He'd learned a thing or two growing up in the tender care of Victor Halloran. Control was essential. The second he let someone know they'd gotten under his skin, he lost his position of power within the conversation. That went doubly so for his brother. *Fear or love*. Those were the only two things that forged loyalty, and his brother wasn't showing a whole lot of either for him these days.

Ricky crossed his arms over his chest and raised his chin. "What. The. Fuck?"

So it was going to be like that. James pushed to his feet, slow and controlled, hating that his little brother flinched away from the movement. He deserved it after what he'd done, and the knowledge still stuck in his throat like a chicken bone. Knowing that he was doing what he thought best to keep his people from dying in a war that wouldn't benefit anyone was the only thing that kept his remorse in check. "Where were you?"

"Didn't know that I needed to check in with my keeper before I took a piss."

He wanted to reach across the space between them and smack the shit out of the little idiot. Ricky was all posturing and no brains. He acted when he wanted to act, and didn't stop to think of the waves his actions might cause. Tonight he might have just gone down to the pub with his boys. Or he could have just as easily decided to try for another drive-by in enemy territory. "Tell me. Now."

For a second, he thought Ricky would push more, but something on his face must have scared his brother, because he finally muttered, "We took a drive through O'Malley territory, saw some shit, then went down to the pub for a few drinks."

O'Malley territory—where Carrigan was once again living. The thought of something happening to her... James's stomach gave a funny leap that had him clenching his teeth. "Saw what shit?"

"Dunno." A belligerent shrug. "One of their bitches

walking down the street. Thought about picking her up, but she was gone before we could."

He made an effort to relax his muscles. There was no way of knowing if it was Carrigan they saw, but there was no reason to think either of her sisters would be wandering about unescorted on the same night he knew she'd been out. It was too much to hope for a convenient coincidence.

James sat down and folded his hands on the massive desk. "Stay out of their territory."

"But—"

"I didn't fucking stutter, Ricky. Stay out of their territory or you'll damn well wish you did."

His brother stared at him for a long time, and James held the look, waiting to see what he'd do. There was a confrontation coming, whether he liked it or not. When Ricky cursed and marched out of the room, slamming the door behind him, James allowed himself a silent sigh of relief.

Yeah, there was a confrontation coming for sure. Thank Christ it wasn't coming tonight.

* * *

Carrigan woke up to knocking on her door. She blinked at the clock and mentally cursed. Seven a.m. Everyone in the family knew that it was running the risk of death to wake her up before eight, but the knocking hadn't abated. She cursed again—this time aloud—and struggled out of bed. It took her a few minutes to find a nightgown to drag on, but she wasn't about to answer the knock while naked. Good thing, too. Liam stood on the other side of her door, his face carefully blank as he stared at some point over her shoulder. "Your father requests your presence."

It wasn't a request and they both knew it. But it also wasn't Liam's fault that Seamus O'Malley liked to haul his children before him at the most inconvenient time. She smoothed her hair back. "I don't suppose I have time to get ready?" He might be her father, but she didn't like having these talks without her full armor in place. Ten minutes after waking up meant there was no chance of that...something her father had no doubt considered when he sent his favorite muscle up here to wake her.

As she expected, Liam shook his head. "He said immediately."

Naturally. She glanced down at her long nightgown. It was white and vaguely Victorian and looked like something a virgin out of a historical novel would wear. It would have to do. "Then let's not keep him waiting." She closed her bedroom door behind her, but Liam didn't move out of the way. "What?"

"You went out last night."

She looked around quickly to make sure no one was within hearing range. "I went to church."

The look he sent her told her exactly what he thought of the lie. "Someone is supposed to be with you when you leave the house."

"It's not my fault the other men can't keep up." Liam alone was the one who allowed her to have her occasional excursion. Any of the other men would report it to her father and put a quick end to her tiny bit of freedom. She patted him on the shoulder and hurried around him, wanting to escape this conversation even more than she wanted to avoid the one waiting for her downstairs. "The study?"

"Yes."

She could feel his disapproval at her back as she made her way down the staircase and through the halls to the study. Though her father sometimes held meetings in the library, his study was his preferred place of business. She hadn't had any illusions about what kind of meeting this was, but the location he chose only confirmed that this was business. She closed the door softly behind her and wished she'd taken a few minutes to throw on something other that this goddamn nightgown. "Father."

"Carrigan." He sat behind his desk, and the sheer size of it should have made him look diminished. It didn't. He looked like a king in perfect control of his kingdom—the kind of man who could order someone's head removed without blinking. He showed as little emotion now as his gaze coasted over her, taking her measure just like he always did when they spoke.

She couldn't shake the feeling that he catalogued every new sign of age, every line or less-than-youthful blemish. She was twenty-eight—hardly an old maid—but he never failed to make her feel like she had one foot in the grave. All without saying a single word. She kept her spine straight and her shoulders back, refusing to flinch away from the criticism she saw in his dark eyes.

"We missed you at dinner last night." He glanced at the papers scattering his desk. "Both of your sisters managed to grace us with their presence after your months in the country."

Their exile. Four long months spent in the Connecticut house, theoretically out of danger, while the men in the family took care of the remaining threats. It had never occurred to them to ask her what she thought of the situation, because her opinions and feelings didn't really matter as long as she was obedient. Carrigan swallowed down the old anger. Losing her cool would just reinforce her father's belief that she was too emotional to be trusted. There was no winning with him, but she wasn't going to make things harder on herself. She clasped her hands in front of her. "I was at Our Lady of Victories. It'd been too long."

"I see." He hadn't moved, but she couldn't shake the feeling that he was larger. More dangerous. His cold dark eyes watched her so closely, she straightened on instinct, her heart beating harder in her chest. *He doesn't know. He can't possibly know.* He didn't move, but suddenly the room seemed a whole hell of a lot smaller. "Have you given any more thought to your decision?"

Here it was. She knew all the right answers to get him to hold off, but going through this song and dance was exhausting. "I've been praying."

There was no hint of his thoughts on his face. The only warning she got was a slight lifting of his brows. "I grow tired of this game, Carrigan. Your age is becoming an issue, a fact both you and your suitors are well aware of."

Suitors. Such an old-fashioned word, with more than a hint of romance if a person didn't know better. Carrigan knew better.

Her father continued, "You're not going to take your vows, and we both know it. Which means it's time for you to pick a husband. The list of interested men has been steadily decreasing for the last year, and it's time to stop toying with them. You have until your birthday to make a decision, or I'll make it for you."

Her birthday. December twenty-third. A little less than a month from now.

Her lungs turned to lead in her chest, each breath a searing agony that did nothing to clear the frantic buzzing of her mind. *A blink of time and then it'd all be over.* She'd known it was coming, but some small secret part of her had hoped they'd never have this conversation.

He was obviously waiting for a response, so she forced a small smile. "Of course, Father." She kept her voice perfectly bland, giving no indication to the panic rising inside her with each tortured inhale. She wasn't sure she ever wanted to get married, let alone to someone her father approved of. It had worked out for Teague, but that was a one-in-a-million chance. She wouldn't be so lucky.

"I'm glad you're being reasonable about this." He lifted a paper and motioned for her to take it.

Meaning he was glad she was doing exactly what was expected of her. Carrigan took the paper with shaking hands. It was far harder than it should have been to smile at her father as if she didn't want to be as far from him as the earth would allow.

"Here are the candidates who are left. Choose wisely."

She managed to push to her feet and leave the study without breaking down or showing the slightest flicker of emotion, but as soon as her bedroom door closed behind her, she slumped to the ground and dropped her head into her hands.

All the fighting and scheming, and for what? It was over. Tears threatened, but she pushed them back. Crying wasn't going to do a damn thing for her. It was what weak women did in the hopes of manipulating the men around them. Tears didn't work on her father. They never had.

She raised her head, resolve settling in her, loosening the band around her lungs. She had to pack an entire life's worth of living into a month. There was no other option. And it had to be *good*.

Those memories were going to have to sustain her for the rest of her life.

CHAPTER THREE

Carrigan sat in the library, trying to recapture the feeling of peace she'd once been able to have here. It was no use. Everywhere she looked, she saw evidence of her father and a reminder of her deadline ticking down. He'd given her a *list* of eligible men—a list that was apparently smaller than it had been a year ago. Like it was a shopping list that she just had to go down and choose one to spend the rest of her life with—to put her safety and future in the hands of. It made her sick.

She ran her hand over the soft fabric of the couch. Once upon a time, this place was her sanctuary. She used to lie here and stare at the ceiling and dream about what she wanted to do when she grew up. Back then, it had ranged from a lawyer to a fashion designer to—she snorted to think about it—a marine biologist. And now? What would she do if she hadn't been born a daughter in the O'Malley family?

She traced the pattern with a single finger. It was tempting—far too tempting—to indulge in the fantasy. Here, in this room, she could almost believe being a publicist was actually an option. It was a career that she could have used to the benefit of her family, if only her father would see her as something more than a set of ovaries.

With a bachelor's degree in communications and journalism, she easily could have let the O'Malleys slip into the spotlight a little—just enough to entice the media and everyone who watched it. They could manipulate public opinion and gain more power and influence as a result.

But her father wouldn't even discuss it with her. As far as he was concerned, she had her place, and it was her duty as a daughter to stay in it.

The door opened and she tensed, ready to smile and make some excuse to leave. Company wasn't high on her list of things she wanted at the moment—hell, it wasn't on the list at all. But when Teague appeared in the doorway, she had to bite her lip to keep from throwing herself at him. She held herself perfectly still, but sheer relief at the sight of him made her giddy. Even though she knew he couldn't actually do anything to help her, his presence was a comfort she didn't know she needed until he was here in the room with her. "Teague."

"Hey." He closed the door behind him and crossed to sit next to her. "How was Connecticut?"

"It's good to be back." Even if it meant that she didn't have a choice anymore about the direction her life was going.

His dark eyes, so similar to their father's, searched her face. "Is it?"

Words and worries and fears welled up inside her, desperate to be put to voice. She couldn't, though. If she started talking, it would be too slippery a slope into something as dangerous as tears. Carrigan refused to cry. *Refused.* "You know how this goes. Choice doesn't come into it."

His mouth tightened. "Carrigan—"

If she let him, he'd offer her a shoulder to lean on... and she'd never be able to stand on her own. Teague had always been too willing to act as shield to her and their sisters. It was a crying shame that he couldn't save her from her inevitable future. "How was the honeymoon?" As soon as her brother had been released from the hospital, he and Callie disappeared for a few weeks to somewhere in the Caribbean.

"We're not talking about me." He gave her a half smile. "But it was wonderful."

"Good." Even if her life was falling apart around her, at least one of her siblings was genuinely happy. She leaned back. "Did you come to offer me congratulations? Father has me set to be engaged before the end of the year."

His expression grew thunderous. "That's less than a month."

"Well, you know I'm twenty-eight. My value is only diminishing with time. And let's not even talk about my eggs." The flippant comment struck something deep inside her. She wasn't sure she even *wanted* children, but if she ever decided that she did, she didn't want to bring them into a world where their sole purpose was to be pawns in a game not of their choosing.

Like she was.

Like all her siblings were.

Teague sighed and put his arm around her shoulders. "Say the word and we'll fight him over it. We'll get you and the girls out of here." *We* being he and his new wife, Callie. "You can be free. Make your own choices. This isn't all there is to life. *He* isn't God, no matter what our father likes to think."

The worst part was Carrigan knew he meant it. He'd ship her and the others off and willingly take the heat. And, good lord, there'd be heat. Their father wouldn't take the loss of prime marriage material lying down. He might be pleased that Teague consented to marry the Sheridan heir—even if no one was happy that they snuck off to the courthouse without telling anyone— but that wouldn't mean he'd so much as pause before he razed them and their territory to the ground for crossing him.

She couldn't let him take the risk. Not for her.

"You know what happens if you do that, Teague. You and Callie end up dead, and he hunts us down, drags us back, and then I marry some man on his list anyway."

His smile was bitter. "You don't have much faith in me."

"I have all the faith in the world in you. But that doesn't mean I'm going to let you take the fall for me. I make my own choices." Between death by marriage and death by convent. Not much of a choice when she looked at it like that—especially since it looked like her father was no longer willing to consider the convent as a choice—but she wasn't about to let someone else fight for her.

Not when she knew they'd lose.

She'd already lost too much to power games and war.

They all had. She wasn't willing to lose anyone else. "Promise me, Teague. Promise that you won't do anything to piss him off."

"Carrigan..." Teague sighed. "What can I do? If I can't get you out of here, and I can't save you from this, what the fuck can I do?"

There was nothing to do, but if she told him that, it would crush him. The only thing Teague had wanted more than getting out of this life was to get her and their other sisters out as well. That he hadn't been able to do either killed him. Seeing her walk down the aisle, delivered to a man he knew she didn't love, would deal a wound that would fester over the years. He knew she wouldn't have chosen this path for herself. He knew she wanted out as much as he did.

And *she* knew the cost was too high to risk their father's wrath.

"The same thing you've always done. Be there for me." She dropped her head onto his shoulder. He was as solid as a rock. He always had been. The contact centered her, and it must have done the same thing for him, too, since he relaxed a little.

"That seems like a cowardly choice."

There had to be some way she could get through to him. "*My* choice, Teague. Please don't take it away from me. I've already had that happen one too many times." A low blow, but Carrigan wasn't above hitting him where it hurt in order to keep him safe. He had a chance at happiness. She might be a selfish bitch, but even she wasn't selfish enough to take that away from him.

He hissed out a breath, the barb striking true. "Damn it."

Needing to change the subject and put them back on more familiar—and safe—ground, she said, "How goes the wedding planning?" Both their parents and Callie's father refused to acknowledge that their marriage was legitimate until they did things "right." Carrigan found it darkly amusing that there was no end to the sins her father could commit and still sleep at night, but seeing one of his children married without an actual wedding was one he couldn't live with. But then, she'd always known he had skewed priorities—and that wasn't even getting into their mother. She took their courthouse marriage as a personal insult, and as a result she was determined to plan the largest and most extravagant affair she could to make up for it.

For her part, Carrigan was just happy the wedding planning kept her mother's attention elsewhere. The last thing she needed was her other parent meddling alongside her father's determination to match her up with someone on his list.

This time Teague's sigh was less agitated. "For all her protests, Callie's taken the whole thing well in hand. She's gone head-to-head with our mother a few times, from what I understand, and come out on top at least half the time."

"Half? Impressive." She was surprised their mother had conceded *anything* let alone multiple anythings. But then, she already knew Callie was something else. The woman had held herself together in the face of certain death and managed to work with Carrigan to get them both to safety. If there was going to be someone to put Aileen O'Malley in her place, it would be Callie Sheridan.

She smiled at the thought. "I like her."

"I like her, too." Teague grinned, some of his worry melting away. Love did shit like that.

Carrigan stamped down on the envy threatening to take root. Teague was lucky, and she didn't begrudge him that, though part of her wished she'd be able to find the same connection with someone. She knew better. If she agreed to marry one of the men on her father's list, it wouldn't be a love match.

"Do you think..." He hesitated. "Do you know which way you're going?"

She didn't need him to clarify. "I don't really have a choice." The convent hadn't really been an option for her. It was a bargaining chip she'd used to keep her father's ambitions at bay. That was it. Her life would have been a lot simpler if she had a higher religious calling. *Or if I'd been born with a penis*. Maybe then her opinions and plans would actually have had merit in their father's eyes. "All that's left is to pick the groom."

"Don't make any hasty decisions."

She laughed. "Teague, I have a month. The only thing left to me is hasty decisions."

"Just remember—all you need to do is say the word and I'll get you out."

She hugged him. "I know." Just like she knew she'd never say the word. Teague had stood as protector between her and problems in the past. Or tried to. It never quite worked out like either of them wanted it to, and she wasn't about to place bets that this time would be the exception to the rule.

All that was left to her was to go on the expected dates and pick the least horrible one of the bunch. Then it was a matter of hoping for the best. She could stack the deck in her favor to make up for the lack of choices, but in the end it all came down to whoever she chose to hitch her wagon to. There was no reason to expect that she'd enjoy spending time with any of the men, since she fully expected her father to pick men similar to the caliber of man he was.

God, she hated this.

Carrigan patted her brother's hand and rose. The longer she procrastinated, the less time she'd ultimately have. It was better to bite the bullet now and get this shit started. "I'll talk to you later."

"Sure."

She felt his worried gaze on her all the way out of the library and into the hallway. It was only when she shut the door behind her that she breathed a temporary sigh of relief.

Now, to deal with her father.

She found him in the formal living room, looking bored as her mother pored over some kind of photo album—something to do with the upcoming wedding, no doubt. It would be held in just under two weeks, so most of the details had already been taken care of. It stood to reason, though, that little last-minute things were bound to pop up.

She stood in the doorway, waiting for them to acknowledge her. Her father looked up first, almost comically pleased for the distraction. "Carrigan."

It was far too tempting to make small talk—about anything other than the real reason she was here. That was the coward's way out, though. "I'm going to meet the men you have on this list."

Her mother finally looked up, green eyes narrowing. "What list? I haven't seen any list, Seamus."

"It's none of your concern." He spared one of his rare smiles for Carrigan. "I'm glad you've decided to be reasonable."

"Anything for the family, Father."

Besides, if the man she married turned out to be a monster, she could always take a page from Callie's book and shoot the bastard dead.

* * *

Sloan floated through the hallways of her childhood, feeling more like a ghost than a woman. The feeling had been there in their giant home in Connecticut, and she'd wandered the house at all hours of the night, driven from her bed by the treacherous thoughts of what could have been. If she'd made different choices the night Carrigan was taken. If her brothers hadn't drunk themselves stupid and walked home. If her father hadn't been so willing to risk all of them in a grab for power.

She didn't like the answers she came up with.

They didn't really matter. The past was dead and gone, just like Devlin. She pressed a hand to her chest, stopping at the top of the stairs, feeling like she'd just run ten miles. *Devlin*. One of her brothers was dead, and everyone was going on as if nothing had changed—as if their world hadn't turned to dust around them.

It wasn't fair, and she knew it. Life went on, whether they wanted it to or not.

She took a deep breath and kept walking, her bare feet padding over the cool wood floors. She wasn't a child.

She *knew* life had to go on. It couldn't come to a full stop just because her heart was so broken she didn't think it'd ever recover. Devlin had been only twenty, three years younger than her, and growing up they'd always been close. Of all her brothers, he hadn't expected her to change. He'd been perfectly content to share the comfortable silences she was so fond of, broken only to bring up something interesting that one of them was currently reading. And he'd managed to accept the weight of the burden their family placed on them, while still striving for more.

And now his dreams were ashes in the wind, whisking hers away with them.

Their father liked to say that great privilege brought great responsibility with it. He was a liar. He hadn't been the one forced to make compromise after compromise. He was completely content to move his children around like pieces of furniture, aligning them to his satisfaction to keep the O'Malley clan strong. What did their individual happiness matter in the grand scale of the family's safety?

Not even a tiny bit.

Her stomach lurched, leaving her lightheaded, and Sloan paused to lean against the wall. She might have gotten away with her midnight wanderings in the old redone farmhouse, but there were too many people here. It was only a matter of time before one of her well-meaning siblings guided her back to her bedroom. Or the guards reported her to her father.

Imagining how pleasant *that* conversation would be had her picking up her pace. She passed Keira's door, hearing strains of some hard rock song on the other side of the door. It was selfish to think Sloan was the only one suffering. Her youngest sister had taken Devlin's death just as hard—if not harder. She'd started drinking. A lot. Sloan knew that Carrigan chalked it up to her age, but she wasn't so sure. Keira drank like she was trying to escape the thoughts in her head. That kind of thing didn't simply disappear over time.

It got worse.

She touched the door, hesitating. Should she say something? Try to get Keira to talk to her? Sloan had always been good at listening, but broaching this subject was going to reopen wounds that hadn't even had a chance to close, much less heal.

So she kept walking.

Carrigan's door opened as she approached, and her older sister stepped into the hall, wearing a sheath dress that left little to the imagination. She froze when she saw Sloan. "You're up late."

"I couldn't sleep."

For a second she thought—hoped—Carrigan would let it go. She obviously had plans to sneak out, and her skin nearly twitched with impatience. But then she stepped back into her room. "Let's talk."

More talking. Sloan let loose a silent sigh and obeyed. The sooner they got this over with, the sooner she could retreat into her room and lose herself in a book. It was the only escape that worked these days, the only thing that took away the harsh edge of reality.

Carrigan perched on the edge of her bed and gave her a long look. "Father's decided that he's tired of waiting for me."

She'd known this was coming. They all had. Her sister's ability to hold him off for this long was something to be commended, but it couldn't last forever. "How long?" It felt curiously like she was asking how long Carrigan had left to live.

"My birthday."

Her breath stalled in her chest. "But..." Sloan looked down at her hands, fighting to get the words past the concrete block in her throat. "*Marriage*."

It was on the tip of her tongue to point out that it had worked out for Teague—to maybe even suggest that Carrigan would get the same results—but she stopped. Their brother had been fortunate to the point of unbelievability. Lightning never struck the same place twice, and those were the odds for Carrigan to make a love match from the list of men their father had provided.

"I know." Carrigan took her hands. "I didn't drag you in here so we could have a pity party. Things are the way they are. I just wanted to give you as much of a heads-up as I could."

Because she was next.

The realization settled inside her, turning her blood to ice and her brain into a worthless buzz. As soon as Carrigan was safely carted away into a marriage, their father would turn his eye on *her*. She'd never pretended the Catholic devotion that her sister had, not to the point where it would be believable that she was considering joining a convent. Even if she had, their father wasn't likely to fall for the same ruse twice. No, he'd strike quickly, while she was still young enough to be valuable. *Pliable*.

"It doesn't matter if I see it coming or not. It's inevitable." It seemed like her feet had been set on this path from birth. She'd never put much thought into it before, and now her time was up. *What am I going to do with a husband?*

"Sloan..." Carrigan hesitated, and then seemed to change what she'd been about to say. "I'm sorry."

She managed to squeeze her sister's hands back, even though her fingers were numb. "Don't be sorry. Go enjoy your night."

"Do you want to come with me?"

She would have laughed if she had the breath for it. "You know how much I hate those clubs. Don't worry about me. I'll be okay." A lie, but one Carrigan let her have. Sometimes it seemed there were more comforting lies than truths between them now.

"We'll talk more soon."

What was the point? They could talk for days on end, but it wouldn't change their circumstances. Helpless fury rose inside her. She was well and truly trapped, up to her neck in quicksand and sinking fast.

God, what am I going to do?

CHAPTER FOUR

Carrigan stepped into the club and tried to tell herself that she was here for the right reasons. It had nothing to do with looking for James, and everything to do with proving to herself she wasn't afraid. Because she wasn't. The only reason he'd gotten the best of her was because he kept catching her off guard. That wouldn't happen tonight. Even as the thought crossed her mind, she scanned the crowd, searching for that towering blond figure.

Nothing.

Ignoring the feeling that might have been disappointment souring her stomach, she wound through the dance floor and headed for the stairs leading to the VIP area. She needed a drink and to get her head on straight, and then she'd go dance until she forgot what she'd agreed to earlier today.

Just like she always had.

And maybe she'd finally break her four-month-long dry spell...

She shook her head and climbed the stairs. No. Not tonight, and not a guy from here. It hadn't worked out so well last time, and she sure as hell wasn't looking for a repeat kidnapping. At the top of the stairs, she paused and let her eyes adjust to the dim lighting. Up here, there were no strobe lights or black lights or anything other than tiny lamps on each of the tables, throwing off just enough illumination so that someone could walk the entire floor without tripping over something. In theory.

She headed for her favorite booth, but drew up short when she saw that it was occupied. Her brain took precious seconds to catch up to her eyes. There he was, the asshole, sitting in *her* booth with his legs stretched out in front of him, wearing those jeans that hugged his ass and thighs and a smug smirk, with his arms stretched out across the back of the booth. Challenging her.

In case she missed all that written all over his face, there were two drinks in front of him—a beer and, if she didn't miss her guess, a dirty martini. *Her* preferred drink. How the hell did he even know that?

Oh yes, this was a challenge all right.

Every intelligent cell in her brain demanded she turn around and walk away. *Run* away. But then the bastard raised an eyebrow, as if daring her to sit down and drink with him, and she threw common sense right out the window. Carrigan strode across the distance separating them, putting a little more swing into her step and smiling to herself when his gaze tracked the movement. Album or not, tangled history or no, he wanted her.

And she wasn't above using that against him.

"Two nights in a row. I must have pissed off Lady Luck somehow." She sank onto the cushioned seat across the small table from him. The bartender appeared half a second later, and Carrigan smiled sweetly at her. "A dirty martini, please."

The woman looked at the table, looked back at her, and shrugged. "Sure thing."

If anything James just seemed more amused. "Too good for my drinks?"

"I'm not stupid enough to take a drink I've left unattended . . . and I've never laid eyes on this one until I got here. Party Girl 101."

"Now, lovely, why would I need to drug you? You came here of your own free will, just like I knew you would." He leaned forward and propped his elbows on his knees, drawing her gaze to the way his black T-shirt clung to his shoulders and how his dangling hands seemed designed to frame the bulge between his legs.

Her body zinged to life in a way it hadn't in months. It was all too easy to take a walk down memory lane and feel him lifting her against that wall and shoving his cock home, growling filthy words in her ear in that same tone of voice he was using now.

Shit.

She held his gaze even though all she wanted to do was look away. James wasn't pretty. He was far too masculine for that. The first time she'd seen him, she thought he'd look perfectly at home on the back of a Harley, and that perception hadn't changed with time. Everything about him screamed *danger* in a way she wasn't used to. The men in her family were dangerous—there was no doubt of that—but it was a polished danger. James's wasn't. He was gritty and primal and...She really needed to stop. Right now. "I wouldn't put anything past you at this point."

"You wound me."

"You kidnapped me. I'd say we're nowhere near even." Something she had to keep reminding herself, though the fact she kept forgetting annoyed the hell out of her. Only a weak woman would get all aflutter over a man who obviously meant her harm. A weak woman or one with a death wish.

Carrigan wasn't either.

So why was she here, sitting across from him as if they were best pals? She leaned back and recrossed her legs. "Why are you stalking me?"

"If you'd remember, *you* are the one who came to me. I was just sitting here, minding my own business, enjoying a drink." His cocky grin said otherwise. He'd known she would come back—that she wouldn't be able to resist. The knowledge that he'd read so much in her personality in such a short time set her teeth on edge.

"Enjoy it in a different bar. Hell, in a different city." She had to get a handle on her attitude. As it was, she was practically waving a giant sign telling him that he got under her skin. There was no reason to hand him over more power than he already had—and he already had too much.

"Now, lovely, don't be rude. I'm buying you a drink." He nodded at the bartender as she handed over a duplicate of the dirty martini already sitting on the table.

"I can buy my own damn drink." She sounded surly and childish and hated it. *You can do better than this. So do it*. She watched a trio of girls who couldn't possibly be twenty-one pass their booth, hips swinging wildly and sending come-fuck-me looks at the man across from her. He didn't even glance their way, which only aggravated her further. "What do you want, James?"

"You already know the answer to that question."

Did she? Because she was starting to wonder, even though she knew better. *He wants the album back. Plain and simple.* She'd have to be a damn fool to think he actually wanted *her*. "Pretend I don't."

Instead of jumping right on that, he snagged his beer and drank deep while he watched her with those unnerving blue eyes. She couldn't shake the feeling that he saw more than she wanted to reveal. Carrigan took a sip of her own drink—perfect, as always—determined to wait him out and not speak again first.

The silence stretched out between them like a live thing, twisting and snapping and full of too many things best left unsaid. *Why? Why did you do it? Why did you make me feel so much and then turn around and betray me in every way that counted?* They were questions she'd never allow herself to ask because even the asking showed him that she cared in some small way. She *didn't*. She looked away, doing her damnedest to ignore the way her hand shook when she brought her drink to her lips.

"Why did your father bring you back to the city?"

It was so unexpected, she almost answered truthfully. She caught herself at the last minute. "It doesn't really matter."

"It does." He shifted, once again drawing her attention to his big thighs. Powerful thighs. Every part of him was built powerfully, like he was a gladiator from ancient times. She had no problem picturing him wielding a sword in an arena somewhere, cutting through his enemies with the same determined look on his face that he wore now. "Word has it that your father is arranging a marriage for you."

"Gossip is bad for the soul," she said in her most prim tone, even as her mind raced. She hadn't expected the news to be kept secret—her father had no reason to hide his intentions for her—but hearing it from a man who was both an enemy and something more was disconcerting, to say the least. She'd only been back in town for three days—either James had an inside man, or her father had put together that damn list of his long before she drove back into Boston. A thought struck her, and she blurted out, "You aren't thinking of throwing your hat into the ring, are you?"

His gaze sharpened on her face, searching for an answer she wasn't sure she had. "It would almost be worth seeing the look on his face when I did."

Her brain caught up to her mouth. Finally. She pressed her lips together, as if that would really do anything to help her maintain control. Control was one thing she'd always prided herself on having—if not over her life, then at least over herself. Being this close to James, even with a table between them, was making it hard to focus. "You wouldn't dare."

"Wouldn't I?"

Yes. He so would. And her father wouldn't hesitate to shoot him, tentative truce or not. Carrigan stared at her drink, tilting it this way and that in the low light. After everything that happened, it shouldn't concern her if James Halloran had a death wish. It should serve him right to take a bullet the same way her little brother had—even if he wasn't the one who gave the order—but the thought of the world no longer holding him in it...it was a cold one. "Don't do it."

"I think I'm insulted. The thought of marrying me is enough to shut you down completely."

"Funny, you don't sound particularly insulted." She had to get them off this subject—the sooner, the better— so she went on the offense. "If you're hoping for a repeat of that night, you're in for the disappointment of a lifetime. I'm never letting you touch me again."

A strange smile pulled at the edges of his lips. "Liar."

She jerked back, her heart beating too hard. He wasn't flustered or worried or anything, except arrogant. "You're an insufferable jackass." Now was the time to get up and walk away, and put him in her rearview for good. But Carrigan had always had a nasty habit of playing with fire, and James was scorching hot.

"Guilty." He stood and moved around the table, slow and purposeful, to sit next to her, entirely too close. She started to shift away, but his heavy arm dropped around her shoulder. The feeling of his bare skin against hers made her whole body clench up. Torn between wanting to bolt and wanting to crawl into his lap, she froze.

James had no such problem. He wound a lock of her hair around his finger. "You want me, lovely. You want me so bad you burn with it."

With every turn of his finger, he brushed her bare shoulder with his knuckles, the gentle touch making things low in her stomach coil tighter and tighter. She dug her nails into her palms. She wasn't weak and she wasn't afraid, and she sure as fuck wasn't going to melt into a puddle at his feet just because he'd casually touched her. "You're wrong."

* * *

James wasn't wrong. Across the careful distance he'd created between their bodies, he had no problems picking out the signs of desire. Her pulse fluttered, heart beating too hard; her pupils dilated, and her nipples pressed against the thin fabric of her sad excuse for a dress. The damn thing barely covered her from breasts to ass, and the fit was enough to tell anyone who cared to look that she wore nothing underneath. It wasn't the same one she'd worn they night they hooked up, but it was close enough to make his mouth water. The fire in her eyes as she did her best to take him out at the knees only made him want her more.

He leaned closer, still keeping the precious inches between their bodies. He might want this woman more than sanity, but she was like some kind of wild creature that'd wandered into his life. One false move and it was over. Letting her go last night was the right thing to do. He'd piqued her curiosity, added a healthy dose of anger and, maybe, she felt even a sliver of the desire that threatened to take his common sense and turn him into a goddamn fool.

But he had to play this right or she'd be gone for good. It'd be better for both of them if she was. Smarter. But taking the safe and smart road didn't stand a chance with a woman like her looking at him with *that* expression in her eyes. His lips brushed her ear, her rose scent teasing him. "I'm not wrong, lovely. You crave me the same way I crave you."

"I don't." The words were barely more than a whisper, almost lost in the demanding beat drifting up from the dance floor.

"You do. And if I slipped my hand up your dress, I'd find you wet and wanting." Fuck, he wanted to do just that. Only sheer stubbornness kept his free hand away from her when she shivered. "It wouldn't take much, would it? A few strokes to make your eyes slide shut and your head fall back. Circle that sensitive little clit of yours and feel you come apart around me."

Her back arched, so slight that he would have missed it if every fiber of his being wasn't focused on her. "No..."

He had to get the fuck away from her before he did exactly what he'd just described. The VIP room was far from packed and, even if it hadn't been, no one would blink an eye at two people hooking up in the shadows. But it wouldn't get him anywhere with Carrigan, aside from a few moments of pleasure. Then she'd be gone, and he had the feeling he wouldn't be seeing her again in the near future—if ever.

That didn't suit his purposes one goddamn bit.

So he pressed a soft kiss to the sensitive spot behind her ear and backed the fuck off. When she turned and blinked those big green eyes at him, he almost threw caution to the wind and kissed her. Only the knowledge that it wouldn't stop with a kiss, wouldn't stop until he was buried between her thighs, kept him from giving in. "I'll be seeing you, Carrigan O'Malley."

Still holding her gaze, he grabbed his beer and drained

the rest of it. He'd already taken care of the tab with the bartender, so he stood and, with one last look at her, walked away. It felt unnatural to do it, but it was becoming increasingly clear that the fire in his blood for Carrigan wasn't going away. He'd been so sure it would, that seeing her again would be enough to bring common sense rushing back and remind him that she was the enemy and he'd done the right thing when he'd chosen his family over her.

Except that certainty hadn't come last night. And it sure as fuck wasn't here tonight, either.

All he could think about as he strode down the stairs to the main club floor was that he'd well and truly fucked up. She was within her rights to never forgive him. Hell, *he* wouldn't forgive him if he was in her position.

And wanting her forgiveness had nothing at all to do with the damn album.

"Fuck." He settled into an empty spot at the bar and waited. Just because he was giving her space didn't mean he was going to leave before seeing her safely into a cab. She wouldn't thank him for the babysitting detail, but he'd never forgive himself if something happened to her because he wasn't watching. *What the hell am I thinking? Something* is *happening to her.* He'd hoped against hope that the rumor he'd heard about her old man selling her off to one of his allies was false.

The look on her face had told him otherwise.

Knowing she was destined for a political marriage was like watching a hawk get its wings clipped, or a tiger be declawed. While it was possible that she'd maintain the fiery personality and streak of wildness that called to him on a level he wasn't prepared to deal with...it was just as likely that her future husband would kill that part of her, leaving a dead-eyed Stepford wife in her place.

The thought burned. Beating some sense into Seamus O'Malley sounded satisfying as fuck, but ultimately it wouldn't change anything. *Nothing* James did would change anything.

And hell if that knowledge didn't stick in his throat.

The minutes ticked by, but it wasn't too long before Carrigan appeared at the top of the stairs like some kind of fallen angel. He couldn't see her eyes from where he stood, but he imagined her a queen surveying her kingdom. The moment her gaze landed on him, her body went tense. He waited, curious to see what she'd do. She marched down the stairs, her hips swinging with each step. But instead of coming to give him a piece of her mind, she shot him a look and disappeared onto the dance floor.

That shit was a dare if he ever saw one.

He was moving before he made a decision to, stalking after her. People took one look at him and parted like the Red Sea. He walked through them without pausing, stopping when he caught sight of her, her hands above her head, her eyes closed, her body moving with the writhing beat of the song.

She was the most beautiful thing he'd ever seen. His plans to keep his distance went up in a puff of smoke and he closed the space between them, needing to touch her more than he needed his next breath. James slipped behind her, resting his hands on her hips. It took all of three seconds to pick up her rhythm and match it, fitting himself behind her. She arched back against him, her arms

looping around his neck and her head resting on his chest
as they ground together.

Stupid. This wasn't part of the plan, wasn't part of
keeping control of the situation. Because if anyone was
in control right now, it was Carrigan. She guided him
with the rolling of her hips, her ass against his cock, the
heat of her searing through his clothes as if they didn't
exist.

Unable to help himself, he coasted his hands up her
sides to frame her ribs, his thumbs brushing the under-
sides of her breasts with every other beat. She moved
closer in response, rotating in his grasp until they faced
each other, her chest pressed against his chest and her
fingers twined in his hair. She went onto her tiptoes,
dragging her body up his, and he groaned in response.
"James?"

"Yeah, lovely?" A little voice tried to pipe up to point
out that he'd give her damn near anything with her moving against him like this, but he ignored it, waiting for
her answer.

"I might want you…" He tightened his grip on her
hips. She laughed, a sound he felt more than heard. "But
you try that manipulative shit on me again, and I will
go for your throat." And then she was gone, slipping
through his arms like smoke. He stood there like a damn
fool, sporting a hard-on for the record books and watching her walk away. He shook his head and followed.
Head games or not, his needing to see her safely to a cab
hadn't changed.

Fuck, he was almost proud of her for turning the tables on him so efficiently, even if he was going to suffer
for it physically. He could weather a little suffering and,

to be honest, he'd seen a whole hell of a lot worse. James grinned. He followed her out of the club, letting her pull ahead, and leaned against a wall as she flagged down a cab. Only once it veered back out into traffic did he turn and head for his ride.

Damn that woman, but he only got more intrigued with each interaction. He looked forward to seeing what the next one brought.

That small voice in his head tried to pipe up again, tried to remind him that she wasn't his and never would be, but he ignored it. She wasn't married yet and if she was willing to play, he was more than willing to go the distance.

CHAPTER FIVE

James's phone rang when he hit Southie. He glanced at the clock on the screen. Two a.m. Nothing good came from calls at this hour. With a curse, he answered, "What?"

"Trouble."

No shit. Michael wouldn't be calling him for anything else. "Tell me."

"Tit for Tat. Ricky's there."

Well, shit again. There wasn't a need for more goddamn information. Their brother, Brendan, had been killed in that strip joint four months ago. James had never liked the place, and that went double since it used to be the front for human trafficking of the young and pretty variety. He'd put a stop to that shit the second he took over the Hallorans. Now the only women who worked there were there of their own choice. If they turned tricks on the side, that was up to them, but they traded a percentage for his protection. It was as fair a deal as he could offer them, and most were more than happy with the arrangement.

There was no goddamn reason for Ricky to be there that wouldn't send James's blood pressure straight through the fucking roof. "When?"

"They left fifteen minutes ago."

At least this time he could nip this shit right in the bud instead of dealing with it hours later. He turned right at the next light. "Meet me there."

"Will do, boss."

He hung up and floored it. There was no rational reason to think that his brother was up to something . . . other than every other fucking time he turned around, Ricky was finding ways to undermine him. Whatever familial bond they'd had as kids, it was gone now.

My brother would happily see me dead and out of the way now.

James blew out a breath. It was a truth he hadn't wanted to deal with before, but it *was* the truth. He let it settle inside him as he pulled up in front of Tit for Tat. The building looked damn near indistinguishable from the ones around it, aside from the neon sign out front advertising full nudes. Only its patrons knew exactly what was offered on the inside—them and the few cops he had on the payroll to keep his ass out of the fire.

He hated dirty cops. There was something fundamentally wrong with a man who put a price on his honor, no matter how useful they were when it came to keeping his people out of jail. But then, honor wasn't something James had the luxury of holding close. He didn't have an inch of high ground to stand on. Not anymore.

Inside it was hot and dark—aside from the brightly

lit stages—and stank of lust and greed. James headed for the bar, ignoring the scattering of men watching Echo swing herself around a pole, her dark hair flying behind her. He nodded at Tawna, noting at how shaken she looked. Her wide blue eyes made her look younger than her twenty-something years, and she actually seemed grateful to catch sight of him. If he had any doubt that Ricky was here, it vanished then. The sins of their father seemed to be something both his brothers had inherited.

Some days he thought it hadn't really skipped him, no matter how much he wanted it to. "Where's my brother?"

She pointed a shaking finger to the stairs, and he mentally cursed in every single fucking way he knew. He hadn't been up there since Brendan's death, and he could have spent the rest of his life without doing it again. *Goddamn it.* It took simultaneously too much time and not nearly enough to get up those rickety-ass stairs. They needed to be torn out and replaced, but no one would ever do it. That wasn't the kind of place Tit for Tat was. At the top, the hallway of doors stretched out, all of them closed. This was where the girls brought men for lap dances or the other side of their business. The thin doors let out more sounds than they concealed, but his destination wasn't in any of them. No, it was the final door—the one containing what passed for an office.

He found Ricky sitting behind the massive desk, deep in conversation with two men James didn't recognize. If that wasn't a giant-ass red flag, the fact his brother had managed to clean up his shaggy blond hair and find a button-up shirt somewhere was. He was crashing a business meeting—one he wasn't supposed to know about from the flash of worry that appeared on his brother's face. Ricky shot to his feet. "James."

There wasn't a damn thing he could do until he knew what the hell was going on, but he didn't need to let his little brother know that. He jerked his chin at the door. "Out." Ricky hesitated, but James had too much practice using his cold stare to manipulate people. His brother didn't stand a chance. He slunk through the door like a beaten dog with his tail between his legs. James waited several long seconds to make sure he didn't change his mind, and then took the seat behind the desk. "Gentlemen."

The two men were anything but. Oh, they cleaned up well enough with their cheap suits, but there was no mistaking the glint in their eyes. Killers, both of them. What in the ever-loving fuck was Ricky doing meeting with these guys? They exchanged a look, and the man on the right, a redhead with hands the size of hams, leaned forward. "Since you didn't seem to be aware of the meeting taking place, I'll bring you up to speed. We're not interested in the internal power games the Hallorans have going on—all we care about is getting paid."

That was a relief, though he doubted he'd get lucky next time. "Then we're on the same page. What's the merchandise?"

Another shared look between the men. "We heard you were down on your inventory." The redhead motioned at the club around them. "We have a crop hitting the harbor two weeks from now. They're good stock, so we're commanding top price."

Girls. They were shipping in more girls, and Ricky had been Johnny-on-the-spot to buy them up. Just like

Brendan used to. It was official—when James got his hands around his fool brother's neck, he was going to strangle the fucking life out of him. They were *out* of the flesh trade.

But if he didn't buy up these girls, some other piece of shit would.

For a second he almost let it go. It wasn't his problem. He had more than enough to deal with without adding this to the mix. He eyed the men, both who James would bet had been in this business for years. They didn't care if he agreed to this purchase. There were plenty of buyers, even in this day and age. If he turned them away, they wouldn't blink at supplying someone else. Someone who would be more than willing to sell unwilling women to men who didn't care about consent. *Godfuckingdamn it.* He smiled through gritted teeth. "Let's talk money."

As much as he wanted this done and over with, he took the time to haggle with the men. There was no telling if he would have to deal with them again, and it set a shitty precedent for him to give in to the first price they named without bargaining. But, fuck, he hated every second of it. By the time they settled on a price that was respectable but not insulting, he felt like he'd been hit by a truck. They arranged to have the *merchandise* dropped at an agreed-upon location on a date two weeks from now.

He watched the pair walk out of the office, and seriously debated grabbing the gun fastened beneath the desk and putting two slugs in each of them. It wouldn't do a damn thing to help either the situation or how fucking filthy he currently felt. Slave traders were like cockroaches. You managed to kill one, and three more popped up in its place. Taking out these two wouldn't help the girls on that boat coming in, or the ones that would undoubtedly follow.

Fuck. He pinched the bridge of his nose, wishing he could just douse himself in bleach and be done with it. He couldn't save the world. Hell, he couldn't even save his little corner of it. The best he could do was figure out some place for those girls where they weren't forced to be little better than sex slaves. They would get a choice. They would have some sort of income from a job. He'd make sure of it.

But first he had to deal with Ricky.

James looked up to find his brother standing in the doorway, puffed up like he was ready for confrontation. Too fucking bad. He wasn't going to get one. "Sit."

"You can't just—"

"Sit." He didn't raise his voice, but he didn't have to. Ricky had been conditioned from a very young age to respond to that particular icy tone, just the same as James and Brendan. His older brother hadn't ever bothered to learn the trick of speaking like that, because his sheer size and personality got his way more often than not. James was a firm believer of stocking his arsenal with every weapon available to him. Their father's furious tone was one of them.

Ricky shut the door and dropped into one of the vacated chairs. "I was taking initiative."

"You were trying to undermine me." *Again.* He couldn't let this go on any longer. He'd tried to reasoning with Ricky. He'd tried intimidating. He'd tried damn near everything. Nothing worked. Every time he turned around, his brother was doing something else to sow dissent and fuck up James's life. The longer he let it go on, the weaker his position became.

God damn you for making me do this.

James typed out a text, never taking his gaze off his brother. "You know what happens next."

Ricky's blue eyes, so similar to his, went wide. "James—"

"Don't you dare play the fucking innocent. You knew what you were doing—deal with the consequences." The door opened again, and this time Michael and Jake came through, one of the other men James was reasonably sure of. They hauled Ricky out of his chair, and out of the room. To his credit, he didn't yell or fight.

But the look he sent James made him cold right down to his bones.

He'd known his brother hated him. He hadn't wanted to admit it, but he'd known all the same. It was a truth he'd made as much peace as he could with. Now he had to deal with Ricky blatantly wanting him dead.

Well, fuck.

He waited for the door to close and then slumped into his chair. He'd known this shit wasn't going to be a picnic from the moment he lost Brendan. Being heir was never something James wanted, but he'd done his damnedest to step up and do right by the family. Naive as it apparently was, he'd never expected his remaining brother to turn on him.

Truth be told, he hadn't expected a lot of things.

He sighed. As much as he wanted to get the hell out of here and wash off the stench of this place, since he *was* here, he needed to check in with the manager and make sure things were still going smoothly. He hadn't heard anything recently, but he was learning the hard way that just because information didn't come directly to him didn't mean it wasn't happening. And Ricky taking an interest in Tit for Tat was a red flag he couldn't ignore.

A quick phone call brought Lisa Marie up. She was an old battle-ax who had worked her way up from waitressing to the pole to running the whole damn place. She had to have put sixty in the rearview mirror years ago, but she hadn't missed a beat. As he watched, she snubbed out a cigarette and lit up another one. "Whatcha need, honey?"

"I haven't been in here in a few weeks. Bring me up to date."

"You want to know what that brother of yours is up to." Her shrewd gray eyes saw too much. "He's been in here five days out of seven, sniffing around. He takes over the office and has people coming and going. Don't know what he's up to, but I'd bet my left tit he's up to something." She exhaled a plume of smoke. "The little shit told me we're starting up with those girls again."

"We're not."

"Good. Made *my* girls nervous." She tapped the cigarette into the ashtray on the desk. "Ever since that other brother of yours died—God rest his soul—business is up fifteen percent."

Probably because Brendan scared the living shit out of everyone smart enough to know what trouble looked like. It kept those men and their money away from Tit for Tat. James tapped his fingers on the desk. Ricky seemed all too ready to step into Brendan's shoes, and that was something he couldn't allow. Like it or not, they'd taken a hit when he put a stop to the flesh trade. They needed the bump of legit money. "Are the other clubs seeing the same increase?"

"More or less." She leaned back and crossed her legs, stick thin and covered in pants made of something like spandex. "Having willing girls makes a difference. Johns can tell. And the ones who liked the fear...well, I don't want to deal with that shit."

Neither did James. He waited, seeing from the tension in her shoulders that there was something more. People didn't like silences, especially uncomfortable ones like this was quickly evolving into. Lisa Marie knew the tactic—it was one he'd seen her use before—and she gave him a sardonic smile. "You're not a puppy anymore, James Halloran."

Maybe not, but he still felt like a small fish in an ocean full of sharks. Every time he turned around, another threat was rising at his back. It was fucking exhausting. Still, he waited.

She sighed, smoke drifting out of her nostrils. "That Ricky..."

The seconds stretched into minutes. Finally, he relented. "Tell me."

"I know he's family."

Her sudden hesitance set his teeth on edge. "If there's something I need to know, spit it the fuck out."

That got her moving again. She snubbed out her cigarette. "He's been taking a family discount with the girls—and them saying yes isn't necessary."

Her words left him cold all over. *Fuck, fuck, fuck*. He kept all expression off his face through sheer force of will, but it was a battle. He'd known his little brother was teetering on the edge, but apparently he'd already reached the point of no return. *Fuck*. And James had sat idly by while his brother played fox in the henhouse. It didn't matter if he hadn't known. Those women were under his protection, same as every other person in Halloran territory.

And he'd failed them.

"I'll need a list of names." His voice was so cold, it was a wonder the bottle of beer in front of him didn't ice over.

"Sure thing."

"That's all." He waited until she was almost to the door to say, "And, Lisa Marie."

"Yeah, honey?"

"My brother is no longer allowed in this club—or any of the ones in Halloran territory." He couldn't let this go on unchecked. Ricky wasn't trustworthy, and James wasn't about to let his brother near people they were supposed to be protecting until he could be sure he wouldn't have to protect them from *Ricky*.

She fumbled a new cigarette out of her pack, cursing when it fell to the faded carpet. "But—"

"It's not open for discussion. Inform the bouncers. If he gives you trouble, you call me, you understand?"

"I understand." She scooped up the cigarette and fled the room, shutting the door softly behind her.

Goddamn it. He hated playing the monster. The more often he put on the mask, the less like a mask it felt. Making Lisa Marie scurry from the room left a bad taste in his mouth. No one seemed to notice or care that he was trying to do the right thing. That knowledge shouldn't surprise him, and it sure as hell shouldn't sting.

It did.

He pushed to his feet with a sigh. Once he had the list of girls, he'd figure out his next step. He couldn't just throw money at them—it'd be insult to injury—but there had to be *something* he could do. There was no making something like this right, but fuck if he was going to ignore it.

No one approached him as he walked down the stairs and through the club. He was used to people being wary of him, but there was actual fear in the air. It clung to the back of his throat, a taste he wished he didn't know. He had to struggle to keep his pace even and walk out of there like nothing was wrong. The cold night air didn't do shit to keep him from feeling like the world was closing in on him. James made it to his car and climbed in, locking the doors and starting the engine.

Only then did he lean back against the seat and close his eyes and concentrate on breathing. *Inhale. Hold for one, two, three. Exhale.* And again. By the fifth time, the static hovering at the edge of his thoughts retreated and he was able to put the car into gear and get the hell out of there.

He wished...

But no, there was no point in wishing on stars or any of that shit. His life was the way it was, and so was his current situation. It was sink or swim. If he sank, he'd take down too many people with him. Ricky had more than proven that he wouldn't protect the weak under his domain. Even if James was willing to leave the Halloran name and responsibilities behind, he couldn't leave the people who needed him.

It would just be so much easier to handle this shit if he was sure that the kernel of evil that seemed to flourish in his old man and brothers wasn't doing the same damn thing inside of him. He wasn't a good man. He had no illusions about that. But there was a long haul between "not good" and "fucking monster."

He hoped.

He grabbed his phone before he could think better of it, and dialed the number he'd had for months but never used. It rang and rang, and right when he was about to hang up, she answered, "Hello?"

Carrigan's voice was like a soft ocean breeze, washing away all the shit of the last few hours. James took his first full breath since he'd left the strip club. "Hey, lovely."

CHAPTER SIX

Carrigan sat up in bed, blinking into the darkness. She had to be dreaming. It was the only explanation for hearing James's voice growling in her ear. But no, it couldn't be a dream because she hadn't been sleeping. She checked the clock. Four a.m. She'd left him at the club a little over two hours ago. He should be...hell, she didn't know. Doing anything else but calling her right now. "What do you want?" Instead of coming out harsh, the words were barely more than a whisper. *Needy*. Damn it.

He took a long time to answer, his breathing the only thing breaking the silence between them. "It's the damnedest thing, Carrigan, but I don't fucking know."

It might have been the realest thing he'd ever said to her. She stared into the darkness, her mind frantically paging through possible responses—everything from making a joke and turning things sexual to actually responding in kind—but James spoke again before she had a chance to settle on a choice.

"Right now, though, I want you."

There they were—back on firm ground once again. She knew how to verbally spar with this man, how to keep him at a distance while still wanting him closer, how to dance on the dangerous edge of the attraction that licked between them like the hottest flame. She didn't know how to deal with the soul-deep weariness he'd just shown her.

So she ignored it.

"Like I haven't heard that before."

"This is different." His growl sent delicious shivers through her body.

She settled back against her headboard, allowing a small smile. It wasn't like he could see it. "How do you figure?"

"Because all those other men who have said it to you before weren't worthy."

Big words. "Oh, and I suppose you are?"

"Yeah. More than that, I'm the only one who's going to truly have you."

Carrigan laughed because it was the only appropriate response to the sheer cockiness of his words. *He* was going to be the only one to have her? The man was even more delusional than she could have guessed. "I don't know if you noticed it that night, but I was hardly a blushing virgin when we met." She found herself holding her breath, waiting for the inevitable demands to tell him how many men had been there before him. Or maybe he'd assume there had been only one, and the sheer magnitude of his masculine presence had been enough to stir her almost-virgin heart. In her experience, men fell into only one of those two categories. They constructed their own beliefs about an experience—about *her*—and when faced with evidence that they were wrong, they looked at her like she was either a whore or a virgin in disguise. There was no middle ground.

"They don't matter." He said it totally dismissively, as if it was actually true.

She blinked. "What?"

"They're the past. We all have a past, lovely. It doesn't matter who they were or how many or if you loved or hated every single one of them."

She didn't know whether to laugh or cry or just hang up. Damn him to hell and back for blocking off all the things she'd done with a few short words. If he was trying to mindfuck her, he was doing a hell of a job with it. "I'm not ashamed of what I've done."

"Why should you be?" His voice dropped an octave. "Those choices led you to me, after all."

The *nerve*. "I number you among the mistakes."

"No, you don't." He sounded amused again. *Ass*.

"God, you're completely insufferable." It didn't seem to matter what she said, because he always had a comeback ready. Worse, he sounded like he actually meant them. Carrigan shook her head. What she should do was hang up the phone and block this number. To do anything else was just encouraging him, and that was the last thing she should want.

Right?

"I want to know something."

"What's that?" She really had to work on her mouth getting away from her. Maybe she wouldn't be in this sit-

uation if she had better control. If her father found out…
She glanced at her bedroom door and took a minute to
pad across her room to make sure it was locked. The cell
phone had been a gift from Teague several years ago,
something that she could have without fear of the family
monitoring every call and text.

Though she seriously doubted he'd approve of the
way she was currently using it.

"Why did you come back to the club tonight?"

She froze in the middle of climbing back onto her
massive bed. To answer that was to strip bare a small
part of her. It wasn't anywhere near her center, but it
was still closer than she wanted to let James. *Then hang
up, idiot.* But she didn't. Instead, she answered. Honestly. "Curiosity."

"You know what they say about curiosity and that
damn cat."

Yeah, she did, and that hadn't stopped her. Her days
were numbered as it was—if she didn't use what was left
of her freedom to take chances, she was wasting precious
time. "Are you planning on hurting me, James? Maybe
finishing what your father started?"

"Fuck, no. The world would be a darker place without
you in it." Before she could fully process that comment,
he moved on. "You're not being strictly honest, though.
It was more than curiosity that drove you to sit down
across that table from me."

He was right. It had been a number of things that she
didn't want to give voice to. This conversation was already strange enough—it was almost intimate to sit here
on her bed in the darkness and exchange words with him.
Which meant she had to do what she'd been shoring her-

self up to since the moment she realized he was on the other end of this call. "Good night, James."

"A little too close to the truth, huh?" He sounded like he was smiling. "I can take a hint—on occasion. Good night, lovely."

And then he was gone, leaving her wondering if maybe it really had all been a dream. She went so far as to check her phone to see if she'd actually received a call, and there it was. James's number. Before she could think too closely about what she was doing, Carrigan saved the number under *J* and set her phone aside.

She lay back in bed, going over the conversation even as she cursed herself for doing it. She wasn't sixteen anymore, dancing home from school after the popular boy talked to her. Hell, she hadn't even done that when she *was* sixteen. And James Halloran wasn't some harmless jock. He was a *Halloran*. More than that, he was now the man in charge of all Halloran territory and everyone under their control. One could argue that he was as powerful as her father, though she'd never be stupid enough to say as much where Seamus O'Malley could hear her.

She rolled over and buried her face in her pillow. Sleep. Sleep was what she needed more than anything right now. Maybe in a few hours things would look clearer.

* * *

Cillian stared at the untouched drink in front of him. He could almost taste the whiskey on this tongue. The sensory memory made him want to lick his lips and puke, all at the same time. He hadn't touched the stuff in months—not whiskey, not Guinness, not anything else with a drop of alcohol. Guilt was his new drug, and he excelled at it. If he hadn't been so shit-housed, Aiden wouldn't have decided that they should walk home from the bar that night. If they hadn't walked home, they wouldn't have been vulnerable, and that bastard Halloran wouldn't have had a chance for a drive-by. If he hadn't had the chance, Devlin would still be alive. Cillian had been more concerned with chasing skirts than chasing grades in school, but even he remembered that old logic equation—if A equaled B and B equaled C, then A equaled C.

It meant that Cillian was responsible for Devlin's death.

There was plenty of guilt to go around, or that was what both Teague and Aiden had told him time and time again over the last four months. They could keep believing that if it made them feel better. Cillian knew the truth. He might not have pulled the trigger, but he was the reason they were there in the first place.

He glanced at the table where they'd shared their last drink. The memory of the night was hazy at best—at least before they hit the street—but he vaguely recalled needling Teague about marrying a Sheridan. They'd all been laughing and shooting the shit. For a second, it'd almost been like the good old days. Before Aiden grew up and got serious about his role as heir. Before Teague took it upon himself to save every one of his siblings. Before Cillian recognized the noose around his neck and resolved to live life to the fullest before it yanked tight.

Before.

With Devlin's death, Cillian's entire life devolved into Before and After. He barely recognized the man he was now, the hard son of a bitch he was turning into. A wall of ice had started around his heart, and it only seemed to get thicker with each passing day, freezing him from the inside out.

"Is this seat taken?"

He barely glanced at the man. "Nope." None of the seats at the bar were. There'd been a rowdy group in here earlier, but this close to last call, the place was damn near deserted. Which didn't explain why the hell this guy felt the need to sit directly next to him.

"Buy you a drink?"

It took a second for him to place the accent. Russian, but a little different. Maybe somewhere eastern European, like the Ukraine. He wasn't going to ask—it would just mean opening up a conversation that he didn't want in the first place. Cillian motioned at the full drink in front of him. "I have one."

"You've been staring at it for three hours. It's no longer drinkable." The man leaned forward and caught the bartender's eye. "Two vodka." His accent turned the *v* into a *w*.

Since the man obviously wasn't going anywhere, Cillian finally gave him his full attention. He was in his mid-thirties and had one of the best suits Cillian had ever seen. There was nothing crazy or loud about it, but it managed to scream money nonetheless. It was more than that, though. *Cillian* had expensive suits in his closet. Fuck, he was wearing one right now. But he was conscious of the cloth against his skin and the pull of the fabric every time he moved.

This man wore his suit like he'd been born to it.

Cillian frowned. This didn't feel like a pickup, though. There was no interest in this guy's dark eyes—or at least no interest that had anything to do with sex. In a way, it was a relief—it saved him from having to explain that he didn't swing that way—but it also opened up the question: What the fuck was this guy doing?

When the bartender, Benji, dropped the vodka off, the man lifted his. "I'm Dmitri."

"Cillian." The exchange of names was so automatic, his was out of his mouth before he had a chance to think better of it. Then again, he highly suspected this Dmitri knew exactly who he was. Nothing about this indicated it was anything but planned. The knowledge sat like a burr in the back of his throat. "What do you want?"

"Direct. I like that." Dmitri took his shot without flinching. "We spend too much of our days wasting time making small talk. You and I, well, we know there is nothing guaranteed in this world."

He didn't like this guy lumping them in together, especially when he still had no fucking idea what his game was. "For the second and final time—what do you want?"

Dmitri seemed to be considering him. "It's bad luck to turn down a drink."

"I don't drink anymore." It didn't matter if his hand itched for the glass. He wasn't touching the damn thing. Cillian had been weak too much of his life. It stopped now.

He nodded like Cillian had admitted to something entirely different. "I understand. As for what I want… perhaps I want a friend."

"A friend." He put every ounce of his derision and disbelief into the last word.

"Is that so hard to believe? Men like us don't have many friends. We have pawns and enemies and family—and sometimes those circles even overlap."

That was true enough, but that still didn't answer the question. The small hairs on the back of his neck stood at attention. "Trust issues go with the territory."

Dmitri laughed, a deep rolling sound that instantly made him want to join in. That laugh was a weapon, and one he'd bet the man had honed to perfection. He shook his head. "Let's be frank then, shall we?"

Somehow, he doubted there was anything about this conversation that would be frank. The man talked in circles, and he couldn't shake the feeling that he was giving Cillian enough rope to hang himself with. It didn't matter that he hadn't done anything or agreed to anything to merit the feeling. It was there nonetheless. "Let's."

Dmitri ignored the sarcastic tone. "Your father is keen to marry off your oldest sister."

He knew that. Hell, everyone knew that. "I'm aware."

"I'm one of the men in the running, such as it is." Dmitri shrugged, as nonchalant as if he was talking about the weather. "If I'm going to become family, it wouldn't hurt to get to know her brothers. And you're a kindred soul of sorts."

He blinked. This guy had a set of steel balls to come in here and chat him up like his sister was a sure thing. He sat back. If Carrigan had settled on someone, he would have heard about it. Most likely. He hadn't exactly been playing dutiful O'Malley minion recently. It was possible he'd missed the announcement.

But Cillian didn't think so.

There would be no reason for this guy to come cozy up to him if he thought Carrigan was a sure thing. No, this was something else altogether. He turned the shot glass, eyeing the writing on the side. It was the bar logo, one he'd seen a million times. He watched Dmitri out of the corner of his eye. The man didn't seem impatient or worried or scheming—which meant he was even more dangerous than Cillian had originally guessed. Dmitri was a player in this game of power, and it would be stupid to underestimate him.

So he didn't tell him to get lost. "Sure, I get that." If this man had his eye on Carrigan, Cillian had to figure out what his game was. He didn't seem like the normal power-grabbing sort their father liked to string along by their noses. Dmitri practically *reeked* of power.

Not to mention, Cillian had never seen him before. If he was someone of note in the Boston scene, he would have before now. All of which added up to the conclusion that the man was from out of town.

What the fuck did you invite into our lives, you old goddamn fool?

Dmitri plucked the shot glass out of his hand and downed that vodka, too. "Perhaps next time we'll manage a meal."

It wasn't a question, but he answered it anyway. "For sure." He didn't want to spend another minute in this man's presence. If Devlin were alive, it would just be a matter of a few hours on the computer and they'd know where Dmitri was born, everything about his childhood, and what he ate for breakfast that day. Cillian was learning software and had fledgling hacker skills, but he was nowhere near as good as his little brother had been.

Devlin.

The loss reached up and sucker punched Cillian. He took a careful breath, all too aware of Dmitri's attention on him. He had to get out of here. Showing weakness wasn't acceptable in front of his family, let alone in front of a man who might very well be an enemy. He pushed to his feet, weaving slightly. "I'll see you around." He was aware of the man's gaze on him as he walked around the tables between the bar and the door.

"You can count on it."

It sounded more like a threat than a promise.

CHAPTER SEVEN

Carrigan stared at the list her father had provided, not sure if she should be grateful or insulted. There were six names and phone numbers and...nothing else. No information. No pictures. Nothing. She resisted the urge to crumple the paper and throw it across the room. Barely. "Nothing an Internet search can't fix."

She grabbed her rarely used laptop and brought up the Internet browser. The first name..."Chauncy Chauncer. Wow, your parents must either have been mad at you when you were born or presumptuous beyond measure." With a name like that, there couldn't be that many out there in the world. Thankfully—both for her and any potential Chauncy Chauncers—the one that popped up in half a dozen articles on the first page seemed to be the one on her father's list. She pulled up a picture of him and sighed. He was exactly what his name had led her to expect—middle-aged with a comb-over to do Donald Trump proud.

Gross. She might be staring thirty in the face, but that didn't mean she was willing to spend even a second of thinking about what sex with him would be like. It was bad enough that she'd have to go on one date with him. Carrigan shuddered and moved onto the next name.

Adam Marrow.

This one had a wider field of range. She paged through site after site of different Adams, eventually narrowing it down to two. One was old enough to be her grandfather. The other was in his early forties and, if the news articles were anything to be believed, had apparently been under suspicion for killing his wife a little over a year ago. They hinted at his criminal background and listed his rap sheet. She pinched the bridge of her nose, fighting off a headache. That had to be the one.

So far they were batting a thousand.

Next up, Charles Pope.

Her phone rang and she was so pathetically grateful for the distraction, she answered without checking the ID. "Hello?"

"Were you waiting by the phone for me to call?"

James.

She huffed out a breath, though something in her chest gave a warm lurch. "You again?"

"Don't act like you don't want to hear from me." He laughed, low and intimate. "Unless you don't, in which case I can go..."

"No!" The word was out before she had a chance to take it back. "Even talking to you is better than what I was just doing." Husband shopping. Her stomach twisted in on itself. This was what her life had come to.

"How can I refuse a woman in need?"

"You can't." Except the one time she'd actually needed rescuing, *he'd* been the one to put her in that position. Desperate to think about something else—*anything* else—she said, "What are you wearing?"

A pause, as if she'd shocked him. "You're hitting on me."

"Are you complaining?" She twisted around in her chair and stared into the mirror on the wall across from her. When he didn't immediately respond, she kept going. The only alternative was to back down, and Carrigan was so goddamn tired of backing down. The only reason she kept taking James's calls was because of the distraction he offered her. If he wasn't going to play, there was no reason for her to stay on the phone.

She really wanted him to stay on the phone. "Shy? That's okay, I'll go first. I'm wearing a thin white tank top and a pair of black panties." She was a liar, but it would take all of five seconds to make it the truth.

"Lovely, you're testing me." His voice gained an edge.

Good. At least someone was feeling as out of control as she was. "I suppose you'd like photographic proof." She stood and shimmied out of her long skirt, and then pinned the phone between her ear and shoulder while she unhooked her bra and took it off. "Hold, please."

Ignoring his cursing, she adjusted her angle so he would have to be blind to miss the faint outline of her nipples against the fabric of her tank top, and snapped a picture. She knew she was playing with fire. Good lord, of course she knew. But she wasn't about to stop. She grinned as she sent the picture.

Carrigan put the phone back to her ear in time to hear his sharp inhale. "Your turn." She held her breath, waiting to see if he'd actually do it. Receiving pictures was one thing. Putting them out in the world was entirely another. Really, she shouldn't have taken the risk in the first place. There was no telling what he would do with them—they might show up on the Internet. Then who would want to marry her?

Funny, but the idea of countless men checking out her rack didn't bother her nearly as much if it meant she dodged the marriage bullet. The shame on her family might be enough that her father would send her away permanently. She'd like to spend some time in New York or LA or even New Orleans. Maybe Rome or Paris or Tokyo. The world was so damn big and she'd only seen a little slice of it.

Her phone beeped, pulling her out of her thoughts. She glanced at the picture he'd sent and started to shake. *Oh my God.* James was shirtless, wearing only those goddamn jeans she couldn't seem to get enough of. And they were unbuttoned—a clear invitation if she ever saw one. An invitation she desperately wanted to accept. "Damn, James. Somebody taught you how to selfie."

"Maybe I'm a natural." His voice was little more than a growl. "You started this, lovely. Tell me what's next."

The strange mix of command and handing her the reins got her head back in the game. She walked over to her bed and climbed onto it, trying to ignore the trembling in her legs. She could be in charge. She *wanted* to be. "I'm lying on my bed."

"What color are the sheets?"

The question seemed to carry far more import than it should. "White."

"They don't suit you. Red is your color. Go on." He sounded so damn imperial, as if he actually knew her. He didn't. No one did, really. She wore so many masks, sometimes she worried she'd forget the woman at the center of them all.

But this time he was right. She would have chosen red for herself.

Carrigan pushed the thought away and focused on the now. "You talk too much."

"My mistake." He didn't sound the least bit sorry. *Good.* She wasn't, either. "How do you want it, lovely? Rough, I'd bet. You're not fucking breakable, and I think you love to be reminded of that fact." Something rustled on his end of the line. "Close your eyes."

She obeyed without thinking, and then instantly snapped them open. "I thought I was in charge."

"You let me know if I get something wrong." His laugh told her how unlikely he found the possibility. "Close your eyes."

"Fine. Fine." Shutting out the sight of her room narrowed her world down to his voice in her ear, and it was all too easy to imagine him here with her, a single breath away from touching her. Any second now he'd reach out and haul her against him.

"I'd drag you to the edge of that bed and spread those sweet thighs. Spread your thighs, lovely." Once again, she obeyed without thought. James hissed out a breath. "I like the picture you'd make, those amazing breasts straining against that pathetic excuse of a tank top, and those tiny panties. I want to rip the fucking things off. But not yet."

She was picturing it, too. Picturing him standing over her, with *that* look in his blue eyes—the look that made her feel possessed...owned. Like he'd never get enough of her and he never wanted to. He'd looked at her the same way on that night four months ago, when he'd been buried inside her. She shivered at the thought, her breath catching in her throat, her nipples pebbling.

"Yeah, I thought you'd like that. But a pussy like yours...it's meant to be worshipped. You'd take me to my knees, ready to do damn near anything to hear that sweet little whimper you make when you come. Touch yourself, lovely. Slowly. Trace a single finger over that goddamn lace. Are you wet for me?"

Her panties were soaked. Carrigan moaned as she circled her clit through the wet fabric. "James, God, I'm so wet." She hesitated, desire dragging words from her mouth she had no intention of letting free. "For you. I'm wet for you."

"And needy. I hear it in your voice." It was in his voice, too.

They were poised on the edge of something she had the sudden fear she couldn't take back. It was silly—they were miles away from each other, connected only by a phone call. She had control. And if she could feel it slipping through her fingers...well, James never had to know. "Are you touching yourself?"

"Lovely, I'm so hard, it won't take much to get me there."

She slipped her hand into her panties, stroking herself. "I'm close, James." Every time she said his name, he made a sound that was almost pained. She liked it. She liked it a lot. "Come with me."

"Circle your clit, just how you like it." He cursed long and hard, but she heard a zipper being dragged down.

She obeyed, moaning, the sounds of his desire only stroking hers higher. "You're close."

Another curse. "Come for me, lovely. I want to hear that whimper."

She pressed down on her clit as her body spasmed, that horribly weak and needy sound coming out of her mouth despite her best effort to keep it inside. She stroked herself twice more, unable to resist the delicious aftershocks of pleasure, and then dragged her hand out of her panties. "Shit."

James laughed, the sound free of the darkness he seemed to carry around inside himself. "Yeah, that about sums it up."

She opened her eyes and stared at her ceiling, reality crashing over her. Whatever came next, she didn't want it. James wasn't on the list. He was so off-limits, it wasn't even funny. He was the only man she could be found with that might make her father actually hurt her.

And she wanted him more than she'd ever wanted a man before.

"I have to go."

"Wait—"

She hung up before he could finish the sentence, before he could say something that would give her the excuse she desperately wanted to curl up around her phone and cling to the lifeline of his rough voice. She couldn't afford the weakness and, even more, she couldn't afford for him to realize he *was* a weakness.

Though if he didn't know that after this conversation, he was an idiot.

James Halloran might be many things, but stupid wasn't one of them.

Damn it.

* * *

James stepped into the shower, his mind whirling. He didn't make a habit of having phone sex—why go for a substitute when you could have the real thing?—but...fuck. With Carrigan that had been hot as hell. His nerve endings were still snapping with the strength of that orgasm, and he wanted more.

Now.

He ducked his head under the spray and scrubbed a hand over his face. He'd known she wanted him, but knowing in theory was one thing—hearing her coming as a result of what he was saying was totally another. Their having sex again had moved from the "if" category to the "when."

She was spooked. He got that. He was feeling pretty goddamn spooked himself. So he'd give them both time. She had to come to him now. That was the only way this thing would play out with both of them satisfied. James washed his hair, pointedly ignoring the little voice inside him that muttered that he'd never be satisfied with a piece of Carrigan as a replacement for *all* of her. "All of her" wasn't on the table. Even if it was, there were their families to consider.

The thought of his family was enough to wash away the last of the feel-good he had going. He needed to deal with Ricky, sooner rather than later. Right now his brother was cooling his heels in the room in the basement designed to hold people the Hallorans didn't want walking off the property without permission.

Really, both Callista and Carrigan should have been in that room when they were here. It would have stopped their escape before it started. And one of them—if not both—would have died. Had he known as soon as he hauled Carrigan up to his room that she'd find a way to escape? What if he hadn't given her the chance? What if he'd gone with the normal protocol?

He shook his head. It was pointless to focus on the past and play the what-if game. He had plenty of problems in the here and now to focus on. So he forced himself to close out the part of his mind that wanted to revel in the recent conversation with Carrigan. That lighthearted feeling that he hadn't been sure he was still capable of had no place here. Not now.

Ten minutes later, he was toweled off and dressed and heading downstairs. Michael met him at the landing on the main floor. "He's asking for you, boss." He made a face. "Demanding, more like."

"I'll take care of it."

Michael didn't immediately move out of the way. "With all due respect, I'm going with you." He hesitated, and then charged on. "That kid is a rabid dog. He'll go for your throat without a thought and deal with the consequences later."

James wanted to argue, to say he was wrong, that he and Ricky were family. But family wasn't the loving and cozy heartwarming made-for-TV movie that so many people believed. It was the poison in his veins that he could never bleed out, and the weight around his neck, dragging him into the deep.

So he nodded and let Michael follow him into the basement. It felt darker here, danker, as if it really was a dungeon. It used to be his old man's favorite part of the house before his arthritis made navigating the basement stairs impossible. After that, rather than admit weakness, he just burrowed into his office and, for all intents and purposes, never came back out again.

I wonder if he's warm enough in prison.

James set the thought aside. If Victor hadn't gone off the goddamn deep end and decided to declare war on the O'Malleys *and* Sheridans over a stupid insult, he wouldn't be behind bars right now. Discretion was the name of the game. Staying below the FBI's notice. He snorted. Those bastards had too much time on their hands. They noticed everything. But up until four months ago, they hadn't bothered to swat the fly that was the Halloran family. Victor was the reason that had all changed.

Now Ricky had taken it into his fool head to follow in their old man's footsteps. James stopped outside the door and took a breath, steeling himself for what came next. He could scream to the moon that he didn't want this— didn't want to have to take these steps—but it changed nothing. Ricky was a threat—worse, he was a stupid threat.

That was unforgivable.

James walked into the room, aware of Michael following him, and waited for the door to shut behind them. Ricky was zip-tied to a chair bolted down in the middle of the room. The boys had done a good job, and he didn't have any bruises visible. He turned his head and spit on the ground at James's feet. "Bastard."

"You directly disobeyed an order."

"It was a shitty order." Ricky's blue eyes, the one thing all the members of their family shared, glittered in hate. "Bringing in more girls is good for business."

It didn't matter if it was or not. That wasn't the point. The point was his dumb-ass brother was putting himself and everyone around him in danger. And no matter how potentially profitable it was, they were *out* of the fucking slave trade—for good. "Except it's not. If you bothered to do some fucking research before you charged blindly ahead, you'd know that business is up since I disbanded the flesh trade."

Ricky spit again. "Your stomach's just too weak for what needs to be done."

That wasn't his problem and they both knew it. "What else have you been doing?"

"Nothing."

Damn it, he should have played this better. James crossed his arms over his chest, hating how his brother flinched at the sudden movement. He'd tried with Ricky. He'd tried reasoning with him. He'd tried restricting him. He'd even gone so far as to take a page out of their father's book and beat the shit out of him. Nothing worked. If there was some magical way to get through to his brother, he sure as hell didn't know what it was. Hitting Ricky might feel satisfying in the moment, but it wouldn't change anything—anything except pushing James closer to monster territory. "You'll stay down here until I figure out what to do with you."

Ricky's head snapped up. "What the fuck?"

"You heard me." He turned, giving his brother the insult of his back. "And if I hear about you taking a woman without permission again, I'll kill you myself." He walked out of the room to Ricky's cursing and locked the door behind him. James passed the key to Michael. "He gets a meal a day. That's it."

"Sure thing." Michael slipped the key into his pocket. "How long you going to keep him down here?"

"As long as it takes."

CHAPTER EIGHT

Carrigan chose her clothing with care. She always did—too much of her life depended on other people's perceptions of her—but tonight was especially important. Tonight she was going out with the poorly named Chauncy Chauncer. Short of a miracle, she didn't expect to see him again, but she still had an image to uphold.

An image she despised.

She grabbed a long dress from the back of her closet. It was—naturally—white, and the only thing daring about it was the square neckline that allowed a little cleavage. The rest of it would cover her from wrists to ankles—a straitjacket of her own choosing. She kept her makeup light, and styled her hair in careful waves.

Stepping back from the vanity, she sighed. "I look like a virgin sacrifice." The first part was laughable. The latter was all too accurate.

She stopped in front of her dresser, her hand going

to the drawer where she'd stashed James's album. She hadn't touched it since she got back into Boston. After running into him, and then talking to him...and then letting him command her into an orgasm over the phone, it felt like a betrayal to dig through his personal property.

Besides, she'd already practically memorized its contents.

There was only one person the blond woman in the old photos could be—the three boys of varying ages she always had her arms around only confirmed it. James's mother. Carrigan didn't know much about her beyond that she was dead and had been for years, but the way the woman looked at her sons...there was love there. A whole hell of a lot.

And she'd taken the reminder of that love from him.

She should give it back. It was the right thing to do. But if she did, there was no guarantee that he wouldn't live up to his word and leave her alone. *That*, she didn't want. *Maybe I'll just hang on to it for a few more days. It's safe enough here. I'll give it back. Eventually.*

Satisfied, she glanced at the clock on the nightstand and confirmed that she was almost late. There was nothing left to do that she could pretend wasn't stalling. *Damn it.* She slipped on her heels and headed downstairs. As expected, her father waited at the front door. He took her appearance in with a single sweep of his gaze. "Excellent." He gifted her with one of his rare smiles.

That smile used to be something she strove for. When she was a kid, she'd lived for her father's approval. She'd bent over backward with piano lessons and good grades and anything that she thought would impress him to get that smile. Now? Now she saw it for what it was—his approval of having a possession polished up to show off for a peer. He didn't see her as a real person. He never had. If she'd been a son...

Well, she'd stopped wishing for that right around the time she accepted that she'd never be enough for Seamus O'Malley, no matter how *good* she was. It didn't matter how good her grades were in college or how worthy her ideas for the family were. All that mattered was her value as a trading piece with his allies—and her ability to give them heirs.

She stopped at the bottom of the stairs, feeling like a prize cow he was about to put on the market. The comparison made her stomach turn over, because it wasn't too far from reality. Her father finally nodded. "The car's waiting outside."

Carrigan waited a half second before she realized he wasn't going to say anything else. Disappointment soured her stomach, made worse because she knew better than to expect anything else. Twenty-eight years, and hope still got the better of her on occasion. Determined not to let anything show on her face, she walked out of the house and down the steps to the waiting car. Liam held the door for her, and she pretended she didn't see the pity in his eyes.

The ride was far too short for her peace of mind, and her nerves were still raw when they pulled up in front of La Coupole. It was a French restaurant that got its kicks from mimicking its famous cousin in Paris. She'd never been there before, mostly because the whole thing gave off a stink of new money, and Carrigan had better things to do with her limited free time than have men and women parading around like peacocks, each determined to prove that he really deserved to be in Boston's upper crust. Chauncy obviously numbered himself among them, which wasn't giving her high hopes for the meal.

One meal. You can do one meal.

She let Liam help her out of the car and stepped onto the sidewalk. A deep breath did nothing to shore up her failing courage. The whole thing was suddenly so much more *real*. The truth that she'd been fighting off since her father handed her a list of names hit her in the face. He was really selling her off in marriage, even though he'd have to be blind, deaf, and dumb not to see the value she could bring to their family and its various businesses. He didn't care that being forced into this would kill a part of her she'd barely let off the leash, didn't care about anything but the bottom line. Carrigan had thought herself beyond the point of being able to be hurt by her father and his ambitions.

She was wrong.

"Miss O'Malley?" She did her best to wipe any expression off her face, but something had to show through because Liam looked distinctly more uncomfortable when she faced him. He cleared his throat. "If you want to go somewhere after this, I'll fudge the times for you."

There it was again. Even her father's muscle pitied her. She wanted to throw his pity back in his face, to insist that she was *fine*, that she was totally in control of her life. *Lies*. So many lies. Worst of all, she couldn't afford to do that—not when Liam was offering her an unexpected escape.

Just get through the dinner.

She managed a smile. "Thank you."

He opened his mouth like he was about to say something, and then reconsidered and strode around the car to climb behind the driver's seat. With nothing left to keep her from the restaurant, she walked inside. The heat slapped her in the face as soon as she made it through the door, just this side of sweltering. She shrugged out of her coat and handed it to the hostess hovering just out of reach. "I'm meeting—"

"Mr. Chauncer. Yes, we know. Please, follow me." She turned without another word and marched deeper into the building, leaving Carrigan to follow her or be left behind. She was forced to hurry to keep up, nearly tripping over her stupidly long dress in the process. The hostess wove through tables, finally stopping in front of one in the middle of the room. Carrigan would have preferred something a little more private. As it was, the place was packed even for a Saturday night and her skin twitched at the feel of people's eyes on her, real or imagined.

To distract herself, she focused on the man sitting at the table. He grinned at her like he'd just won the lottery, revealing teeth that were too white and straight to be real. It took her a full five seconds to realize he wasn't going to stand or try to get her chair. Every single man in her family would have done it, from her father down to...

No, she wasn't thinking about Devlin right now. She needed to be strong and have her walls firmly in place in order to deal with this prospective husband.

Carrigan sank into the seat across from him...and he still didn't say anything. To buy herself time, she glanced at the menu. She wasn't opposed to driving the conversation, but this was passing strange and shooting straight into Looking-Glass territory.

A waiter appeared at her elbow, and she set the menu down. Before she could speak, Chauncy cut in. "She'll have a Riesling, and I'll have scotch—the most expensive you have."

She barely tolerated wine as it was, and she despised white wine. Especially *sweet* white wine. The waiter nodded and moved off, and Chauncy took that as his cue to actually speak *to* her. "You're just as beautiful as your father promised. A little thicker than I'd like, but there are personal trainers for that kind of thing."

Carrigan stared, too shocked to be pissed. He was no prize, his skin too orangey from excessive tanning, his teeth too perfect, his comb-over not doing a single thing to hide the fact he was balding. He was carting around a thick middle that was more barrel than six-pack, and he was going to criticize *her* body? She took a sip of water, more to buy herself time than because she was thirsty. What was she supposed to say? Half a dozen careful responses flitted through her mind, but what came out of her mouth wasn't anywhere near polite. "With all due respect, I don't know if I'd be willing to take personal trainer recommendations from you."

He turned a mottled shade of red. "You have a mouth on you." But then he smiled. "Good. I like them spirited."

Good lord, she could actually feel her blood pressure rising by the second. She wasn't a horse to be broken. The waiter appeared with their drinks, and she gulped hers down, doing her best to ignore the sticky sweetness clinging to the back of her tongue. "So, Chauncy, you invest in real estate?" Maybe if she could get him talking about himself, he'd stop saying things that made the hair on her arms stand on end.

"Yep. Us Chauncers have an eye for a good investment, especially when there's land attached to it." He chuckled like he'd made a witty joke. "Don't you worry your pretty head, my dear—I have more than enough money to keep you decked out in diamonds and whatever you could possibly want."

Carrigan finished her wine and resigned herself to a hellish evening. Once Chauncy got talking, he didn't shut up. Part of her was grateful she wasn't expected to do more than make inquiring and agreeing noises when he paused for breath, but the misogynistic comments he kept tossing her way made it hard to keep the bland expression on her face. By the time he told the waiter that no one at their table *needed* dessert, she was ready to throw her drink in his face. Hell, she would have, but the Riesling had stopped tasting like shit two glasses ago, and she was loath to waste good alcohol on a pathetic excuse for a man like Chauncy.

She pushed to her feet after he paid the bill, doing her best to ignore the head rush that accompanied the movement—and Chauncy's hand touching the small of her back. When James did that, it made her want to arch into his touch like a cat demanding to be stroked. With Chauncy, all she wanted was a bleach bath. They made their way back to the entrance, and she used the excuse of putting on her coat to create some distance between them.

He'd apparently decided he approved of her, though, because he was hot on her heels when she hit the door. "Carrigan."

She gritted her teeth and turned, an unforgivably weak gasp flying from her lips when he grabbed her arm and pulled her close. She smelled the scotch on his breath a second before he kissed her. She went completely still, her mind buzzing with white noise at how *wrong* this was. He forced his tongue into her mouth, licking her teeth.

That snapped Carrigan out of it. She pushed on his shoulders, trying to get some distance between them. Despite being on the soft side, Chauncy held her against him with apparent ease. *Stop panicking and think, damn it*. She willed her body to go soft, letting him back her against the wall.

Then she kneed him in the balls as hard as she could.

He went down like a chopped tree, making a high-pitched noise that was far more satisfying than it should have been. She gasped out a breath of air that felt a thousand times fresher than it had been when she walked out onto the sidewalk. This piece of shit thought he could put his hands on her? How many women had he tried this with before? She went cold at the thought. Not every woman was capable of defending herself, especially against a large man. *Bastard*. She used her toe to tip him onto his back and glared down. "I'm only going to say this once, you piece of shit. You touch me—or any other unwilling woman—again, and I'll take great pleasure in slitting your throat while you sleep." She stepped over his writhing body and looked up to find Liam in the middle of running toward her. "I have it taken care of."

He ran a hand over his short dark hair. "I can see that."

Thank God, because she was doing everything in her power to hold it together. She lifted her chin. "Shall we?"

Liam jumped to it, ushering her to the car. Only when he put it in drive did she finally lean back against the seat and give in to the shakes. She'd been in shitty positions before, but this seemed so much worse. Maybe it was because of her circumstances. It didn't really matter. All that *did* matter was scrubbing away the memory of his hands on her body and his tongue in her mouth as quickly as humanly possible.

Before she could think too much into it, she reached for her phone. It barely rang once when James answered. "Did you miss me, lovely?"

She knew she should play coy and keep the minuscule distance between them from shrinking any further, but she just didn't have it in her tonight. "I need you."

* * *

James had thought he'd imagined the fear in Carrigan's voice when she called. If she was in actual trouble, she sure as hell wasn't going to call *him*—no matter how much he liked the idea of being the one to swoop in and save her from her problems. He liked the idea too much.

But then she walked into the quiet little pub where he was waiting, and he realized he hadn't been wrong the first time. There were faint bruises beneath her eyes, like she'd been sleeping even less than he had, and she held herself like a woman who'd been beaten for the first time. He was on his feet before he made a conscious decision to move. "Who hurt you?"

"No one."

"Don't play that martyr bullshit with me, Carrigan. Who the fuck put that look on your face?" She'd gone through hell and back because of *him* and it hadn't put that haunted expression in her green eyes. He clenched his fists, trying and failing to get control of his temper. She wasn't his to protect. Hell, even if she was, he had a pretty shitty track record of keeping people in his care safe. There was no reason why she'd be any different.

Except that he wanted her to be different.

She brushed past him, drawing his attention to her clothing. "What the hell are you wearing?"

Carrigan spun and glared. "I don't need your shit right now."

"You called me, lovely, so my shit is exactly what you're going to get." She looked like an angel—one that had had its wings clipped. He wasn't sure what gave him that impression, but the long white dress was opposite of everything he'd found the woman to be in the short time they'd known each other. She was wild and impulsive and free. She wasn't...this virginal almost-bride. He didn't like the change. He didn't like it one bit. "Sit your ass down. I'll get us drinks, and then you're telling me what the fuck is going on."

"Hold your breath on that."

He wouldn't have to. She might be prickly as all getout, but she wanted to talk. She wouldn't have called him otherwise. The bartender met him halfway, a nervous little mouse of a guy. James made an effort to speak softly because the man looked half a second from pissing himself. "Whiskey for me. Dirty martini for the lady."

"Yes, sir, right away, sir."

He'd known there was a decent chance he'd be recognized here on the outskirts of Halloran territory, but short of dragging Carrigan out of Boston, there weren't many options. So James slipped the guy a few hundred bucks. "For your discretion." He let a little threat into his voice.

"Of course."

Satisfied that the bartender wouldn't go telling tales, he made his way back to where Carrigan had picked a booth. Ignoring the empty side, he slid in next to her. "What's going on?"

She didn't look up. "What makes you think something's going on?"

"How about because you won't meet my eyes for the first time since we met? Or this...I don't even know what to call this getup." He tugged on the white fabric pooled on the booth seat between them.

Her green eyes flashed, a welcome show of anger. "There's nothing wrong with the way I dress."

"You're right. This isn't you. This is some scared virgin who's looking for her white knight. If I've learned anything from our time together, it's that you'd have no problem slaying dragons on your own."

Her mouth formed a little O of surprise, but she recovered quickly enough. "You don't know me."

"Not nearly as well as I want to, no. But you don't grow up the way we did without learning to read a person." The bartender appeared with their drinks, and James waited for him to scurry away before he spoke again. "Talk to me. I can't help you if I don't know what's wrong."

"No one can help me." She didn't say it like it upset her—more like it was a truth of her life that she'd come to terms with years ago. It made his chest ache. Carrigan took a long drink of her martini. "I'm almost thirty."

He blinked. "What's that got to do with anything?"

"Biology, my dear Watson. How in God's name can I pop out half a dozen kids if I'm past the age of safely being able to do so."

There was so much wrong with what she just said that he didn't know where to start. So James just went with the first thing he thought of. "Do you want kids?"

She froze with her drink halfway to her mouth and slowly set it back down. "You know, I don't think anyone's ever asked me that before."

The raw pain in her voice made him want to comfort her, but that was one skill James had never learned. Maybe if his mother had lived...but there was no room in this world for *what if* and *maybe*. So he did the one thing that he knew how to do. The single thing guaranteed to distract her.

He kissed her.

Carrigan went rigid for half a second, but he waited, his lips on hers, and let her choose. That hesitation was all it took for her to melt, turning to fire in his arms. He wanted to haul her against him, to let this feeling consume him until none of the bullshit mattered anymore. Right now, in this moment, there was only her. They could be the last two people in the world for all he gave a fuck. Hell, part of him hoped they were. As her tongue stroked his, a small, treacherous thought wormed into his brain and took root.

With this woman by my side, I'd be content to let the rest of the world burn.

CHAPTER NINE

Yes, this, this is what I need. Carrigan twined her arms around James's neck, trying to get closer. Every second he spent kissing her, the memory of Chauncy's wormy lips on hers moved a little farther away. She pulled back enough to say, "Touch me."

For a second, she thought he might tell her no, but then he shifted, lifting her into his lap and scooting closer to the wall. To the shadows. His big body dwarfed hers, his arms easily cradling her against his chest. The position was all wrong to ease the aching between her thighs, but it would do. For now.

She kissed him again, needing the escape it seemed only he could give her. He sank his hands into her hair, tipping her head back and devouring her mouth as if it was the best thing he'd ever tasted. She could feel him hard beneath her ass, and she rolled her hips, wishing this booth was somewhere more private.

He must have been thinking the same thing, because he rested his forehead against hers. "As much as I'm enjoying this, lovely, I'm not about to fuck you in this booth, and if we don't stop, that's exactly what's going to happen."

That didn't sound like a bad thing, which just proved that she was out of her damn mind. She shivered, her hands compulsively clenching his hair. He closed his eyes and growled, so she did it again. "Carrigan—"

"Take me somewhere." Anywhere, just as long as it meant she didn't have to come back down from the contact high his mouth gave her. Reality could wait. Right now she wanted an escape more than she wanted anything else in this world.

Again, there was that hesitation, like he thought he should refuse her. She'd never taken James for a gentleman, but that was the feeling she got when he looked at her with those pale blue eyes that were like the hottest fire. He caught her chin in a painless, unforgiving grip. "I'll give you what you want, what we both want— on one condition. You tell me what the fuck happened tonight."

She didn't want to. He'd chased the memory away, and she didn't want to do anything to bring it back to the forefront of her mind. And definitely not to confess it to this man.

But who else could she tell? Teague? If he knew, it'd only make his guilt worse. Or he'd decide to put everything he'd worked so hard for in jeopardy by doing something unforgivable to Chauncy. Not unforgivable as far as she was concerned—the man deserved a good beating—but there were consequences. There were *al-*

ways consequences. And if she told Sloan…No, it wasn't even an option. Her sister already looked like a woman with one foot in the grave. Carrigan refused to be the thing that pushed her over the edge.

James alone didn't have a horse in this race. He might be too arrogant for his own good, but he was a Halloran. When it came right down to it, they'd always be on opposite sides of the line in the sand.

Not to mention the carrot he dangled in front of her was one she'd commit unmentionable sins to get. "Okay, fine."

He hauled her out of the booth and tossed a handful of cash on the table. "Let's go." He took her hand and led the way through the back door. In the alley, he paused. "You have a man with you?"

It took a second for his words to penetrate. "Right. Liam." She dug her phone out of her purse and typed out a quick text. The bodyguard wouldn't be happy, but there wasn't much he could do. And, really, he was rarely happy with the stunts she pulled.

They stopped in front of a cherry red muscle car. She raised her eyebrows, but there wasn't much to say. It fit James perfectly, all coiled strength beneath a rough exterior, ready to unleash at a moment's notice. He held the door for her and she slipped into the passenger seat. "What would I have to do to get you to let me drive this thing?"

His unexpected grin sent her heart hurtling into her stomach. "For you, lovely? All you have to do is ask. Scoot." He tossed her the keys and nodded to the driver's seat.

That was all the encouragement she needed. Carrigan

hauled her dress up to her thighs and hopped the gearshift to settle behind the wheel. She turned over the engine, a stupid smile spreading over her face at the responding roar it gave.

"You know how to drive a stick?"

"Yeah." Her oldest brother, Aiden, had taught her when she turned sixteen. She hadn't had a chance to use the skill much in the intervening years, but it was like riding a bike. She hoped.

"Then take her down 93 south and open her up."

This car had the feel of something well loved and completely pampered. She didn't get the feeling he let many people behind the wheel...and he was letting her. Carrigan glanced over to find him watching her, an unreadable expression on his face. Like he didn't know what to think of her. Considering she didn't know what the hell she thought of him, she should find it comforting.

She threw the car into gear and pulled onto the street. It took twenty minutes to get out of Boston, and she kept expecting James to start his interrogation. To be perfectly honest, she would have told him damn near anything he wanted as long as he let her drive this thing. Behind the wheel she felt totally and completely in control, like she could do anything she set her mind to. The only downside was that it was too cold to roll down the windows and really *feel* how fast they were going.

The comfortable silence continued as she drove south, getting off 93 and working her way by memory through the smaller highways. It was only when she turned into the access road that led into World's End park that James spoke. "Are you planning on taking me out here and murdering me?"

She laughed. "Just your virtue."

"Thank fucking Christ for that." But he didn't immediately jump her when she put the car into park and turned off the engine.

The darkness felt more absolute here, as if they were the only two people left in the world. "This park used to scare me." She wasn't sure where the words came from, but she kept talking. "My family isn't big on camping—as you can imagine—but my brothers dragged me out here when we were in high school. Nothing particularly traumatic happened, but being surrounded by trees with no noise from civilization still makes my skin crawl."

"Totally makes sense why you brought us out here, then."

She glanced at him, but the lack of light made his expression indecipherable. It was easier to talk to him this way, without those blue eyes that seemed to take in too much drilling into her. Strangely enough, a perverse part of her missed them all the same. "The stars seem brighter out here." She opened her door and climbed into the night. The cold hit her hard enough to make her shiver, but there was something about it that was almost as cleansing as James's kiss. She inhaled deeply, letting it scour away the last traces of her date.

James followed, meeting her at the front of the car and leaning on the hood. He tilted his head back, revealing a throat she wanted to nibble on. "They're bright." Without looking at her, he snagged her wrist and towed her closer. The warmth of the engine battled the cold that made her breath ghost in front of her. The circles he traced on the sensitive skin of her wrist only heated her further. "Now, lovely."

She looked at the stars because they were easier to face than the man next to her. "My father gave me a list of men he decided were eligible. Tonight was my first date." She shuddered at the memories pushing against her. It didn't make any sense. Nothing particularly horrible had happened. She'd had unwanted men kiss her before, had been forced to pull similar moves, and it had never brought up the core-deep revulsion currently leaving an acrid taste in the back of her throat. She'd never lost it like she almost did tonight. Not once. "He got handsy. I was forced to defend myself, though Liam would have taken care of him if I hadn't been able to." But she'd needed to be the one to do it. She was so goddamn tired of being forced to rely on the men in her life for every little thing.

This, at least, she'd been able to do for herself.

James was so tense beside her, he seemed about to erupt into violence at the drop of a hat. She braced herself for him to demand the name of the man who touched her without permission, or to throw out threats that he may or may not even plan on following through with.

But he surprised her again. "Did you hurt him?"

She sure as hell hoped so. "He'll be singing soprano for a few hours, at least."

"Good." And that was that. His thumb continued those circles that both soothed and made her skin prickle.

She waited, but he didn't seem inclined to ask any more questions. The man never stopped surprising her. She wasn't sure what she thought about that. Letting the subject drop was fine with her, though, because she was more interested in the other half of their bargain than she was with treading over things she couldn't change and would rather not think about. "Make me forget for a while, James. Please."

* * *

How could he resist her?

James couldn't. He might be seeing red and determined to figure out who the fuck "got handsy" with her so he could go rip the man to pieces, but the desire for her undercut all that. She needed him. That's why he was here tonight, and that was a gift so priceless, he knew beyond a shadow of a doubt he didn't deserve it.

Because there was no way he wouldn't fuck this up.

He pulled her into his arms and kissed her with everything he had. She smelled like summer, even in late November, a reminder that this wasn't forever and he'd be a damn fool to waste a single second. He ran a hand down her spine, fitting her against him, letting her feel exactly how much he wanted her.

Christ, he wanted her.

She arched against him, soft in all the ways he was hard, offering herself to whatever he had in mind. To have this woman, who was all fiery passion and strength, yield to him, was enough to make his head spin. It made him want to be a better man, a man who might deserve such a woman. It was a pipe dream, a stupid fucking thought, but he couldn't shake it.

James backed them around his car and yanked open the passenger seat. He'd never been so happy that he'd gone with a '70 Chevelle rather than the '67 Camaro he'd had his eye on all those years ago. He guided her into the backseat and followed her in. It wasn't enough space, but with the residual heat from their drive down here, it was better than the cold outside the car.

He kissed her again, but he didn't stop at her mouth. Instead, he worked his way over her neck, pausing there to savor the softness of her skin as she quivered against him. A quick yank on the shoulders of her dress exposed her bra, a sheer lace thing that was completely at odds with the rest of her getup. *This* was the true Carrigan, the woman who loved pretty things and dressed herself to the nines. "Get this fucking thing off." He pulled again, sliding it down her body. She lifted her hips to help him, jerking her arms out of the dress and kicking it off.

Then there was only her, a few scraps of cloth all that were between his hands and mouth, and her body. "Christ, lovely." Faced with the fact this was actually happening was like hitting a brick wall. He wanted her. Fuck, he wanted her so much it was everything he could do not to rip those panties from her body and fall on her like a starving animal. The last time—the only time— he'd surrounded himself with her had been the closest he'd come to losing himself.

But this wasn't about him.

He'd promised to help her forget, and going from zero to sixty in five seconds flat wasn't going to cut it. James blew out a long breath, fighting for control. He'd barely touched her and he was teetering on the edge. There had to be a better way to go about this, because he didn't trust himself.

The answer hit him right between the eyes. He sat back, shifting them around so she lay on the seat and he took the space between her spread thighs. There wasn't a ton of room, but that hand's width of space between their bodies would have to be enough. She lifted her head, looking down her body at him. He couldn't see her face clearly, but the flash of her green eyes was enough. His cock was so hard, it was a wonder he could string two thoughts together. "Take your bra off."

She opened her mouth, and then seemed to reconsider. "James—"

"We're doing this my way or not at all. Choose."

"Fine," she snapped. But her movements were slow and steady as she arched her back and reached beneath herself to unhook her bra. Then she lifted her arms and pulled it off slowly, giving him a tease before she finally dropped it onto the floorboard.

His heart slammed in his chest, need demanding he reach for her this fucking instant. He clenched his fists. "Now the panties."

"Bossy." She lifted her hips and brought her legs together to slip the fabric off. Then she resumed her position, leaving herself completely open to him. "Any more commands?"

"Yeah." He licked his lips. "Touch yourself like you did the other night."

This time there was no hesitation. She slid her hands up her sides to cup her full breasts, toying with her nipples until they were puckered and practically begging for his mouth. One hand stayed there, fingers still busy, while the other traveled down the center of her stomach, teasing them both, before stopping just above her pussy. "You like to watch."

It wasn't something he'd indulged in often. He usually

just saw what he wanted and took it. There were plenty of women willing to throw themselves at him over the years, but none that he'd ever done more than fuck. This thing with Carrigan was different. He wanted to crawl inside her mind the same way he wanted her body. It was complicated and uncomfortable, and he sure as fuck didn't want to talk about it right now. "One finger, lovely. Trace that sensitive little clit of yours."

She obeyed, making that sexy whimper at the first contact, and he couldn't contain it any longer. He slid his hands up her legs, starting at her ankles, bracketing the fine bones with his hands, and then moved up her calves to stop halfway up her thighs. He spread her further, wishing the light was better so he could see every single detail. "Show me how you like it."

"Taking notes?" Her voice was breathy as her finger kept up its circling movement.

He massaged her thighs, enjoying the way her muscles played beneath her skin and her breath caught in her throat. "No point in doing something if you don't do it well. Now, lovely. I want to see you finger fuck yourself."

This time there was no hesitation. She slipped first one finger and then two into herself. He could *feel* her gaze on him, though he couldn't tear his eyes off the sight of what she was doing with her hands. "Slow and steady."

"No." Her back arched, and her other hand joined the one between her legs, starting up where it'd left off on her clit. "I want it hard. Rough. More."

He grabbed her wrist. "Don't forget who's in charge." His hand moved like it had a mind of its own, tracing over her soft skin and following the line of her fingers to her pussy. He allowed her to pump two more times, his hand shadowing hers, and when she slipped hers away, his stayed. *Take your goddamn hands off her while you still can.*

But he didn't.

Instead, he mirrored her circles around her clit, damn near groaning when she whimpered again. "Yes, James. Just like that. Please don't stop touching me."

He didn't stop. He needed to hear her make that whimpering sound again because of *him*. James ran his free hand over her stomach, marveling at how soft her skin was while he took his time exploring her pussy. She was warm and wet, and when he crooked his fingers inside her, she clenched around him. "You like that."

Carrigan reached over her head, baring her body completely to him. "Do it again."

He did it again, twisting his wrist so he could circle his thumb over her clit. Each time his fingertips ran over that spot inside her, she cried out and arched up, her body so tight it was like it might explode into a million pieces. "Let go, lovely. I'll be here to catch you when you fall."

Three more strokes and she was there, her scream ripping through the closed space of the car and her body shuddering with the force of her orgasm. James never took his gaze off her face as he worked her, drawing it out until she was limp and panting. "Oh my God...I mean...holy shit."

He leaned down and kissed her. It didn't matter that he was so hard, he thought he might split the seams of his jeans, or that his mouth watered for a taste of her, or that he'd give his left nut to keep going, to know that he was the one making her come until she couldn't come anymore. That's not what tonight was about. He kept the kiss light, even when she arched into it, and then sat back. "Let's get you home."

That was the last thing out of his mouth before Carrigan moved. She grabbed his shoulders, leveraging herself up to straddle his lap. "Nice try, but I'm nowhere near done with you yet."

CHAPTER TEN

Carrigan recognized what James was trying to do—
back off before they had sex because part of her was
still reeling from her earlier encounter. That wasn't what
she wanted from him. With only the shadows between
them and their breath fogging the windows of his car,
she couldn't shake the feeling that she might never get
another chance like this. It was about escape, sure, but
it was more than that. She'd spent the last four months
pretending that she wasn't jonesing for another shot at
James Halloran. Lying to herself.

She'd be damned before she let this opportunity pass.

His hands rested on her hips, the light touch completely at odds with the tension of his body. He wanted
her. She knew he did. But he just as obviously wanted to
set her aside and get the fuck out of the car. She had no
intention of giving him the opportunity to run with this
unexpected honorable streak.

Carrigan kissed him, pressing her entire body against his. He resisted her for one heartbeat, two, three, until the fear rose in the back of her mind that maybe she'd read the situation wrong and he *didn't* want her. That he'd just given her a pity orgasm. She was half a second from pulling away when he growled against her mouth.

As if that sound released him, his grip tightened on her hips, hands sliding down to cup her ass and drag her even closer. His cock was a hard ridge beneath his jeans, and he didn't hesitate to line it up with her still-sensitive clit. The friction made her moan, and he ate the sound, his tongue diving into her mouth and taking control the same way he'd taken control of her hips.

Needing to feel his skin against hers, she reached for the bottom of his shirt and dragged it up over his head. Her hands smacked the roof of the car, but she didn't care. All that mattered was getting James as close to her as he could possibly be. And then they were chest to chest. The shock of having no barrier between her and another person had her going still, wanting to savor every second. She'd had lovers before, but they were always hurried fucks in less-than-convenient locations.

Oh God, I've never been fully naked with an equally naked man. How pathetic is that?

He sensed her hesitation, though he chalked it up to the wrong cause. James gripped the back of her neck. "Second thoughts?"

"No. Fuck, no." She couldn't tell him the real reason, not without baring a part of her she didn't share with anyone. Carrigan rolled her hips. "Fuck me, James. Please." And she would soak up every second of it like a flower seeking the sun.

"I tried to do the goddamn honorable thing."

She reached for the button of his jeans. "That's not what I want from you."

"Yeah, I'm getting that." He knocked her hand away and undid his pants. She had to shift to the side so he could get them off, but then he hauled her back to straddle him again. "I want to see you ride my cock. And when you come, you're going to know that I'm the one you're coming for. You understand, lovely? Only me."

There was the possessive streak again, the one that had spooked her so badly before. She bit her lip, doing her damnedest to beat the panic back. *It's not forever. I'm promised to someone else and we both know it.* She slid against his cock, her conscious mind taking a backseat as the primal part of her roared to the fore. Tomorrow was another day. All that mattered was how good he made her feel right this second. She moved up, angling until his cock notched at her entrance.

James stopped her with a punishing grip on her hips, holding her in place. "As much as I want to sink into that tight pussy of yours without a fucking thing between us, it's not happening. Condom. Now."

She froze, irrational hurt slapping her in the face. "You think—"

"I think that you deserve better than that." His grip lightened, but not enough for her to actually move. "I'm clean, but I don't expect you to trust me, and I don't expect you to take a risk that might result in a kid. I don't want there to be a damn thing about this that you regret, lovely. Not a single thing."

There was that feeling again, the one that fluttered in her chest—like panic, but not at the same time. She smothered it, though it took more effort this time. "Where?"

"Center console."

Carrigan wasted no time twisting around to scramble for the latch. There were a handful of condoms in there, and she grabbed the first one she came into contact with. She tore it open and rolled the condom over his cock, trying to slow down when he cursed. But she wasn't in a teasing mood. Not anymore. No, she needed it hard and fast and *now*.

He seemed to be feeling the same way, because he urged her up and then slammed her down on his cock, filling her completely. The breath left her lungs, her thoughts left her head, and there was nothing except James's ice blue eyes on hers. He ran his hands up her sides, pausing to cup her breasts. He ran a single finger over the tattoo curving around her left one. "Ink?"

She shifted, biting back a moan, and then did it again. "Do you really want to talk about this right now?"

He hesitated, as if he really did want to talk about it, but finally shook his head. "Later."

There wouldn't be a later. She didn't want to trade secrets. The things they'd talked about tonight were already enough to leave her feeling raw and vulnerable. She didn't need more. So Carrigan leaned down and kissed him. He growled against her mouth and shifted them, laying her down on the backseat. The new position shoved him even deeper inside her and she moaned. *Yes. This. This is what I need.*

He knew it, too.

James hooked her leg over his arm and spread her wider, so he could grind against her clit. "This is what you want, lovely." He pulled almost all the way out and thrust hard enough that she had to reach over her head with one hand to keep from sliding into the side of the car. He jerked her back down and did it again. "You want my cock, you want the way it feels when I fuck you."

Yes. Oh God, yes. But she clamped her mouth shut to keep the words inside. She wouldn't give him more than she already had. "Stop. Talking. And. Fuck. Me."

The bastard laughed. "Struck a nerve, didn't I?" He dug a hand into her hair and held her close as he did exactly what she demanded. James fucked her like this was his heaven, like each stroke might be his last, like he'd never get enough. "And you damn well know how much I like to talk when I'm inside you." He kept going, never breaking stride, though his voice had dropped an octave. "You make me crazy, lovely. You're so wet and tight, and the noises coming out of your mouth make me never want to stop."

She never wanted him to stop. She bit his shoulder. "Harder."

"Hell, lovely, I'd give you damn near anything you wanted if you demand it in that voice."

Take me away. Once again, she managed to stop the words before they left her lips. That wasn't what this thing with James was about. He was here to make her forget for a little while. Not forever. There was an expiration date on what they were doing, and she'd be a fool to forget that. So she gripped his hair and held him tight. "Make me come, James."

He kept up that delicious rhythm that had her spiraling closer and closer to the edge with each thrust. "Next time you'll be coming against my mouth. I'm going to fucking worship your pussy with my tongue until you're begging." He slammed into her. "You want that."

It wasn't a question, but it didn't matter. She answered anyway. "Yes. Oh God, *yes*." Her mind shattered into a million pieces, scattering to the wind, and she clung to him as he kept going until his rhythm faltered and he followed her over the edge with a curse.

She slowly came back to herself one sense at a time. The sound of his rough breathing. The intoxicating smell of sex and leather. The way he held her like she was something precious. Her heartbeat picked up. *I've just made a terrible mistake.*

* * *

Everything had changed.

James rolled over, taking Carrigan with him, so that she was sprawled across his chest—as much as a person could sprawl in this backseat. She'd gone tense, so he figured it was only a matter of time before she bolted. Though, considering where they were, she wasn't going to get far. He stroked a hand down her hair. "Breathe, lovely."

"I *am* breathing." She started to move off him but stopped when she must have realized there was nowhere to go but the floorboard. "You're not going to toss me into the trunk, are you?"

Guilt threatened to choke him, but he forced it down. "Don't throw that in my face. We're past it."

"You might be. Maybe I'm not." She reached around and came up with her dress. "Please take me home."

She was lying. Just like it had before, this thing that

flared between them scared the shit out of her. He'd seen it on her face the first time they had sex, which was why he'd demanded her name—so he could find her again. How things played out after that…yeah, it was shitty. But she *was* past it. She wouldn't have called him tonight if she hadn't finally accepted that he never would have let his father and brother hurt her. Which meant she was in panic mode again right now. He could force her to sit here and talk it out.

Or he could let her go.

Really, it wasn't much of a dilemma. If he'd learned anything about Carrigan, it was that she'd go for a person's throat if they backed her into a corner. People had been putting her in cages her entire life. He wasn't about to be one of them.

So he sat up. "Okay."

She froze in the middle of shimmying into her dress. "What?"

"I said okay. I'll take you home. Just give me a second to get my pants." He didn't want tonight to end with her running from him, because he wasn't done with Carrigan O'Malley. Not by a long shot. James pulled on his jeans and shoes and then pushed the front seat up so he could climb out into the night. He offered his hand to help her out, but she ignored it. So that was how it would be. Fine. He pushed the seat back into place and held the door so she could take the passenger seat. It was going to be a long ride back if the way she crossed her arms over her chest was any indication. He'd need the distraction of driving.

Once he got the Chevelle started and the windows defrosted, he headed back toward the city. He didn't speak, and neither did she. James could actually feel her building up walls between them. Retreating. A part of him even understood. He'd had sex before. Hell, he'd gone out of his way to keep things at *just* sex in the past. It was simpler. His life didn't lend itself to being able to build a healthy relationship—he wasn't even sure if he was capable of it. Easier to keep things at a strictly physical level. That way both parties left satisfied, and the chance of someone getting hurt was virtually nonexistent.

That being said, this thing with Carrigan wasn't just sex.

He'd known that four months ago, and it was only becoming clearer the more time he spent with her. He admired her fire. He liked that she never hesitated to get in his face and put him in his place if she thought he was out of line. He liked how nothing her family had done to date had broken her. Fuck, he just plain liked her.

He took the exit that would spit them out near Beacon Hill, and wound his way up to the block just down from her town house. "You want me to—?"

"This is good." She already had the door open.

"Carrigan." He waited for her to look back. "Next time you need to forget—or need anything, period—I'm here."

She flinched like he'd raised a hand to her. "I don't think that's a good idea."

"How much time do you have before you need to make a decision?" He kept his tone low and even, though all he wanted to do was haul her ass back into the car and get the hell out of here—spend a week lost in each other and ignoring the call of the real world.

"A month. Less than that now."

Not long enough. Fuck, he was beginning to think that twenty years with this woman wouldn't be close to enough. But he'd take what he could get. "Every time you go on one of these dates, the noose is going to tighten around your neck. I can help you forget, lovely. You know it and I know it." He didn't wait for a response, needing to get this out before she bolted. "So when the pressure gets too much to handle—and it will—call me. I'll be there. I promise."

She hesitated, and then shut the car door and walked away. He waited until he saw her enter a brownstone down the block, and then he put the car in gear and drove away. She'd call. She might tell herself that she wouldn't—she might even convince herself that she was through with him—but when her back was against the wall, she'd call him again.

He was sure of it.

James headed back into Southie, the upper-crust neighborhood that Carrigan lived in slowly replaced by smaller and smaller houses, each in worse repair than the next. Even the ones that obviously had owners who cared about upkeep showed decades of wear and tear. The O'Malleys and Hallorans might fight like dogs over the bone that was Boston, but they really came from different worlds. The outward evidence of it in the neighborhoods they lived in was just the beginning.

But none of that seemed to matter when he was with Carrigan.

He forced himself to set aside the feel-good sensation being around Carrigan brought him. There was nothing he wanted more than to dwell on how amazing she'd felt squeezing his cock, and how much he wanted to get inside her again at the soonest available opportunity. But he couldn't afford to be any more distracted right now than he already was.

And he was seriously fucking distracted.

But Ricky was waiting, and so was the real world.

CHAPTER ELEVEN

Carrigan spent the next week keeping busy and avoiding all the things she didn't want to think about. The list was getting kind of ridiculous. She'd had a hell of a time keeping a straight face during Mass on Sunday while the priest went on about original sin. Her mind kept going back to the feeling of James's hands on her skin and his voice in her ear. If that was a sin, she had no interest in being a saint.

She knew she should get the rest of the dates out of the way, but Monday slipped by while she wasn't paying attention, and she spent nearly all of Tuesday with Callie, hiding out from Aileen and her last-second wedding plans. And then she blinked and it was Friday and she'd managed to get through six whole days without picking up the phone and dialing James.

He had a lot of nerve saying he'd be there for her. She'd have to be a fool to trust him. It was more than their shared history, though that should be more than reason enough. She didn't trust anyone beyond family— and she didn't even trust her family half the time. People had a nasty tendency to put themselves first when she needed them most.

The only person she could trust to take care of her was *her*.

Which meant it was time to stop dragging her heels and get through these dates. Her fate wasn't going to magically change in the next few weeks, and the longer she waited for the initial dates, the less time she'd have to actually make a decision. Holding off wasn't going to hurt anyone but her, so she wasn't going to wait any longer.

She moved on to the next two names on her list. Kellen O'Neill. Dmitri Romanov. An hour of Internet searching later, she had little to no information on either of them. Kellen O'Neill was a pretty common name, and the only Dmitri Romanov she could get a bead on was some Russian prince who may or may not be fictional. Probably not her guy.

Resigning herself to not knowing a damn thing about these men before she met them, she dialed the number next to Kellen's name. Ten minutes later she had a date for dinner that evening. He hadn't even hesitated. It was hard to tell on the phone, but he sounded young and eager. Neither one was a turn-on, but it might mean he was easy to manipulate. She filed that away in the back of her mind and dialed the next number.

"Dmitri Romanov."

She blinked. She'd expected someone Russian from the name, but he sounded... She shook her head. "This is

Carrigan O'Malley. I've been given to understand you're interested in linking your assets to my father's." Such a careful way of prettying up what this really was—her father selling her off to further his business.

"You understand correctly."

"I'd like to meet with you, this afternoon if possible." Knocking off two of the names today would keep her busy—and keep her mind off James.

Dmitri chuckled. "I'll clear my schedule. Shall I meet you at three?"

"That would be perfect." This Dmitri didn't sound like the type of man to paw at her uninvited, so there was absolutely no reason she should so much as talk to James today. Good.

"I look forward to meeting you, Carrigan." His accent gave her name an exotic roll, and she couldn't stop a shiver. *Damn.* "Enjoy your day." And then he was gone, leaving her feeling vaguely unsettled.

Dmitri Romanov wasn't a man to be underestimated.

She frowned. They'd exchanged a handful of words. He'd canceled his plans to meet her. There was absolutely nothing in what he'd said that should be making her skin twitch like she was surrounded by danger she couldn't see. *So why is my stomach in knots and my heart beating too hard?* She set her phone down next to her on her bed. Growing up in the house of a powerful and ruthless man, it made sense that some part of her instinctively recognized it in this stranger, even over the phone. That had to be it.

Chauncey had been a pig. She got the feeling that Kellen was a puppy. Dmitri...well, Dmitri was something else altogether.

A knock on her door was all the warning she got before her mother swept into the room, her dark hair perfectly styled, her makeup flawless, and her pantsuit looking like she was ready for brunch. Aileen took in the space with a critical eye, and finally settled on Carrigan. "You had a date last night with one of your father's candidates."

It was a fight to keep her face perfectly bland. She could still feel him pawing at her, and the anger over his asshole commentary hadn't dimmed with time. Her interlude with James had made the memory bearable, but she wouldn't hesitate to knock that slimy fuck on his ass again if she ever was forced into his presence. "Yes. Chauncy Chauncer."

Her mother made a face. "New money." As if that summed up everything worth knowing about him. Unfortunately, she wasn't wrong in this particular case. She moved to the dresser and started straightening the pictures there. "How did it go?"

"He's no longer in the running."

Aileen looked over sharply. "What did he do?"

She should have known that her mother would pick up on the underlying anger that Carrigan still couldn't shake. Every time she so much as thought Chauncey's name, a slow-burning rage rolled through her. He'd insulted her, and then he'd touched her without permission—*assaulted her.* She picked at a nonexistent thread on her comforter. "He had problems taking no for an answer."

It wasn't something she'd ever admit aloud to her father but, as rarely as she and Aileen saw eye to eye, she knew her mother would understand *this.* Sure enough,

her perfectly lipsticked mouth tightened. "You took care
of it." There wasn't any doubt on her face that Carrigan
was more than capable of putting the pig in his place.

"I got my point across." She just wished she'd hit him
again. Or kicked him while he was down. Her shoulders
tightened at the memory of him shoving her against the
wall. "He's a fool, so I doubt it had any lasting effect, but
he won't be touching *me* again."

"Good." Aileen hesitated and then went back to
straightening pictures. "You'll let me know if you need
to take further actions."

Even if she didn't, her mother would find out anyway.
She might not be as flashy about it, but Aileen had as
many—if not more—people reporting to her as Seamus
did. "Of course."

"Good. Now that that's taken care of, show me this
list of your father's."

She handed it over because there really was no other
option. Besides, even though her mother was as willing
to sell her off as her father was, at least Aileen would
take more factors into account than just his potential
alley value. *I should have asked her before going out
with Chauncey.* The realization had her straightening her
spine. She'd made a mistake. Maybe this would help her
to keep from repeating it.

*I don't want any of them, though. There's no way they
can make me feel as good as James does.*

She shut that thought down *real* fast. But it was no
use. It wormed its way into the back of her brain, its
presence small but nagging all the same. It didn't matter how good the sex was with James, or how he never
seemed to react the way she expected during their con-

versations. Even if she'd been willing to consider...
anything...with him, it was a moot point.

He wasn't on the list.

End of story.

Aileen picked up the paper, a tiny line appearing between her brows as she looked it over. "Take both the
Marrow boy and Atcherberg off the list. I can't believe
your father would stoop so low." Her green eyes flashed.
"Marrow just buried his third wife. And Atcherberg has a
gambling problem that is already beggaring his family."

She didn't ask how her mother knew these things.
There was no point when she was, in all reality, most
likely right. Carrigan fought back a sigh. "Then my potential list is down from six to three." After today it
would shrink even further. She looked at her mother, all
the things she couldn't say pressed against the inside of
her lips. *Please don't make me do this. Please don't make
me marry some stranger to further the family's interests.
Please, please, please.* It was a little girl's cry into the
dark, begging the monster not to be real.

If Aileen saw what she was thinking—and the way
she pressed her lips together said she sure as hell did—
she ignored it. She set the list back on Carrigan's bed.
"That will make things simpler. Now, this wasn't why I
came looking for you." She straightened and smoothed
her hands over her perfectly pressed green dress. "You
haven't been in to get the final fitting for your brides-
maid's dress yet."

The wedding. Of course. She should have known it
wasn't concern for her well-being that had her mother
searching her out. These days everything seemed to boil
down to Teague and Callie's wedding. "I'm surprised

you need me in there at all. Don't you know our mea-
surements by heart?"

"Carrigan, don't be cheeky. The wedding is a little
over a week away. Make it a priority. I won't have you in
an ill-fitting dress."

Since the wedding was more about what her mother
wanted than what Callie wanted, she'd take it as a personal insult if Carrigan didn't do exactly as instructed.
She glanced at the clock beside her bed. "It'll have to be
this afternoon, then." She'd take care of it after her date
with Dmitri.

"See that it is." Aileen nodded, turned on her heel, and
marched out of the room. Probably off to terrify one of
Carrigan's other siblings. They all loved their mother, but
she was almost scarier than their father was. She never
seemed to be involved with his darker decisions, but anyone who believed that wasn't looking hard enough. She
might not take part in the business publicly, but she stood
as their father's partner in every way that counted.

Carrigan pushed to her feet and headed to get ready.
She'd barely started her makeup process when her treacherous mind wandered back to James. What had he been
up to this week? Was he grinning and feeling superior because he got what every man seemed to want from her?
She shook her head. No, that wasn't James. Maybe she was
naive, but very little he'd done to date could be grouped in
with "other men." He played by rules that she didn't understand, and when he looked at her with those blue eyes,
she was tempted to throw caution to the wind and do whatever it took to spend a few more hours in his bed. Which
would be a nice change of pace, because they hadn't actually made it to a bed yet.

But it simply wasn't possible.

His words from last night rolled over her again. *Every date you go on is going to be tightening the noose around your neck. Call me. I'll be there.*

He would, too. He'd more than proven that since she got back into town. She paused in the middle of swiping mascara over her lashes, her gaze landing on the phone next to her on the counter. She could call him right now. Would he drop everything and come get her? Maybe rev up the engine of that car of his and take her anywhere she wanted to go?

Before she could talk herself out of it, she snatched up her phone and dialed. Carrigan held her breath as it rang, telling herself that this was dangerous and stupid and half a million other things that all added up to a terrible idea. It didn't matter. All that mattered was the unexpected lifeline he'd offered her.

The phone rang. And rang. And rang. It clicked over to voice mail, and she was so shocked, she almost didn't hang up before it got to the beep. Carrigan stared at her phone, half convinced that it had malfunctioned on her end. She carefully set it down and forced herself to see the truth. All that night had been was pretty words. When it came down to the wire, she couldn't lean on James. She'd forgotten that for a moment.

She wouldn't forget again.

* * *

James ignored the buzzing of his phone in his pocket as he carefully rolled up his sleeves. "You know why we're here, Joe."

The big black guy raised his chin, but his nostrils were flared and too much white showed around his eyes. He was fifteen seconds away from pissing himself in fear. *Good*. Hopefully this shit wouldn't have to go to extremes for James to get the information he wanted. He finished his right sleeve and started on his left. "Ricky's been taking meetings without my permission." He needed to know exactly who he'd talked to, and his little brother wasn't talking.

"You'll have to take that up with him."

He should. Fuck, he knew he should. But a part of James was still unwilling to go that final distance and bring torturing information out of his little brother to the table. Call him crazy, but that seemed like a line that, once crossed, he'd never be able to find his way back over again.

His thoughts took a hard right turn and settled on Carrigan. What would she think of what he was about to do? Of what he was threatening to do to his own flesh and blood?

Ricky would have hurt her. He would have done his damnedest to make her scream and he would have loved every second of it.

He shook his head. *Not helping*. But if he could get Joe to talk, he could simplify his life. "I'm taking it up with you." He moved to the table Michael had set up next to where the man was tied to a chair in the center of the room. The harsh light directly above Joe's head was positioned in such a way that he was partially blinded, and most of the rest of the room was in shadows. Victor Halloran knew a whole hell of a lot about intimidation tactics—he liked to say that half the interrogation session happened before he ever laid hands on his victim.

James fought back a shudder. He could shout that he wasn't his old man until he was hoarse, but the proof was in his actions. He picked up a set of pliers. "These don't look like much. Most houses on this street have a set or two." He stepped up close to Joe, letting him get a look at the rusted metal. "My old man didn't take good care of his tools, but he loved the shit out of them. Would you like to see what he taught me?"

Joe's entire body went tense, his gaze glued to the pliers. "Look, man, you really need to talk to Ricky. I was just following orders."

"His orders." James turned the pliers, picking a piece of something he really didn't want to think about off the tip and flicking it at the other man. "You should be following mine."

"We didn't think you were going to step up." The words were barely more than a whisper. "Ricky talks a good game, and he gets shit done."

Shit that didn't do the Hallorans a single bit of good. But this man didn't see that—and neither did the others who followed his little brother. All they saw were the actions. Not the consequences. He couldn't say that aloud, though. The second he tried to reason with these men was the moment he lost them completely. They'd proven time and time again that they didn't respect anything but brutal violence.

Love or fear. That's the only way.

Love would never be enough. It didn't matter what he did, or how well he took care of the people in their territory, or how much their legal businesses had increased in the last few months since he'd taken the reins. *Nothing* mattered but becoming a monster even the monsters feared. It was the only way to keep them in line.

Fine. He'd give Joe his goddamn fear. "Who runs the Hallorans, Joe?" Despite trying to muscle every single emotion down to where he could lock it away for what he needed to do next, he sounded so goddamn tired.

The man in the chair started to sweat. "You do, boss."

Too little, too late. He moved closer, his feet feeling like they weighed a thousand pounds. "Me, Joe. Not my brother. You learned that lesson a little too late." He forced the man's fingers apart. "But you won't forget it again."

An hour later it was done.

James walked out of the room, his skin feeling too tight. *Fuck, fuck, fuck.* He stopped next to where Michael leaned against the wall, a toothpick in his mouth. "Get him cleaned up and home. He can figure out how to splint the fingers himself." The words were foul in his mouth, and he had to resist the urge to spit.

"Sure thing, boss." Michael pushed off and took two steps before he stopped. "You did the right thing."

That's what he was afraid of.

Once upon a time there'd been a right and a wrong and a clear line between them. Now everything was upside-down and backward. He lived in a reality where torturing a man was the right thing to do—the lesser of two evils—and he'd never hated himself as much as he did in that moment. But there was no getting off this crazy train—the doors had closed and they'd left the station. The only thing to do was ride it out to its conclusion and hope there were enough people left standing to make the whole thing worthwhile.

He wanted to talk to Carrigan. Just being around her was enough to hold all the shit he didn't want to deal with at bay, but he couldn't bring himself to call her with another man's blood on his hands and his cries for mercy still ringing in James's ears. No, he'd shower, go down to the weight room, and then shower again.

Maybe if he punished his body enough, he'd be able to bear the new stain on his soul.

CHAPTER TWELVE

Cillian sat across from his father and oldest brother, waiting for the guillotine blade to fall. He damn well knew that they'd been waiting these last four months for him to pull himself out of his spiral and step into the slot they'd created for him. The family bookkeeper had been making noises about retiring for over a year now, and it was finally time for Cillian to go through the necessary training to bring him up to speed so he could take over.

Once upon a time, he hadn't cared about the future. He'd known where his place would be, and he'd been content with that—as long as he got to experience as much as he possibly could before he was forced to take up the mantle of family responsibility. It was never something he railed against like his brother Teague, because he actually liked the work he'd be doing.

But he was having a hell of a time getting excited about it—getting excited about *anything*—now.

His father sat behind his massive desk, and Cillian couldn't help thinking he looked small. Seamus O'Malley had always been larger than life, but the events of the last few months had affected him just as much as they had every other member of their family. There were new lines on his face, and his shoulders bowed as if carrying the weight of the world. For the first time in living memory, he looked *old*. Not that anyone had the balls to point it out.

Seamus steepled his hands. "Enough is enough."

Ah. They weren't here to talk to him about stepping up to be the bookkeeper. This was about Devlin. Cillian sat back and stretched his legs out, crossing them at his ankles. They could do this now, but he wasn't about to make it easy on them. *I'm not the only one who's walking wounded, but I'm the easiest to focus on.* Maybe it was better this way. If their father was determined to nail his ass to the wall, it gave his little sisters a chance to find their feet. *Not Carrigan, though.* "I don't know what you're talking about."

"Yes, you do. Don't play stupid." This came from Aiden. He actually took a step forward, his fists clenching, before their father held up a hand to stall him.

"We've all mourned Devlin—"

For fuck's sake. Cillian straightened. "Really? Because it seems to have been business as usual. Real nostalgic." No one was saying what they were thinking—that it would have been better if *he* had been the one to take the bullet.

The shock of the thought nearly took his breath away. It was a truth that he'd been dancing around for months, and there was something cathartic in finally letting himself think it. *It should have been me.*

Devlin was the one with the world at his feet. Cillian was just going through the motions, dicking around as much as possible. Even with his destined role as accountant, he was expendable.

And they all knew it.

Aiden crossed his arms over his chest. "And getting shit-housed drunk every night of the week is honoring our brother? Please. Don't play the martyr to cover up that you're doing what you've always done—skipping out on family business when we need you the most."

"If I need to drink to deal with shit, then I'm going to goddamn well drink." If they thought that's what he was doing, he wasn't going to set them straight. Alcohol had become the enemy the same way the Hallorans were the enemy. He'd been so fucking weak his entire life, had always chosen the easiest path. He was done with that shit now.

"*Enough.*" Seamus didn't raise his voice, but he might as well have roared by how the single word cut through the room. He waited, but neither Aiden nor Cillian made a sound. Apparently satisfied, their father sat back. "We all mourn Devlin in our own ways. You, of all people, should know that, Cillian. Cut down your drinking and take one of our men with you when you go. I refuse to lose another son to carelessness."

God forbid another one of your beloved assets slips away. The thought wasn't fair, but Cillian could give two fucks. Maybe their father loved them. Maybe he didn't. But if he did, then he had a hell of a way of showing it.

But Seamus was letting him get off easy this time, and he damn well knew it. "I'll take an escort." *For now.* He pushed to his feet. "If we're done here—"

"Sit."

His legs went out from beneath him before he made a conscious decision to obey.

"Bartholomew is retiring. You will begin training with him next week. Once he's satisfied you know what's necessary, you will take over his position."

Next week. He'd known it was coming up fast, but he'd had no idea *how* fast. *Fuck.* It wasn't that Cillian didn't like the idea of keeping the family's books. Ever since he'd shown an aptitude for numbers and the morals required for creative accounting, it was assumed he'd step into that role when the time came. Hell, a part of him had even looked forward to it. He might never run the O'Malleys—and, seriously, that wasn't a position he aspired to—but with their finances within his control, he'd have the keys to the kingdom, so to speak. Every cent that filtered through their businesses—both legit and illegal—went through the bookkeeper.

But then Devlin died, and Teague was married off and helping to run things on the Sheridan side now. And Carrigan...

Every time he thought about the lost and terrified look on her face when she told him she was going to have to marry a stranger, it made him want to hit something. If that Dmitri guy was any indication, the sharks were already circling, scenting blood in the water. He couldn't imagine his strong-willed sister married to someone like that. But she didn't have a choice any more than the rest of them did.

He was getting off easy. He knew that. He'd always known that. Once upon a time, he'd even reveled in the knowledge.

Not anymore.

But that had more to do with him than the job he was expected to step into. There wasn't much he got excited about these days, and it sure as fuck wasn't going to be keeping the books with a side of computer hacking that convinced him that the night Devlin died hadn't been a horrible case of fate making a mistake.

He blinked, realizing that both his father and brother expected a response from him. A harsh laugh slipped free. "I'll be there." He stood again. "If there's nothing else…"

His father waved a hand. "Go."

"Gladly." He turned on his heel and marched out of the room before Aiden could chase him down and yell at him for being disrespectful.

It used to be that he didn't lose sleep over his siblings' fates—not when he always knew *his*. Now he couldn't stop thinking about them—about what Devlin would be doing if he wasn't six feet underground. He'd have started his junior year of college in the fall, going about school with the same enthusiasm he went about life. It wasn't the same way Cillian had always lost himself in the partying and good times. Devlin genuinely enjoyed everything from his morning coffee to the lectures from his professors to whatever book he was buried in at the moment. At twenty, part of him had just been so…young. Full of potential.

Potential that had been cut short because he was in the wrong place at the wrong time.

And his other siblings?

Teague was fine. Hell, Teague was better than fine. He had a banging-hot wife who seemed to genuinely care about him. If anyone in their family was living the dream, it was Teague. They didn't see him nearly enough these days, what with his attention being focused solely on solidifying the Sheridans' hold on their portion of Boston. Cillian didn't blame him for that. His theoretical future kids would be as much Sheridans as O'Malleys—more, really.

Keira and Sloan... He didn't even know. He'd barely seen them since they got back from the house in Connecticut, and that was indication enough that something was off. Keira was normally in the middle of everything, and for her to be playing least in sight wasn't a good sign. And Sloan was probably half a day from slitting her wrists in angst.

I'm going to need to talk to her sooner rather than later.

Aiden didn't seem too torn up about being heir and preparing to step up and take over the family. Cillian had never pegged him for a clone of their father, but then he'd been wrong about a lot of things. What did he know?

And Carrigan... fuck.

He turned the corner and picked up his pace, heading for the door. There wasn't a damn thing he could do to help Carrigan. There wasn't a damn thing he could do to help *anyone*.

* * *

Carrigan walked into the restaurant and stopped cold. It was totally and completely empty. She glanced back at the door she'd just come through. Surely if it was closed, it would have been locked? She'd been to Sling-shot countless times in the last ten years and it didn't matter the day of the week or the hour, it was always damn near packed. She looked around again, wondering what the hell was going on.

A flustered girl who couldn't be more than eighteen hurried up. "Ms. O'Malley?"

"Yes..." The hairs on the back of her neck stood on end. Was this a trap? Dmitri was on her father's list, so she'd assumed he was safe enough to meet. Surely she hadn't assumed wrong? *Damn it, I know better than this. Where's Liam?* He'd gone to park the car, so he'd be here in just a few minutes. She touched her purse. The Taser was still stashed in the bottom of it. She could use it if she had to—it wouldn't kill anyone, but it'd give her a chance to run. If there was a legitimate threat, Liam was more equipped to deal with it than she was, no matter how much she hated relying on someone else to ride in and save the day.

"It's safe." The Russian accent rolled over her like the best kind of vodka. The man who stepped out from behind the column matched it perfectly. Carrigan had the wild thought that he'd been standing there with the sole purpose of making an entrance, but then he took a step closer and she was too busy staring to speak. He was...well, he was gorgeous. Dark hair styled perfectly. Cheekbones sharp enough to cut, which should have made him look feminine but didn't in the least. And those gray eyes. Good lord, the man was sex on a stick.

If you didn't mind that the stick was more likely to beat you to death than fuck you.

Other women might miss it, but there was a coldness in his eyes that his smile didn't touch. She had a feeling those eyes never warmed up. Not to mention everything about this meeting was orchestrated to put him in a position of power for their exchange. He'd shown up first, made sure one of the most popular restaurants in the neighborhood was empty, and had waited until she had her guard down in the confusion to make his entrance.

If she was taking bets, she'd bet that he never went into any situation without first making sure he would be in control of every aspect of it.

Dangerous. Very, very dangerous.

She cleared her throat. "Dmitri Romanov, I presume."

"You presume correctly." He motioned at the empty restaurant behind him. "I thought our meal would proceed smoother if we didn't have an audience."

Either that, or he wanted as few witnesses as possible to take care of after he murdered her. She glanced back at the door again. Where the hell was Liam?

Dmitri caught her look. "If you're uncomfortable, we can go somewhere else."

Damn it, she was so flustered, she wasn't bothering to mask her expressions. Carrigan took a careful breath and smiled. "No, this is fine. It's just unexpected." And strangely thoughtful, though she was still more inclined to look at it through the potentially violent lens than the romantic one.

"Shall we sit?" He motioned to a table set back from the windows, where no one from the street would have a clear view of them.

With a nod, she moved to the table and took a chair

that put her back to the wall. Maybe this Dmitri wasn't a threat to *her*, but that didn't mean he wasn't dangerous. She already knew he was. The problem was that people tended to present the best versions of themselves when they first met strangers. It was up to her to dig through the bullshit to the meat beneath, and she couldn't do that until she got the conversation rolling. "So, Dmitri, tell me about yourself."

He sank into the chair across from her with an effortless grace she envied. "First-date questions, Carrigan?"

Ignoring the heat of embarrassment rising up her neck, she lifted her chin. "Do you have a better idea? I'm on a compressed timeline, which I'm sure you're aware of. I have to start somewhere."

"Then why don't we start with why I'm on this list of your father's?" He looked completely relaxed, as long as she ignored the eyes. Those eyes watched her like she was a deer and he was a wolf, just waiting for her to twitch in the wrong direction before he pounced. "I run a very prominent empire in New York. You father wisely sees the value of allies outside Boston."

New York.

Which most likely meant she'd be required to move down there, because he certainly wasn't going to relocate up here. Her lungs turned to lead, and she gripped the edge of her chair as she fought lightheadedness. Somehow, even in the middle of all this, she'd never once considered that she might have to leave Boston. "I see." There were days when she wanted to burn the city to the ground around her, but it was *home*.

A waitress appeared next to their table, giving Carrigan a much-needed breather, and set down two glasses of water. She poured them each a glass of red wine, and then left as silently as she'd come.

This Carrigan could focus on. "High-handed of you." Why did every rich man in the world think that drinking wine was required? At least he'd ordered red instead of white—a tiny silver lining.

"I like to go into business meetings having the upper hand." His smile was more shark than sheepish. "Forgive me, but I did a bit of research."

If he'd done as much research as he claimed, he'd know she preferred dirty martinis to wine any day of the week. *James* had figured that out all on his own. *Thinking about him right now is a mistake. Focus on the man across from you.* She took a cautious sip of the wine and nearly melted into her seat. It was light and a little fruity and hands down the best wine she'd ever had. "This isn't half-bad." Since he seemed to want to cut to the chase, she might as well play. "You'll be expecting me to move to your home and play the little wife in between popping out half a dozen children."

"Setting aside the small talk. Good." This time his smile was almost real, though it still didn't reach his eyes. "To answer your question—I'm willing to negotiate. I have no interest in a little wife, as you so eloquently put it. Especially an unwilling one."

Pretty words, but she trusted this man as far as she could throw him. "So what is it you *do* want?"

"A part-time partner. I have no need of someone to help me run my various business ventures, but there are times when having a wife on my arm would make or break a deal. It also creates stability, because my people see me as settling down and providing heirs that will prevent a civil war. Stability, Carrigan, is key. So, yes, I will need children, though half a dozen seems excessive—no offense to your parents, of course."

"Of course." She took another sip of wine through numb lips. "You say a part-time partner. Should I take up knitting when you don't need to dust me off, prop me up, and have me entertain guests?"

He shot her a look. "Hardly. I see no reason why you can't spend a good portion of the time here in Boston—as long as you agree to the appropriate protection. I simply ask that you do nothing to bring negative attention. And that you stay faithful."

It was so strange to have it all laid out there in bald terms. Part of her wanted to scream at him for making her feel so...What? If he'd given her romance, she would have called him a liar. All he'd done was tear away the thin curtain between her and reality. She'd known what these men expected of her. Dmitri was simply clearing the air. She sat back. "Do you conduct all your negotiations like this?"

"Only when the situation calls for it. You're a smart woman, and I thought you'd appreciate it if I was frank with you." He frowned, the first time his perfect mask had so much as cracked. "Was I wrong? Would you prefer flowers and romance and pretty words?"

"No, thank you." She could almost feel the room solidifying around her as she found her feet again. He'd caught her off guard, but she found she actually preferred this to the lies people tended to tell when they first met each other.

James hasn't lied to you.

Shut up.

James wasn't her future. It didn't matter how he made her feel or that she said things to him she never would have said to anyone else. She couldn't hold him up in comparison to every man on her father's list. They'd all end up wanting. Dmitri was nothing like him. He was dark where James was light, polished where James was rough, a shark to James's junkyard dog.

Maybe all the differences were a good thing.

She set her wineglass down. "Two children, and I'm in Boston at least six months of the year."

"I'll agree to the two children. I can't promise specific timelines as I don't know when I'll need you." He paused and smiled at the waitress who now brought their food. Reuben for him, and a chicken Caesar wrap for her. Her favorite.

"This one you got right." She snagged a fry and took a bite. Perfection.

"Research allows me to surpass a lot of the unnecessary bits." He pushed his plate to the side. "As I was saying, initially you'll need to be in New York more. I have to establish your place in my home for both allies and enemies. The first year, possibly more, will require the majority of your time to be spent with me."

She didn't like the idea of it, but it was fair—fairer than any other deal she was likely to get. That didn't mean she had to drop everything and jump on it. "I'll let you know."

Dmitri smiled his shark's smile. "I wouldn't expect anything else."

He had her and he knew it. Unless her date tonight went spectacularly—or the one she had yet to set up with Charles Pope—she wasn't likely to get a better offer.

Carrigan rose. "Thank you for your time, Mr. Romanov."

"I look forward to seeing you again, Carrigan."

She turned and walked away, feeling his gaze on the back of her neck the whole while.

* * *

An hour in the gym later, and James couldn't get the feeling of blood off his hands. He stood beneath the scalding spray of the shower and scrubbed and scrubbed and scrubbed. It didn't help. Rationally, he knew nothing would help. The problem was mental—not physical. He looked at his hands, red and raw from the repeated washings. "Damn it."

He turned off the shower and dried off. In the past, whenever he got too close to the edge, he'd locked himself in the room with his mother's photo album and anchored himself by remembering happier days. That option wasn't available—hadn't been since Carrigan took the album. He needed it back, the sooner the better. The thought of carrying on like this without an anchor made him sick to his stomach. This life was a slippery slope, and he was already too far gone. If he wasn't careful, he'd wake up one day and realize he'd turned into his old man.

James grabbed his phone and dialed. He'd meant to call Carrigan back earlier, since his promise to her was still ringing in his ears, but he couldn't with the memory of what he'd done to Joe still riding him so hard. It wasn't going away anytime soon, though, and maybe some time with her was just what he needed to center himself. The longer the line rang, the tenser he got.

What if she's in trouble? She hadn't left a message earlier, but that didn't mean a damn thing. He'd told her to call when she needed him, and then the first time she'd called, he hadn't answered. *Good job, dipshit.*

The call clicked over to voice mail and he cursed. "I'm sorry I missed your call. I'm here now." As tempting as it was to keep talking, to postpone the moment when he had to admit he'd fucked up, he made himself hang up.

A knock on his door made him frown. "What?"

"It's me, boss." Michael poked his head in. "I double-checked that shit you gave me. It's all like Joe said. The first meeting Ricky actually pulled off was with those guys you met at Tit for Tat."

His breath left him in a rush. Thank Christ he'd been able to put the brakes on his brother before he did any more damage. "Good."

"Anything else you need from me?"

"Check on my brother and you can head out." Between Joe and the aftermath, he'd wasted the day away. *Where are you, Carrigan?* He made sure his ringer was on and pocketed his phone. He wasn't going to be able to eat anytime soon, but he couldn't sit up here and mope in his room for the rest of the night. It was important he be seen, both as a warning and a promise to his people. Which meant Mickey's was on the agenda.

He drove down there even though it was within walking distance. It was tempting to just keep driving. Too tempting. He had to remind himself of his responsibilities and what was expected of him more and more often as time went on. As shitty as it was, he dreaded the day where it all became second nature to him. When he finally fully stepped into the man he was required to be in order to run the Hallorans.

The monster.

Fuck, he was a moody bitch today. James walked into Mickey's, ignoring the way silence fell as the men there caught sight of him. He made a beeline to the bar and nodded at Tommy. Tommy actually blanched before he caught himself. *Not you, too.* James forced his shoulders back and nodded. Fear or love. He might have been coming in here since before he could legally drink, but that history didn't matter anymore. What mattered was that Tommy now saw him as someone to be feared. "Whiskey."

He ignored the way the bartender's hands shook as he poured a healthy glass and passed it over. James didn't say thanks—just took the glass and retreated to his customary booth in the back. From here he could see everyone in the place. He sipped his drink as they slowly relaxed, and conversation started back up.

Good. He might scare the shit out of them now, but they weren't completely crippled by it. When his old man came into a room, no one spoke until he left it again. James didn't like to think about what he had to have done in order to command that kind of fear.

Because he already knew.

He checked his phone again. Nothing. This was so damn stupid. James shook his head and downed half his whiskey. He should just track her ass down and make sure she was okay—except that was stalking, and he'd already crossed too many lines when it came to Carrigan. He couldn't drop everything and go rushing to her side when that wasn't what she'd asked him to do. There had to be a line somewhere.

He set his phone aside and concentrated on the whiskey in his glass, letting the low conversation from the pub roll over him. She'd call if she needed him. Simple as that. He just had to make sure he didn't drop the ball next time she did.

If she called again.

CHAPTER THIRTEEN

Carrigan checked her phone for the twelfth time in five minutes. There was no way around it. Not only had James not called her back since the first time, but Kellen O'Neill was late. Extremely late. Over thirty minutes late.

She should have known after the conversation with her mother that the day was only going to go downhill from there, but the puppy had been so eager over the phone that she hadn't really thought he'd stand her up. Another glance at her phone. Yeah, still late. She heaved a sigh. She should just go home. Dmitri had already offered her a legitimate choice, even if it was the best option of a group of truly shitty options. She didn't really *need* Kellen O'Neill.

But she didn't stand up and leave.

A few more minutes. She eyed her empty glass. Another martini wouldn't hurt. It wasn't like she was driving. She smiled at the nervous-looking waiter and ordered. *He thinks I'm being stood up, too. Wonderful.* More to keep her hands busy than anything else, she texted James. *Hey stranger.*

As soon as she pushed send, she regretted it. He hadn't answered her call earlier. Yes, he'd called back— a call she'd ignored—but...really, she didn't have a reason to be hurt or pissed or anything. They'd had sex twice, but they were hardly friends. She shouldn't even be texting him right now. Another glance around the restaurant proved that Kellen was, in fact, still late.

Her phone rang in her hand, startling her so bad, she almost dropped it. "Hello?"

"I'm sorry I missed your call earlier."

She was, too. Though it had allowed her to get through lunch without the distraction he offered—both a blessing and a curse, as it turned out. What the hell was she going to do about Dmitri? She straightened the fork next to her plate. "It's not a big deal."

"It is. I told you I'd be there and then I fucked up. I'm sorry." He went on before she could answer. "What are you doing right now?"

"Being stood up, I think." She forced a laugh.

"Another date with a guy from that list?"

"Yes." This was what her life had been reduced to— and it hadn't exactly been a dream to begin with. She was waiting for a man her father approved of, with the sole purpose of marrying her off, while on the phone with a man that was the enemy as far as the O'Malleys were concerned. "Apparently he doesn't find Ciao to his liking."

Something rustled on the other end of the phone, and she thought she heard a door slam. "He's a fool."

"I'm not arguing that. I've giving him ten more minutes, and I'm bailing. Right now a date with my bathtub sounds like heaven."

James growled. "I like the picture that brings to mind. Bubbles?"

"Absolutely." She smiled and nodded her thanks to the waiter who brought her drink replacement. "Mine smell like roses and suds up like crazy."

"Damn, lovely, I'd like to see that."

He wouldn't be able to, though. He wasn't welcome in her house, and she sure as hell wasn't going back to his anytime soon. Unlike Teague, James didn't keep an apartment somewhere outside the territory of their families. She let herself imagine what it'd be like to have him in a bed, to be able to cozy up with him on a couch while watching a movie, to do any of the thousand little things that people took for granted. It would never happen.

She glanced up to find a young man hustling through the tables toward her. His suit was wrinkled, and he'd obviously been worrying at his tie because it was loose and hanging cockeyed. She'd bet this was Kellen O'Neill. "I've got to go. I think my date is here."

"He's not worth your time."

No, he wasn't. She'd much rather stay on the phone, but this date was a necessary evil. "I'm not arguing that. Good night, James." She reluctantly hung up and slipped her phone into her purse.

The guy stopped next to her table. "Carrigan O'Malley?"

"Yes."

"I am so damn sorry. You wouldn't believe the hell I went through to get here." He dropped into the seat across from hers and scrubbed a hand over his face. "My car broke down two miles away and I had to hoof it."

He wasn't bad looking, though his red hair somehow made him look even younger than he likely was. Pretty blue eyes, though. She raised her eyebrows. His car broke down? It must have been some trek if he somehow managed to get lipstick on his collar in the process.

Another one bites the dust.

She sipped her drink. "You made it, though."

"I did." His smile was kind of sweet, and she was struck by the thought that her world would eat him up and spit him out without hesitation. A puppy, indeed. "Thank you for waiting."

"I almost didn't." If she didn't get this conversational ball rolling, they'd be reduced to commenting about the weather in thirty seconds flat. "So what is it you do, Kellen?" *Why are you on my father's list?*

"I'm in software engineering." He launched into the description of some kind of technological mumbo jumbo that she could barely follow.

She could actually feel her eyes glazing over, but she tried to focus. He might be a puppy, but this guy seemed genuinely *nice*, even if he was a damn fool for showing up for this date with evidence of another woman on his collar. There was no shark lurking beneath his skin, and she doubted he'd have the idiocy to shove her against a wall and force his tongue into her mouth. *I could manipulate a man like this. With some careful planning, I could have him eating out of the palm of my hand.*

But he wouldn't be faithful.

Who am I kidding? None of these men are going to be faithful. This is a business arrangement, not a love match.

She sipped her drink again. "That's fascinating."

He grinned. "It's really not, but thanks for saying so. I'm sure you have much more interesting stuff to talk about than my boring company."

She might, but him nattering on about his company gave her the distance to let her thoughts wander. Carrigan started to ask another question, but movement near the front of the restaurant made her look over. She stared. She was seeing things. She had to be. There was no way that James was now shouldering past the harried-looking hostess and stalking toward her, intent in every line of his body.

He wore a pair of faded jeans and a black shirt and, *holy shit*, an obviously well-loved leather jacket. She pressed her legs together. It was all too easy to imagine what it would be like to swing up behind him on a motor-cycle, with his big body wedged between her thighs, and hang on for dear life as he gunned the engine and they took off. She'd felt free flying down the interstate in his car. How much more so would she feel on the back of a motorcycle?

"Do you know that guy?"

"Huh?"

"He's looking at you like...uh, like he knows you." Kellen sounded uncomfortable, but Carrigan couldn't tear her gaze away from James.

He stopped next to their table and took the seat next to Carrigan. "Hey, lovely."

"Hi..." She finally looked at Kellen, whose mouth was hanging open. "James, this is Kellen. Kellen, James."

James barely glanced at him. "You don't show up for a date with a woman like this with lipstick from another woman on your collar. Fuck, man, you don't show up for a date *at all* with another woman's lipstick on you." He turned back to Carrigan. "You seriously considering this guy?"

No, she wasn't. But there was something like jealousy in James's face, and she couldn't help poking at him a little. "I don't know. He seems nice."

"I'm sitting right here."

"That's your first mistake. There's no such thing as a nice guy. We're all dogs, lovely. Every single one of us." He jerked his thumb at Kellen. "This one just pretties up better than most. Didn't your brothers tell you that it's the so-called nice guys you have to watch out for?"

She *had* had that conversation with Aiden many years ago. It made Carrigan smile to think about. Her oldest brother might be making choices right now that she hated, but once upon a time they'd been close. "I think I remember hearing something about that."

"*Still* sitting right here."

"Pipe the fuck down, kid." James shot him a look. "As I was saying, you don't really want to marry this guy, do you?"

She didn't really want to marry *any* guy—especially the ones her father had chosen. But wailing about it wasn't going to do a damn bit of good and they both knew it. "I'm doing the best I can with the options I have."

"I know. Hell, I know better than most." Abruptly he grinned and held out his hand. "You want to get out of here?"

"Are you fucking kidding me?"

She looked at Kellen, who didn't look all that nice now. Not that she could blame him. He was a mottled shade of red that didn't go well with his bright hair, and he looked about ready to burst a blood vessel in his forehead. "I—"

"Go back to whatever woman you left to come here, kid. This one doesn't want you."

"Jesus Christ. Fine. Whatever. She seems like a stuck-up bitch anyway." Kellen shoved to his feet, nearly knocking over his chair, and gave them one last disgusted look before he marched away.

James snorted. "Now, where were we?"

"That was mean." A laugh bubbled up inside her, and she pressed a hand to her mouth to keep it inside. She should yell at him for his high-handedness and showing up uninvited, but the truth was that he'd saved her from another hour of boring conversation with a man who was barely more than a child. "Really mean."

"You like me mean." He motioned her forward with his fingers. "What do you say?"

She could go home, climb in a bath, and hope that would be enough to soak away her misery. Or she could take this man's hand and run away from reality for a while. Really, it was no contest. Carrigan slipped her hand into his. "Where we going?"

"Crazy, lovely. We're going crazy."

* * *

Knowing Carrigan was marrying another man was one thing. Seeing her sit across the table from some douche who didn't deserve her was something else entirely. It made James see red. He'd wanted to snatch that little shit up and shake him for being so goddamn disrespectful enough to be late, let alone show up with evidence of another woman on his clothes. When you had a shot at a woman like Carrigan, all others paled in comparison.

Except James didn't really have a shot. All he had was stolen time.

He knew that—fuck, it was a truth he couldn't escape—but the thought still soured his stomach. He wasn't sure if knowing she obviously wanted him as much has he wanted her made things better or worse. Carrigan was the calm in the middle of the hurricane that was his life. It didn't make a damn bit of sense because half the time she drove him up the wall, but the second her hand slipped into his, the tightness in his chest loosened, just a little, and he could breathe again.

He led the way out onto the street and waited for her to text her driver. "He's trustworthy?"

"As trustworthy as anyone is. Though if you kill me and dump my body in a ditch, he's going to take it personally."

James snorted. "Lovely, there are half a million things I'd love to do to your body, and not a single one of them includes pain, let alone death."

"That's...comforting." She turned off her phone and dropped it into her purse. It brought his attention to her clothing. He'd been so focused on getting that asshole out of his presence that he had to step back and take a look at the long white dress she wore tonight. It was different from the one he'd last seen her in—there was a definite Grecian feel to the way the fabric fell around her, but it was white and it covered more skin than it exposed.

"White is the last color I'd choose for you."

She shot him a sharp look. "You don't get an opinion."

"Maybe not, but those tiny little excuses for dresses that you wear to the club are more you than *this*." He pinched the fabric that fell from her hips, and lifted it a little before letting it flutter back into place. "What would you wear if you weren't trying to play a role?"

"Maybe one day I'll show you." She moved past him, the dress giving her the illusion of floating over the ground instead of walking on it. "Where's your car?"

"This way." They strode around the corner to the tiny parking lot. He held the door open for her and then took the driver's seat. "You up for a little drive?"

"As if you have to ask." She ran her hand lovingly over the dashboard. "I could spend days in this car."

He pulled out of the parking lot, picturing what a road trip with Carrigan would look like. Would she wear jeans? Maybe kick off her shoes and prop her bare feet on the dash? Would she laugh as the wind whipped her long hair around, her green eyes hidden by a pair of over-sized sunglasses?

He liked the image. He liked the image too damn much.

He drove out of Boston, heading north. The falling night was clear and cold, and the roads were almost deserted. From time to time, he glanced at Carrigan, but she'd pulled her knees to her chest and was staring out the passenger window, obviously lost in thought. James wanted to know what she was thinking. Fuck, he wanted to know *everything*. But he didn't have a right to.

Beyond that, he had a feeling that she got even less time to herself than he did. So he drove in silence and let his mind wander. He'd been so focused on Ricky, he'd almost forgotten about the shipment of girls coming in soon. Just thinking about it made him feel dirty. Yeah, he wasn't going to set them up as slaves for his own purposes, but that was a cold comfort. Because it was just one shipment. There would be others that he couldn't help. Once the flesh peddlers realized he wasn't in the business anymore, they'd take their merchandise elsewhere. James seriously doubted whoever bought those girls would feel as sick about it as he did.

What if I kept buying them?

He tightened his grip on the steering wheel. It wasn't possible... was it? He couldn't just buy the girls and then set them loose. That'd be almost as fucked up as keeping them. They'd each need to be offered a choice, and if they chose to go out on their own, they'd need their own start-up fund. That'd drain resources that were already strained.

But if all his legit businesses started to see the increase that Tit for Tat did...

It was something to think about. The Hallorans put so much evil out into the world. Maybe it was time for him to start balancing the ledgers.

He glanced at Carrigan again. What would she think of the so-called plan? Before he could think better of it, he said, "If you were going to buy up women from the flesh trade and set them free, how would you go about it?" He braced for her to look at him like he was crazy, but she just twined a strand of hair around her finger and frowned.

"That'd require a lot of resources if you wanted to make any kind of impact."

"I know." Resources he didn't have access to without stooping to lows he promised himself he'd never touch.

She frowned harder. "And there's the added complication that you're just creating a demand for a very specific kind of product. You'd have to have something long term in place to take out the main players, otherwise it might actually contribute to the overall problem, rather than helping it."

"I know." He hadn't thought that far ahead, but it was a valid point. He could ship in all the girls he wanted, but he'd just be ripping more women from their lives if he didn't cut the head off the snake, so to speak. *For someone who doesn't want responsibility to begin with, you sure as fuck attract it.* "I have something in mind."

The night that his old man had been arrested had given him the idea. Someone on the other side had been in bed with the feds. While James wasn't willing to go that far, he thought he could work something out where he threw them the information on the sellers he had and let them do their damn jobs.

If it had the added bonus of helping keep them off his back and out of Halloran business, well, he was okay with that, too.

"In that case..." Carrigan snapped her fingers. "Nonprofit." When he motioned for her to continue, she shrugged. "They aren't the simplest things to set up, and there'd be some serious challenges along the way— especially for a family like yours or mine—but as long as you kept the funds collected going exactly where they're supposed to and aboveboard, it would be a valid option."

Maybe for her. She moved in the circles of society who liked to whip out their checkbooks for that kind of thing. In his neighborhood, most everyone was struggling just to get by. "Hmm."

She turned to face him fully. "Are you seriously considering something like that? I thought you guys dealt in the sex trade."

"Sex trade is different than slave trade." He knew he sounded furious, but it was hard to rein it in when he'd worked so fucking hard to get them out of it, only to have his brother trying to drag them back to hell. "I got us out of the involuntary flesh trade."

"And now you're thinking about getting back into it for different reasons." Even in the moving shadows of his car, her green eyes saw too much. "You could make a serious difference, James. Even if you did it on a small scale, every person you save is a miracle."

He couldn't have her looking at him like that, like he was some kind of white knight or hero or some shit. He wasn't. He was just a man who'd done more bad than good, a man who wanted to balance the scales in any way he could. "It probably wouldn't work out anyway."

"James..." She trailed off and turned back to look out the window. "I was going to offer to help, but I can't promise anything with my current situation."

Which was the exact thing he'd brought her out here to help her forget. *Great job, asshole.*

He took the exit for York, and wound down to the little seaside town. It was a summer tourist spot, so it was nearly deserted this time of year, and the evening hour only added to that. Which was perfect. He didn't have the patience to deal with other people right now. All he wanted was some one-on-one time with Carrigan away from Boston. He parked next to the beach and climbed out of the car.

She was out before he could come around to open the

door for her, and she wasn't looking at the ocean behind them. Instead, she was focused on the house at his back. "I know this house."

If she'd spent any time looking at that album, she would. "It was my mother's." The only thing that had been hers and hers alone in her marriage with Victor. He didn't know how she'd managed to pull that off, but he was grateful. She'd brought them up here—just her and her boys—for a few weeks each summer every year while they were growing up.

She'd passed it to James when she died.

He ignored the dull ache in his chest that always came with thoughts of this place. Some of the happiest times of his life had been spent in this little town, but they were all because of her. She could have taken them to a shack in the middle of the woods with no running water, and he still would have been in heaven.

"I haven't been back here in something like twelve years." Not since he'd come up here after he turned eighteen to set up a maid service to clean the place out once a month after his mother died.

He looked over when Carrigan took his hand and squeezed. "We don't have to go in if you don't want to." Her shiver belied her words. She wasn't dressed for the frigid winds coming off the water.

That got him moving more than anything. He kept a hold of her hand as they crossed the street and walked up the steps. The place still looked the same as it had when he was fourteen. He'd paid for repairs out of pocket as they came up—most recently it had been the roof that needed to be completely replaced. James unlocked the door and stepped back to let Carrigan precede him.

They moved through the entrance to the living room and kitchen, turning on lights as they went. It was like stepping into the past, the cheery beach decorations and bright colors still almost painful after all this time. She stopped in front of the mantel and touched a painting of three boys playing on the beach. None of their faces were visible, but he had no problem recognizing which was which.

"Your mother?"

"She said painting calmed her thoughts and she needed all the calm she could scrape up in a houseful of boys." The bittersweet ache in his chest unraveled a little. His old man didn't talk about Elizabeth Halloran, and James had learned pretty damn fast after her death that to bring her up was as good as asking for a beating. But his brothers didn't want to talk about her, either. It seemed like the pictures of her had disappeared overnight—as if she'd been a figment of his imagination all along and he was the only one still clinging to it. This beach house was the only place left untouched, the only one that still bore the stamp of her years in this world.

James sat on the couch and ran his hand over the knotted afghan draped over the back of it. The thing had more holes than yarn. "She tried knitting, but she was terrible at it." He smiled at the memory of her cursing up a storm as she finally threw it across the room. And how he'd picked it up and brought it back to her and told her that it was the most beautiful thing he'd seen. He'd been maybe all of ten.

"You don't have to..."

"I know." He looked around the room again, seeing the ghosts of so many good memories that he'd locked away. "I didn't bring you out here to whine about my poor dead mother. This was just the one place I figured we could both sit down and breathe for a little bit."

"So you didn't bring me up here to seduce me." She smiled as she sat next to him. "I'm horribly disappointed."

"I think I could sneak in some seduction." He tugged on her hand, pulling her to sprawl across his chest. It felt right to have her here in this place with the wind howling around the house and the memories of a time long gone around them. "Come out with me."

She arched her eyebrows. "I hate to be the one to point this out, but I *am* out with you."

"That's not what I mean." He paused and tried to figure out the best way to go about this. She hadn't signed on for anything, let alone anything beyond sex. But seeing her sitting across the table from that kid tonight had really struck home how fucked up their situations had been since they met. He wanted a slice of normalcy, even if normalcy wasn't *normal*. "Carrigan O'Malley, I'd like to take you on a date."

Her eyebrows rose. "A date."

"Yeah. The whole nine yards."

"But not tonight."

"Nope." He brushed her hair back from her face. "Tonight I swept in and crashed your date with that idiot—you're welcome, by the way—so it doesn't count."

Her lips twitched. "You are a very strange man, James Halloran."

"Lovely, you have no idea." He kissed her, soft and slow, taking his time because neither of them had anywhere to be, and fuck if he'd rush this. For the first time, he had her in a house with walls between them and the rest of the world—not the backseat of his car or, worse, the goddamn storage closet in a club. She went soft as he traced the seam of her lips with his tongue. He pulled back, framing her face with his hands. "Come to bed with me."

CHAPTER FOURTEEN

Carrigan couldn't shake the feeling that this was about to change everything. She could get up and walk away, and he'd let her. She knew James well enough to know that now. Or she could say yes to his question that wasn't a question and jump headfirst down the rabbit hole.

I only have a little less than two weeks left. What do I really have to lose?

Nothing.

But it still felt like a huge step when she nodded. "Yes."

He didn't move. "Yes?"

"Take me to bed, James."

He grinned and pressed a quick kiss to her lips. Then he was up and sweeping her into his arms. She gave a startled shriek. "Hey!"

"Let me have my caveman ways." He strode through the house, not bothering to turn on any more lights and not missing a step despite the shadows. He nudged open a door with his foot and kicked it shut behind them. She sent him a questioning look, which he answered. "Guest bedroom. I don't think anyone used it in the entire time this place has been ours."

He set her carefully on her feet. "Don't move."

His terse orders shouldn't set fire to her blood. She hated orders in every other part of her life, so it didn't make a damn bit of sense that when they came from James, she had to fight not to melt into a puddle at his feet. He turned on two lamps near the bed, bathing the room in a warm glow.

She took the opportunity to look around. There were more paintings on the walls—a large one of the turbulent ocean, a dark storm rolling in. Staring at it, Carrigan could almost taste the sea air and feel the wind on her face. His mother had been gifted. The other painting was of a lighthouse standing guard on a rocky coast. It made her think of James, standing alone against the world.

"You like them?"

"They're beautiful." It was enough to make her want to wander this house and see what other treasures she'd find. She turned and found James inches away, his blue eyes roaming over her hungrily. *Another time*. Her body flashed hot at the memory of what he'd done the last time they were alone. "Touch me."

"Lovely, it would be my fucking pleasure."

But he didn't immediately reach for her. Instead, he circled her once and then stopped behind her. She tensed at the feel of his hands on the bare skin at the nape of her neck, but the tension fled as his thumbs dug into the tight muscles there. She bit her lip to keep from moaning.

"I thought so." He stopped massaging her long enough to unzip the back of her dress and let it fall to the floor. Her bra quickly joined it, leaving her in only a pair of panties. "On the bed—facedown."

Her body obeyed before her mind had a chance to catch up, but what was there to protest? He made her feel good time and time again. Tonight would be no different. Carrigan climbed onto the bed and settled face-down. The comforter was faded from countless washings and smelled faintly of lilacs. She turned her head and watched James strip, his gaze never leaving her body. He shrugged out of the leather jacket and tossed it onto the chair by the bed. Next came his T-shirt, shoes, and jeans. Each move was methodical and precise—and all the more erotic for it. The only thing he left on was a pair of boxer-briefs. His body was roped with muscle from long hours in the gym, but he'd stopped just short of it being overwhelming.

She frowned when he moved closer. There were *scars* on his chest. And not just a few. Nearly every inch of skin was covered with them. She'd felt the irregularities the last time they had sex, but she'd been too distracted to think about *why* his skin felt that way. Those weren't fighting scars, either. They were too perfectly spaced. "James—"

"I've bared all the soul I'm going to tonight, lovely." He climbed onto the bed and moved to straddle her hips. She started to turn over, but his hands on her shoulders stopped her. "Just relax. You need this as much as I do."

The scent of lotion reached her, and then his hands were back on her skin, digging in and working out all the tightness in her muscles. This time she couldn't fight back a moan. She'd known the man had magic hands, but apparently they extended beyond sex. He moved slowly over her, spending precious attention on every inch of her. By the time he reached the small of her back, she was boneless and would have agreed to damn near anything he'd asked of her.

James moved to the side. "Over." She obeyed, rolling onto her back, and he started the process again—this time beginning at her feet and working upward. If his work on her back had left her languid and relaxed, this was entirely different. Her nerves sang to life as he moved up her calf and over her thigh. She dug her hands into the comforter. All the feel-good sensation he'd created shifted, centering between her legs.

He stopped a bare inch away from where she needed him. "Not yet."

Carrigan lifted her head to glare. "I'm ready."

"I never leave a job half-finished." He moved to her other side and dug his thumbs into the sensitive arch of her foot. Against her wishes, her eyes drifted shut and she moaned again. He cursed, and his grip tightened for a single second before he moved to her calf. If she thought his desire would make him rush through this, she was sorely mistaken. He was slow and methodical and, by the time he'd reached her upper thigh, she was damn near panting for him.

"James, please."

"You don't sound relaxed." His wicked grin only stoked her need higher. He used a finger to trace the seam of her panties, dragging over the scalloped lace edge. *Still* not where she wanted his touch most. She lifted her hips, trying to guide him, but he used his free hand to pin her to the bed. "You're wet for me, lovely, aching for what only I can give you." His thumb stopped directly over her clit. With a little pressure and movement, he could send her hurtling over the edge, but he didn't give her either. "It's a damn shame you're going to be needing me for a little bit longer."

"What—*goddamn it*."

He moved before she could, straddling her hips, easily holding her in place when she tried to sit up. James started those maddening circles on her shoulders. "Be good and relax, and I'll take care of you, lovely. That's a goddamn promise."

She didn't *want* to relax. She wanted his hands and mouth on her, his cock filling her until she was lost in a sea of sensation that—damn him—only he seemed able to give her. Carrigan had had good sex before. She'd even had great sex. But what she shared with James was on a completely different level. He didn't let her run things—even when she was on top, there was no doubt that *he* was in control. And hell if that didn't turn her on more than she could have thought possible.

She wasn't winning this—not with a head-on confrontation. So she lay back and stretched her arms over her head, the move designed to draw his eyes to her breasts. "Fine. I'm relaxed."

"Hardly." He palmed her breasts, his rough hands heaven against her skin. "Tell me about this tattoo."

"I think it's self-explanatory."

He traced the words as he read aloud. "I became insane, with long periods of horrible sanity." They were just words but she felt stripped bare beneath his gaze. He frowned. "I've heard that quote before."

"Poe."

"Ah, yeah. I remember now." His thumb moved over the words again, his frown deepening. "Explain."

"You're seriously bossy."

"You like it." He cupped her breasts again, kneading gently. "And you're stalling. I'm surprised. You don't strike me as a Poe fan."

She closed her eyes because it was easier to focus on what he was doing to her body, completely at odds with how closely he watched her face. What was this man doing to her? She licked her lips. "I was an angsty teenager. Poe spoke to me—this quote most of all." It was the bare-bones explanation, but she didn't want to get into how her life was so often jumping the tracks and running out of her control. The feeling only got worse the older she got, when she realized that her father didn't care if she had a brain in her head as long as she did what she was told and didn't talk back. There was no room in their world for a woman with ambitions of her own, even if they would have benefited her family. The so-called insanity was her only escape—her dancing and drinking and men—but the real world was always waiting when she came home.

"I get it. But we'll talk about it again later. Right now I have other priorities." He rolled her nipples between his fingers, and she nearly shot off the bed. James shifted down and took one into his mouth while his hand kept up the assault on her other breast, the twin sensations of his tongue and fingers making her cry out. Each pull of his mouth sent a bolt of desire straight to her core, but it was never enough to take her into oblivion.

"*James.*"

"I've got what you need, lovely." He moved down her body, kissing his way over her ribs and down the center of her stomach as he settled between her legs. "I've been thinking about tasting you since that first night." His lips moved over the lace of her panties. "It's fucking *consumed* me."

Carrigan didn't so much as breathe as he pulled the fabric to the side. His breath ghosted over her and then— *oh God*—his tongue was there, tasting her. Her entire body quivered with the need to move, to arch up, to do *something* to keep the delicious feeling going, but she forced herself to hold still. If she tried to take charge, he might stop, and that wasn't an option.

"Lift your hips." When she obeyed, he dragged her panties off and tossed them to the side. "Better." And then he kissed her there, his mouth moving over her like he couldn't get enough. He growled, the sound vibrating through her as he lashed her clit with his tongue.

All promises she made not to move went up in smoke. Carrigan dug her hands into his long hair, needing him to never stop. She ground against his mouth, driven by the sounds he made and the need spiraling through her. "James, I'm close." If he pulled away now, she might actually kill him.

But he didn't. He shifted, pushing two fingers into her, touching her just the way she liked it, his tongue never moving from her clit. Her back bowed and her vision shorted out as she screamed her orgasm. He worked her until she yanked on his hair. "Too much."

His laugh was music to her ears. "Recover fast, lovely. We're just getting started." But he moved away from her clit and kissed her thighs and then up over her hip bones, and then higher yet to her breasts. It was soft and almost worshipful, and it was all she could do to cling to him while she relearned how to breathe.

* * *

James stretched out next to Carrigan, part of him still marveling that she was here, with him—looking at *him* to fulfill the need in every line of her body. It was a need he was only too happy to take care of. Fuck, he'd take care of her every need if she'd just let him.

Not the time for thinking that kind of shit.

He kissed her, savoring the way she arched up to close the distance between them. "Tell me how you want it, lovely."

"Is this like the phone sex, where you take over almost immediately?" She smiled, not looking the least bit worried if that's what he had planned. And, hell, that's pretty much what he'd been thinking.

Which made it that much more important that he let her take the reins.

He traced a single finger down her sternum. "Tonight, you're in charge."

"Famous last words."

"I mean it." The interest in her eyes caught him, even though she tried to shield it. He'd bet Carrigan didn't get the chance to lead things all that often. She might have with the men she'd been with in the past, but he wasn't those men. He *knew* her. So he could give her this gift.

It might be the only one she'd allow from him. "Tell me what you want, and it's yours."

"Anything?"

He didn't hesitate. "Anything." It wasn't a gift if there were stipulations.

Carrigan rolled him onto his back and climbed up to straddle him. She lightly dug her nails into his shoulders, her green eyes serious. "And if I say I want some pony play, or to peg you?"

It was a fight to keep relaxed. "Is that what you want?" He wasn't into either of those things, but he'd already broken rules for this woman. What were a few more if it meant helping her escape reality for a night? It was no contest.

Abruptly, she grinned. "So serious. God, James, I don't want to stick anything up your ass. I was just teasing."

"Brat." He tickled her ribs, grinning when her laughter filled the room. "You see what kind of sacrifices I'm willing to make for you?"

Her smile disappeared like it'd never existed. "I don't want your sacrifices. I just want you." She leaned down, dragging her breasts over his chest. "What I want more than anything tonight is to ride your cock and have you watching me the way you do." She ran her thumb along his jaw. "And talking. I'm going to need that, too."

He turned his head and captured her thumb between his teeth, pressing down lightly before he let her go. "No complaints about my talking too much."

"Wouldn't dream of it." She kissed him, light and quick, and he let her control it. She teased him until he tightened his grip on her hips, and only then did she open for him making that delicious little whimper as her tongue stroked his. Her whole body moved against his, the sensual slide of skin on skin so much more intimate than he'd ever experienced. But it wasn't really the experience itself. It was because it was Carrigan. She was here and naked and vulnerable, and she felt safe enough with him to let it happen.

He caught the back of her neck. "No running tonight. Stay with me."

"I thought I was in charge." When he didn't release her, she sighed and dropped her forehead against his. "No running. Tonight, I'm yours."

It was a start. He stroked his hand down her back and pressed a quick kiss to her lips. "Good."

"So difficult." She reached over and grabbed a condom from the nightstand.

Watching her rip it open and roll it onto his cock made his eyes slide to half-mast. "The only thing I love more than your hands on my cock is your tight pussy clamping around it." Her breath caught, and he kept going. "I have a request."

"Hmm?" She squeezed him, her gaze on his face.

"Leave the light on. I want to see you while you fuck me."

She considered him, and hell if he knew which way she'd go. Carrigan had proven time and again that she wasn't the least bit shy, but that didn't mean he could take her answer for granted. Finally she gave him one last squeeze. "I think I can manage that." She rose, her body one long line, and positioned his cock at her entrance. He went perfectly still as she sank down, taking him inch by inch.

"Christ, lovely." He kept his grip on her hips loose through sheer force of will. Every instinct clamored for him to thrust up and pull her down, to seal them together as tightly as two people could be. But this was her show. He'd promised, and he'd be damned before he went back on his word. Not tonight. Not with Carrigan. "You squeeze me tight like you never want to let go."

She braced herself on his chest with a hand and tossed back her hair. "You feel so good, I *don't* want to let go." Then she started riding him, rolling her body in a way that made her breasts bounce with each movement and his eyes damn near cross with pleasure. He kept them open, refusing to miss a single second of this.

"You're the most beautiful thing I've ever fucking seen. Your breasts were made to be worshiped, and goddamn it, your skin is so soft it drives me nuts." He hissed out a breath when she reached back with her free hand to cup his balls. "*Fuck.*"

"Keep . . . talking."

He gritted his teeth, silently promising her payback for this exquisite torture. "If you were mine, I'd keep you naked. It'd drive me batshit crazy to know you were always there and available for my cock. Wet and wanting, just like you are right now."

"Sounds like fun."

"You have no idea. I'd take my phone calls with you on my desk, legs spread and pussy waiting for me." *For me alone.* He skated a hand over her stomach. "Let me touch your clit, lovely. I want to feel you come around my cock."

She kept riding him, her gaze never leaving his. Finally she nodded, taking his hand and guiding it between her legs. She kept her fingers lightly resting on the back of his hand, touching him even as he touched her. It didn't take long. He knew what she liked, and he didn't hesitate to give it to her.

Carrigan cried out, her back bowing and her eyes closing as she threw back her head. He tried to hold on, tried to keep his eyes open to experience every second of her coming, but she milked his cock, making him lose control despite himself. James grabbed her hips, pounding into her and following her over the edge.

She slumped to his chest as he finished, and it was all he could do to lie there and just breathe. Carrigan stretched out, making him think of a cat. "God, James. If anyone else talked the way you did, I'd laugh them out of the bed."

"There's no one like me, lovely." He kissed her temple and disentangled himself. It took a few minutes to dispose of the condom and clean up, and when he got back into the room, he found her under the covers with her eyes closed. James joined her, pulling her toward him until her back was pressed against his chest.

She murmured something, twisting a little to look at him over her shoulder. "I don't sleep with people. Not normally."

"I know." He kissed the back of her neck. "Sleep, Carrigan. I'll watch over you and keep you safe while you do." There wasn't much he could promise her—that he could follow through on or that she would accept— but this he could manage. Tonight no one would demand anything of her. He'd make sure of it.

CHAPTER FIFTEEN

Carrigan opened her eyes and yawned. *What time is it?* There was no clock in the room that she could see. She reached blindly for her purse and turned on her phone, still half-asleep. The screen lit up, and the phone immediately dinged to indicate a new message. And then another. She sat up, causing James to tighten the arm he'd slung around her waist. *God, he's so sexy.* He'd woken her up twice in the night for more sex, and she shivered at how thoroughly tired her body felt from the attention. *I could get used to that.*

Her phone rang, startling her, and she hurried to answer before it woke James up. "What?"

"Where the hell are you?"

Aiden. She shoved her hair back. "What's going on?" It was ten in the morning. There was no reason he'd be calling her this early—or at least no *good* reason.

"Where. The. Fuck. Are. You?"

Okay, this was bad. She looked around wildly, but the answer didn't magically pop into existence. There were two options. She could keep avoiding and cowering, or she could try to brazen her way through this. So, really, there was only one option. "It's none of your damn business."

"Wrong answer. Would you like to know *why* it's my business?" A car door slammed. "Because our goddamn father is on a rampage, and our mother is practically breathing fire at the thought of someone, let alone one of her children, ruining this fiasco of a wedding."

The wedding. Shit. She did some quick mental math. "The wedding is tomorrow." *Thank God.* She couldn't believe she'd forgotten about it. Yes, she'd had a whole hell of a lot going on, and technically Teague and Callie were already married, but neither of those were legitimate excuses.

"I'm aware. The rehearsal, however, is this evening, and no one can find you."

She glanced over to where James was now awake and watching her. "There's plenty of time. Calm down."

"There would be, but Aileen has *activities* planned for Callie and the bridesmaids—including *you*—today. Activities that you're not participating in because *no one knows where the fuck you are*."

Carrigan read between the lines. Their mother was furious, and she'd gotten their father riled up, and both of them were taking it out on Aiden. Shit rolled downhill and all that. "I'll be back in an hour." She hoped. Traffic would be heavier than it had been on the way up here.

"You have explaining to do, Carrigan. I'm not kidding."

That's what she was afraid of. But hopefully if she

slipped back in and played her part for the next twenty-four hours, everyone would be too busy to ask her uncomfortable questions. Hopefully. "Just stall a little longer. I'm on my way." She hung up before he could yell at her anymore.

"Trouble?" The sleepy gravel of James's voice made her body perk up despite the stress.

"Not in the way you mean." She slid out of bed and started throwing her clothes on. "Can you drive me back?"

"Yeah, no problem." He followed her to her feet, and she got hung up on how damn good he looked naked. Her gaze caught on the scars on his chest and held when he turned around to pull on his pants. His back was an identical mess, though the scars there almost looked... layered.

"James..."

"Let's get you home before they send out a search party." He yanked on his shirt, not looking at her. "If we leave now, we can swing by a drive-thru and eat on the way."

He didn't want to talk about the scars. She got that. She had plenty of secrets of her own. But that didn't mean she didn't want to know. Even if she could put two and two together—the sheer amount of scars and their placement told her they weren't from some sort of accident. No, every single one of them was intentional. There was only one person Victor Halloran would allow to hurt one of his children like that...and it was Victor Halloran.

She held her dress in a white-knuckled grip. He beat James. He *scarred* James. She wanted to march down to the prison and put a bullet between his eyes. Everyone knew Brendan—and probably Ricky—was a monster. Had they started out that way? Or had their father— the one person put on this world to protect his own children—been the one who broke something inside them beyond repair? Children were to be protected. Yeah, Seamus wasn't exactly father of the year, but he'd never hurt her like that. He'd never so much as lifted a hand or *threatened* that kind of violence. And to go so far as to cut and whip and do whatever had caused the marks on James's body?

Her mother would have killed him on the spot.

She forcibly loosened her grip and finished getting dressed, fury all twisted up with sadness for the boy he used to be. Maybe she was wrong. Maybe it hadn't been Victor who'd hurt his boy. Whoever did it hadn't broken James. The more she found out about him, the more amazed she was that James had grown into the man he was. A man of worth. He might not see it that way—and she was pretty damn sure he thought the exact opposite—but it was the truth.

By the time she made it out of the bedroom, he was flipping his keys around his finger and staring out the window at the ocean. Carrigan paused a few feet away, not sure what the protocol was. Did she kiss him? Touch him? Just smile and head for the car? Throwing herself at him and hugging him and promising vengeance on whoever hurt him wasn't an option, no matter how much it was exactly what she wanted to do.

He glanced at her, his expression shuttered. "You ready?"

"Yeah. Sorry about hauling you out of bed and forcing

you to drive me back." This was so wrong, so stilted. She hated it. She cleared her throat. "Look, we don't have to talk about your scars. I'm sorry I mentioned them at all."

He crossed to her, stopping within arm's reach. "It's fine. It's not something I want to get into."

Maybe it was something he *needed* to get into. But she wasn't a shrink, and he couldn't have made himself clearer if he'd turned on a neon sign that read, *Back the fuck off*. He'd shared about his mother last night. That was unexpected enough. This whole baring-of-the-souls thing wasn't what they were about. It couldn't be. "I understand."

"Okay."

"Good."

"Great." He snagged the back of her neck and pulled her in for a kiss that curled her toes. "Let's get you home."

* * *

Carrigan barely made it through the door when Aiden appeared, grabbed her elbow, and hauled her upstairs. He didn't say a word, and she kept silent because yelling at him right now would undoubtedly bring one—or both— or her parents down on her. Aiden and she might not be as close as they used to be, but his anger was still preferable to Seamus and Aileen's.

As soon as he closed her bedroom door behind them, she shoved him away. "Get your goddamn hands off me."

"Where the fuck were you?" He took a step toward her, but seemed to think better of it and circled her instead. "Those are the same clothes you were wearing last night, aren't they?"

"You're not my keeper."

"Wrong." He ran his hands through his dark hair, making it stand on end. "Jesus, Carrigan, I know you're having a hell of a time with the way things are going, but can you stop being so goddamn selfish for one fucking second and *think*?"

For the first time since he'd towed her up here, she actually *looked* at him. Aiden had always been the classically handsome one of her brothers. Teague was dark and brooding. Cillian was the edgy, too-gorgeous one that made women lose their minds. Aiden was the rock.

He looked like he was cracking under the pressure. There were dark smudges beneath his green eyes, and he'd lost weight recently—weight he didn't need to lose. She reined in the impulse to yell at him like he was yelling at her, and sat on the edge of her bed. "Are you okay?"

"No, I'm not fucking okay." He paced from one wall to the other and back again, each step jerky with barely restrained fury. "You disappeared without a trace from that restaurant and turned off your phone. The only message you got out was telling Liam not to worry."

She was going to have to send Liam a gift basket of whiskey. "It's fine. Obviously I'm okay."

"It is *not* fine." He looked like he wanted to shake her. "Last time you disappeared like this, that bastard Halloran threatened to send us your head in a basket if we didn't comply. He would have, even though Callie turned herself over in exchange for you. Do you have any fucking idea what it did to me to sit here all night, wondering if I'd ever see you again, or if one of our goddamn enemies—who seem to be multiplying by the day—had gotten a hold of you?"

No, she didn't have any idea. She hadn't stopped to think that anyone would worry about her. She'd assumed that they'd be so caught up in their own dramas that she could slip back into the house without a word. "I—"

"You can't keep doing this—the clubs, the men, the drinking. I know how much these little escapades mean to you, but it's not safe."

She knew that. Of course she knew that. But she'd weighed her growing panic over the approaching deadline against what could possibly happen to her while she was out and about.

Nothing's going to happen with me when I'm with James.

She didn't have a right to that belief, but she couldn't shake it. He might have been the reason she was taken the last time, but so much had changed since then. Hell, *everything* had changed. She couldn't say as much to Aiden, though. "I'm sorry I worried you."

"Which isn't the same thing as saying you won't do it again." He dropped next to her on the bed with a sigh. "We might be at peace, but that doesn't mean a damn thing and we both know it. There are more enemies to fear than just the Hallorans."

Considering she'd spent the night with one and was no worse for wear, she believed it. Except… "What other enemies?"

"I don't know." He laughed, but not like anything was funny. "All I'm getting are rumors and things that could be coincidence. Father thinks I'm insane, but I can't help feeling like someone is circling us, looking for weaknesses." He grabbed her arm. "Promise me you won't go out alone anymore, Carrigan. I couldn't handle it if something happened to you." *Again*. The last word might be unspoken, but it still stood between them. The truth was that she was a liability, and her habits made her even more so.

"You know I only have until my birthday to make a decision."

He didn't look at her. "I know."

"And you're still asking me to be good and stay out of trouble, even though this is my last chance at a little slice of freedom?"

"I am." A muscle in his jaw twitched. "I might be a dick, but I think your life is worth more than your happiness."

She wasn't sure if she agreed. Oh, Carrigan didn't want to die. She'd come face-to-face with that fate in the Halloran house and she'd fought tooth and nail to avoid it. But happiness was such a delicate and fleeting thing. She'd gotten a glimpse of what it might feel like last night with James, and she craved more, like a junkie jonesing for her next hit.

She couldn't make the promise Aiden wanted—not without lying. She slipped her arm free of his hold. "Let's get through this wedding, and then we'll talk."

"Carrigan—"

"I've got to shower and get changed. I'll make sure I apologize to Mother for missing the activities she had planned today." Maybe if she kept talking, he'd realize there was no way in hell this discussion was happening today—or ever.

Aiden sighed again. "Fine. You win this time. Get your shit together and I'll see if I can calm down Father before the rehearsal. Don't be late."

"I wouldn't dream of it." She held her breath until he left her room, closing the door softly behind him, and then lay back on her bed and stared at the ceiling. Aiden didn't understand what he was asking of her. He felt bad about it, at least in theory, but he was like Seamus in only seeing the bottom line. The only difference between her brother and father was that her brother would lose his mind if he lost her. Even with all the changes he'd gone through lately, she never doubted Aiden loved her. That love wouldn't be enough for him to defy their father's plans for her, but it was there nonetheless.

But obeying meant never seeing James again. Never seeing those icy blue eyes flare hot with desire. Never losing herself in his arms. Never delving into the secrets he carried around with him like Atlas carrying the world.

She couldn't do it.

It was more than just the deadline bearing down on her. She couldn't give James up. Not yet. Not until she absolutely had to.

* * *

Sloan drifted through the reception hall, a glass of white wine dangling from her fingers. She didn't usually drink, but after the day with her mother, it was a necessary measure. She leaned against the wall, searching the people's faces around her. Carrigan was back. She *knew* that. But she wouldn't be able to breathe easy until she actually laid eyes on her sister.

She's got to stop disappearing like this. Everyone worries so much, and it throws everything into chaos.

The words fell flat, even in her head. The truth was

she envied Carrigan her nights of freedom. They might be small in the grand scale of things, but they were more than Sloan could work up the courage to do for herself. Her only escape lay in the books populating the house's library, and even those were cold comfort these days. Fantasy worlds were all well and good, but there always came the time when she had to put down the book and resume real life. She might face dragons and beautiful men and adventures beyond telling in those pages, but in her day-to-day life she was just a rabbit of a woman. Cillian used to tease her when they were little, saying she was afraid of her own shadow.

He's not far off. Bitterness clawed up her throat, the taste acid on her tongue. If she was braver, she would have taken Teague's offer to get her away. But the sad truth was that she didn't know who she was if she wasn't Sloan O'Malley, fifth child of Seamus and Aileen O'Malley, obedient daughter and…boring. So incredibly boring. *I want more, I just don't know what that* more *is.*

But it was a waste of time and energy to rail at her situation, because the truth was that she wasn't ever going to change. She'd do what her father wanted and, when the time came, she'd marry who he picked for her, slowly withering away like a flower on a vine. At least the flower had a second chance at life when spring came around.

Sloan didn't.

"Hey, squirt. You're looking awfully dark and down over here in the shadows." Cillian leaned against the wall next to her. "Didn't you know that Teague has the market cornered on brooding? You can't take that away from him the night before his wedding."

She looked over to where the brother in question stood in the middle of a group of people, grinning down at his wife like she was the most beautiful thing he'd ever seen. *No one's ever going to—Oh my God, Cillian's right. I'm sitting over here, brooding.* She took a sip of her wine. "I was just thinking."

"Thinking is all you ever do, squirt. You've got to get out in the world and live a little."

She eyed his nearly empty drink—no doubt it wasn't his first for the night. "I think you do enough living for both of us."

"Not how it works." He finished the pale amber liquid in his glass. "Life experience can't be shared, not really. I could tell you stories..." He glanced at her. "Then again, you're my little sister and I think those stories might burn your virgin ears."

Heat crept up her neck and over her face. "There's such a thing as too much information."

"I couldn't agree more. But my point stands—I could go out and do the craziest shit anyone's ever seen, and it wouldn't count any more in life experience for *you* than those books you like to read."

She knew that. Lord, she knew that. But wishing for courage to do something else—something *wild*—with her life was a long way off from actually taking that first step to *do* it. Sloan might only be twenty-three, but she knew herself. She liked her quiet, safe, boring life. Maybe it wasn't always *safe* safe, but if she put herself out in the world, there were no guarantees of even *that*. "I'll take it into consideration."

"No, you won't." He snorted. "You're saying that because you think it's what I want to hear, but in reality you'll be holed up in that nook in the library with a book, reading about someone else's adventures." He seemed to realize how harsh he sounded, because he sent her an apologetic look. "Sorry, squirt. If you can't tell already, I'm not exactly good company tonight."

She could. One benefit to always standing in the shadows was that she saw more than the average person. She'd known the second she got back from Connecticut that something about Cillian had changed. He still pasted on the carefree attitude when he had to, but that wasn't the man he was anymore. Devlin's death had changed him, just like it'd changed them all. She reached out and squeezed his arm. "It'll be okay."

His smile was mirthless. "Well, hell, squirt. I never pegged you for a liar."

CHAPTER SIXTEEN

James spent the day in meetings. It was all shit he knew he'd been neglecting, but his talk with Lisa Marie had driven home just how many things he'd let slip through the cracks. It was time to change that. If he was going to run the Hallorans, he had to stop pussyfooting around and *run* it.

By the time he got back to the house, it was dark and he couldn't remember the last time he'd eaten. But he was confident that there were no more nasty surprises lurking as a result of Ricky's actions while James wasn't paying attention. As for Ricky...

It was time to do something about that, too.

Ten days was long enough to let him stew. He needed to fix this. Now.

He checked his phone as he walked through the door. Nothing. Not that he'd expected Carrigan to call him. She'd made it pretty damn clear that she had a lot going on in the next few days, so there was no reason for the disappointment souring his stomach. He'd just spent the damn night with her. He couldn't possibly miss her. But the thought of going another few days without seeing her again made the feeling in his stomach worse.

Pathetic. He could almost hear his old man's voice in his head, letting him know just what Victor Halloran thought of his son getting twisted up over a woman, let alone an O'Malley woman. *A distraction. That's all she is. Nothing good will come of it.*

He bypassed the kitchen—no point in eating until he dealt with his brother—and made his way downstairs. It was eerily quiet in the basement, the silence broken only by the occasional sound of the house settling. Even though this place wasn't old, it still had the feeling of something tired and exhausted, the history of too many bad memories weighing it down.

I'd like to light a match and leave it to burn.

He unlocked the door to Ricky's cell and walked in. His brother lounged on the rickety old bed, his head propped on his arms as he stared at the ceiling. "James."

"Ricky." He moved to lean against the wall opposite. Ricky didn't look like a broken man, but then, this was the least of what their old man had put them through. His brother had nearly the same scars James did. He opened his mouth, and then reconsidered. There had to be a better way to do this—all of this. "What do you want?"

"Everything." Ricky sat up. "But since that's not on the table, I'd settle for you not treating me like your annoying kid brother and actually showing a little fucking respect."

He had two options. He could leave his little brother

down here to rot, secure in the knowledge that he wasn't causing trouble. Or he could take a risk and see if a little more responsibility would be the thing to get Ricky on track. And it was a risk. But James was all too aware of the whispers that circulated among his men. Plenty of people weren't happy that he was rolling with the peace talks instead of striking directly into the heart of the O'Malleys and Sheridans. If they thought he was locking away Ricky because he was scared of him, it would put James in a precarious place.

If he could somehow get his brother on the same page, it would kill multiple birds with one stone. Not that he was going to trust Ricky—the only reason his brother would suddenly have a change of heart is that he wanted something and had to go through James to get it.

But maybe he could channel that to his purposes.

"I'll show you respect when you earn it." He made a show of looking around the bare room. "Which you're not going to do down here. Are you ready to man up and show you can take orders?"

Ricky narrowed his eyes. "You're letting me out."

"I'm willing to work with you, *if* you're willing to obey."

He seemed to think it over, but there was no masking the excitement in his eyes. Apparently his brother hated this room almost as much as James hated putting him down here. "What do you want me to do?"

Here was the crux. "You're going to run protection duty on the border businesses. If you can manage that without starting shit with anyone, then we'll talk."

"How long?"

Long enough to make sure he was actually, genuinely

wanting this to do right and not just playing James. "Until I say so."

"Fine." Ricky stood and held out his hand. "I'll play soldier."

James shook it, but he held on when his brother would have let go. "And, Ricky, stay the fuck away from Tit for Tat. Your shadow darkens that doorway, and a few days in this room will look like a goddamn paradise."

He hesitated, and then gave a jerky nod. "Sure thing. I was done with the tired-ass tail that works there, anyway."

Sure you were. He couldn't control his brother's actions across the board, but he could at least make sure that the girls who looked to him for protection were actually *protected*. That thought brought him back to the shipment coming in soon. He expected the proprietors to be in touch within a few days, and then he'd have to decide once and for all what he was going to do about them.

I could do some good in this world. Maybe then I'd be able to keep myself from the slow, final slide into being the monster my father was.

He kept coming back to Carrigan's idea of a nonprofit. It wasn't something he could do on his own, but he'd seen the way she lit up with excitement at the idea of running something like that. With her helming that side of things, he could do his part by sliding a portion of the girls into various jobs in Boston. They'd make a hell of a team.

Except we aren't a team. She's marrying someone else, and no man worth his shit is going to let her work with me *on something like this.*

"James?"

He blinked. From the tone of Ricky's voice, he'd said his name a few times. "Yeah?"

"You won't regret this." He turned and walked out of the door without looking back.

Funny, but James was already regretting it. His brother was a loose cannon and he damn well knew it, but letting him out of this room was the lesser of two evils. He had to take a chance, no matter how much he didn't like it. After a few minutes, he left the cell and made his way up to his room. Another glance at his phone showed just as few calls as it had last time. Carrigan was probably still at the rehearsal, or the dinner that had undoubtedly been thrown afterward. She wasn't going to call.

He was a damn fool for wanting her to.

Tomorrow was Teague's wedding. He mulled that over while he showered, scrubbing down his body. He'd gotten an invite only as courtesy and he damn well knew it. They didn't want him there. The strained friendship he and Teague had shared over the years had finally broken under the events of the last few months, and he didn't blame the man for the desire to punch the shit out of James that was written all over his face every time they were forced to interact. Ironically, Callista Sheridan didn't seem to hold his taking her captive against him.

But then, she had shot and killed his older brother. That kind of made it hard to stand on a pedestal.

He ducked under the shower spray, as if something as simple as water could wash away all his sins. Going to Teague's wedding was asking for trouble—trouble he couldn't afford. The peace between the three families was precarious at best, and doing something that might jeopardize it was the height of stupidity.

If he had a brain in his head, he'd leave town tomorrow and avoid the temptation the whole fiasco offered. James shut off the water, knowing damn well that he wasn't going to do it. He craved the sight of Carrigan, and adding more distance between them, even for a limited time, wasn't a goddamn option.

Fuck. Looked like he was going to a wedding tomorrow.

* * *

Carrigan didn't cry. Especially at weddings. Especially at weddings whose planning had been a giant pain in her ass for the last few months and had been arranged by her parents.

But the second Callie started down the aisle in her gorgeous white dress, its train like something out of a fairy tale, and Teague's eyes shone, Carrigan damn near lost it. *He's so happy. That's all I ever wanted for him.* None of her problems mattered today. They could wait. Teague and Callie's happiness took priority, and she was more than content to temporarily shelve her own baggage for a while.

She clutched her miniature bouquet while Callie's father handed her off to Teague and the priest began to talk about love and Christ and marriage. It couldn't be more obvious that neither of the two people at the altar gave two fucks about his words. They only had eyes for each other.

Even Carrigan could admit that the wedding was gorgeous. Her mother had gone all out, and all the headaches and badgering had resulted in a picture-perfect ceremony. The bridesmaids all wore long blue gowns the same color as Callie's eyes, and they all had lily bouquets instead of the traditional roses, which complemented Callie's lily and rose bouquet. All Carrigan's remaining brothers were there, polished within an inch of their lives, and they all looked genuinely happy for the first time in longer than she cared to remember.

It seemed like she wasn't the only one putting aside her baggage for Teague's big day.

Teague and Callie exchanged their vows and were announced as Mr. and Mrs. Teague O'Malley. No one seemed to care that they'd already been married for several months—including them. And then they were down the aisle and disappearing through the huge doors, and Aiden was there, offering his arm to Carrigan. "You managed to be on time, I see."

"Don't be a dick." She spoke through teeth clenched into a smile. Aiden's attitude might stem from legitimate worry about her, but that didn't mean she was going to roll over and play dead for him. *He* wasn't the one being forced into a marriage he didn't want. Oh, she knew their father had his eye on several candidates for her older brother, but the sad truth was that ultimately it'd be Aiden's decision on both the time and the person. Carrigan didn't have that luxury. *I'm not worrying about it today.*

Easier said than done.

They made it to the end of the aisle, and Carrigan walked over to hug Teague. "I'm so happy for you. For both of you."

"Thank you."

And then their mother was there, ushering them all out

of the church and into the waiting limo. It was a squeeze
with all of them, but they managed. Carrigan ended up
sandwiched between Keira and Aiden. He frowned at their
younger sister. "Have you been drinking?"

"It's called celebrating." She reached around to grab a
bottle of champagne that had been stashed in the bucket
of ice in the corner, and took a swig. "We're at a wedding, after all."

From the look of her, she'd been *celebrating* for a
while before they got to the ceremony. Aiden must have
come to the same conclusion. "Keira, we're going to talk
about this."

She rolled her eyes. "Sure thing, Dad. I'll get right on
that."

For the first time, Carrigan wondered if maybe this
was more than their sister just working her way through
grief over Devlin's death. She tried to remember the last
time she saw Keira sober and came up blank. It could be
chalked up to her being busy with her own drama...but
what if that wasn't it at all? She exchanged a look with
Aiden, their earlier bickering falling away in the face of
what might be a real problem. Carrigan shook her head.
Not today. Not on Teague's wedding day.

Aiden nodded and sat back, causing the tension among
the three of them to decrease dramatically. Across from
them, Teague and Callie were lost in their own world,
and Cillian and Sloan were talking quietly. No one had
heard or paid attention to their exchange with Keira. It was
probably for the best. If Teague knew something might
be wrong, he'd set aside everything except for solving the
problem. They'd put it on the back burner so that he could
be happy without strings attached today.

They pulled up to the reception hall—the same one that had been used to announce Teague and Callie's wedding—and everyone piled out of the limo. Half the guests had somehow beaten them there, and the tables were filling up as they made their way up to the main table on the platform. Carrigan gave the crowd a cursory glance, and then almost tripped over her feet when she caught sight of a familiar blond head of hair. *No way*. She touched Sloan's arm. "I'll be right back."

"Okay. Don't be too long, though. I think our mother has dinner set up to go off immediately, followed by the toasts."

One of which Carrigan was giving. She nodded without taking her eyes off the blond man. That was *definitely* James. "I know. I won't miss it." She moved away before her sister could say something else, winding through the tables and trying to get a better look. *This is stupid. Just walk over and tap him on the shoulder and then you'll see that it's not James, because there's no way James could be here.* But then he looked over his shoulder, caught her eye, and *winked*. She changed course, determined to drag his ass out of here before one of her brothers or, worse, her father, realized he was in the room.

James stood and walked toward the door leading deeper into the building—not the exit. *That's it. I'm going to kill him.* Carrigan checked to make sure no one was following, and then ducked after him. She barely made it three steps when an arm wrapped around her waist and a hand over her mouth cut off her curse.

"Relax, lovely. It's me."

She damn well knew it was him. It wasn't like she

was wandering down the hall for her health. She elbowed him and slipped free. "What the hell is wrong with you?"

"Nothing. Why do you ask?" He rubbed his stomach with a grimace. "You sure do like beating me up."

"I don't respond well to being grabbed without warning." She waved it away. "Back to more important things—why are you here?"

He crossed his arms over his chest. "I was invited."

"You were invited." She hadn't realized it was possible to actually feel her blood boil. "You're a smart man, James."

"Why do I feel you're about to use that as a backhanded compliment?"

She ignored the question. "And, as a smart man, you have to be aware that the invitation was a gesture only. No one wants you here, and just by being here, you're upping the chances of causing a conflict that will jeopardize the peace."

"Ah, lovely." He grinned, his total lack of concern making her blood pressure spike. "If I didn't know any better, I'd think you're sweet on me."

"I'm not. I don't believe in caring about idiots who have death wishes." She smacked his arm. "You need to leave. Now."

"Bossy, bossy." He turned and walked farther down the hall, forcing her to chase him like a yippy dog. "Pretty wedding."

"Yeah, it was." She glanced over her shoulder. So far no one had come looking for her, but it was only a matter of time. "James…" What could she say? That it would kill a little part of her if something happened to him? It was nothing more than the truth, and it still pissed her off that he'd taken a risk like this. "Leave."

James peered through a door and then kept it open with his foot. "Not until I get what I came for."

Of course he'd come here for a specific reason. She should have known. Carrigan sighed. "Okay, fine. Hurry up and get what you came for and then you can get out of here." She frowned when he laughed. "What's so funny?"

"Lovely, I came here for *you*." He grabbed her wrist and hauled her against his chest, simultaneously taking a step back that brought them into the room he'd just been looking in. She got the vague impression of a storage closet, and then he shoved the door shut and his mouth was on hers. Shock had her opening for him, shock and the fact that she was hot and wanting just by his touching her.

Torn between shoving him off and yelling at him some more, and kissing him until she forgot all the reasons this was a bad idea, it was no contest. She slid her hands down his chest to hook his belt. "I need you."

"You've read my mind." He pulled at her dress, bunching it up. The further it rose, the greater the barrier between them. "How much fucking fabric does one dress need?"

Too much. She pulled away and turned around. "Unzip me."

He wasted no time in obeying, dragging the zipper down and shoving the offending dress off her shoulders to puddle on the floor. Then he was there, pressed against her bare back, his hand slipping around and into her panties. "You're wet for me."

"Always."

"I think you have a thing for storage closets." He kissed the back of her neck, left bare by her complicated updo. "I like it." And then her panties were gone, joining her dress on the floor. He kicked her legs wider, taking advantage of the position to push two fingers into her. She rolled her hips, moaning, and he growled against her skin. "Quiet, lovely. This isn't some loud-as-fuck dance club. This is your brother's wedding." He fucked her slowly with his fingers. "Someone's going to come looking for you before too long, so you need to be good and quiet so they don't walk in and see you taking my cock like you can't live without it."

She couldn't catch her breath. "Oh God."

He slowed even further, dragging his fingers out of her. "Do you want me to stop?" He circled her clit. "You can put that ridiculous dress back on and walk back to the reception and pretend you weren't about to come all over my hand." His breath brushed the sensitive spot where her neck met her shoulder. "Or I can go down on my knees and lick that pretty pussy of yours until you have to cover your mouth to keep from screaming." He kept going, his words the only thing that penetrated the rushing in her ears. "And then, while you're still recovering, I'll bend you over and fuck you until you're coming again, this time around my cock."

His hand started to slide up her stomach and she grabbed his wrist. "Don't you dare stop." She guided him back between her legs, whimpering when he pushed into her again. "*James.*"

"Fuck, lovely, when you say my name like that, you damn well know I'm not going to stop until I've done everything I promised and more."

CHAPTER SEVENTEEN

James tried to keep an ear on the hallway outside them, but with Carrigan in his arms making that delicious whimpering sound, he lost it. Everything went out the damn window except for his need to bury himself inside her until they both lost control. He kept working her with one hand and used the other to get his pants off. "On second thought, I'm just going to fuck you right now. Every minute I spend without being buried inside you is one minute too many." He grabbed a condom out of his pocket and was forced to stop touching her long enough to roll it on.

Too long.

He ran one hand up her spine, bending her forward, and used his other to notch his cock in her entrance. She was wet and ready for him, so he wasted no time sliding home. James went stock-still, the sheer bliss of being inside her never failing to take his breath away. "The things you do to me." He moved, gripping her chin and maneuvering her so that her back was flush against his chest. His shirt was one barrier too many between them, but he wasn't going to waste the energy to get it off. Instead, he kissed her. "You're mine, lovely. Mine alone." Crazy words. Words he had no right to.

She made a sound of protest, but he wasn't about to let her start thinking right now. James slid his hand down to cup her breast, pinching her nipple even as he slipped his free hand between her legs again, stroking her clit. "Brace your hands on the wall."

The new position allowed him deeper, and he wasted no time taking full advantage of it, fucking her ruthlessly even as he rubbed her clit. "Remember, lovely, be quiet. You never know who might be listening."

There was that whimper again. His balls went tight at the sound, and words came out of his mouth in an unfiltered river. "I want you so much, I can't fucking see straight." He slammed into her hard, the sound of flesh meeting flesh filling the room. "Every time I watch you walk away, all I can think about is dragging you back into my bed, my car, a fucking storage closet. Being inside you is as close to perfection as I'll ever get."

She let go of the wall and slapped a hand over her mouth as she came, and he was forced to grab her hips to keep them both from slamming into the wall. Her pussy milked him, taking away his last breath of control. He slammed into her once, twice, and a third time, coming so hard he saw stars. James caught them both from falling with a hand on the wall, keeping another around her waist. "Shit."

"That about sums it up." She pulled away and turned

around. She had the look of a woman well pleasured, but there was a hint of panic lingering in her green eyes. "This doesn't change anything."

He wanted to argue, to rail at her for being so damn determined to drive herself off the cliff, but that wasn't why he'd come here tonight. He caught her chin and kissed her, moving back almost as soon as he'd made contact. "I wanted to see you. End of story." But it wasn't. Not by a long shot.

"Promise me you'll leave." She rummaged around and found her panties. "We've already been gone too long."

"So determined to see the back of me."

She yanked on her dress and, even in his frustration, he made sure he zipped it up slowly so he didn't damage the fabric. Carrigan turned around as soon as he was done. "Apparently I'm going to have to be the one who has enough common sense for both of us. You can't be here. This can't happen like this. Not where we could be caught."

Her reasoning was sound, but that didn't stop the bitterness on the back of his tongue. "Got it. I'm your dirty little secret."

"Do you *want* a war?" She shook her head. "You know what, no. I'm not doing this. Not now and not like this. If you want to have a conversation like reasonable adults, call me later."

She was right. He *knew* she was right. But that didn't kill the urge to drag her back into his arms and kiss her until she stopped telling him all the reasons they were shitty for each other. He opened the closet door and motioned for her to precede him. "After you."

"You...God, you drive me so crazy." She grabbed the front of his shirt and kissed him, moving away before he could do anything about it. Right into the hallway where two of her brothers stood, shock written across both their faces.

Well, fuck.

Aiden grabbed her arm and the younger one grabbed *him*, slamming him against the wall. "I'm going to fucking kill you." James didn't fight back, just let the little shit shake him.

"Cillian, no!"

Aiden gave Carrigan a shake, too, and *that* set James's temper off. He grabbed the kid and glared at the O'Malley heir. "You can be pissed at me all you want, but you hurt her and I'll take your fucking hand off at the wrist."

Aiden didn't let her go, but he didn't shake her again, either. "I think it's time you left."

Hell, James agreed with him. He caught Carrigan's gaze. *Unfinished business, lovely.* She frowned, obviously worried her brother was going to take him out back and shoot him. "I think you're right." He shoved Cillian away and made a show of dusting off his shirt. "I'll be seeing you around." He turned and made it all of one step before Aiden's voice stopped him.

"My sister might be ready to forget what you almost did to her, but I damn well haven't. You fucking touch her again and it really will be war."

* * *

Carrigan's brothers dragged her back to the reception. Aiden stopped just inside the door, his grip on her arm tight enough to bruise. "You will go to the banquet table, sit your ass down, and smile like nothing's wrong. You will give your planned toast. And then you will sit there like someone who isn't a fucking traitor until it's time to go home. After that, we'll deal with this."

She'd never feared her brother before, but she'd never seen him with another man's murder in his eyes, or with that bone-deep disgust he turned on her. She'd fucked up, and they both knew it. Carrigan gave a jerky nod, and walked to the wedding party's table on shaking legs. Teague sent her a questioning look, and she somehow managed to dredge up a smile for him. "The food looks great."

The rest of the reception passed in a blur. Every time she looked up, she found Aiden or Cillian glaring at her, a physical reminder of the talk she had coming. She tried to dredge up some righteous indignation. Good lord, she tried. But there was nothing.

She'd been sleeping with the enemy.

Worse, she could still feel the imprint of his mouth on her skin, his hands on her body, his cock inside her. Even knowing the trouble that was coming, she still wanted James almost more than she wanted her next breath—which just proved she was too stupid to live.

They saw Teague and Callie off in a flurry of bubbles. Carrigan was an island of misery in the midst of all the joy, her glowering brothers flanking her as she walked to the waiting town car and they got in on either side of her. She barely had time to take a breath before Aiden started in. "What. The. Fuck. Is. Wrong. With. You? James fucking Halloran? *Seriously,* Carrigan? How fucking stupid can you be?"

She crossed her arms over her chest, staring straight ahead. "I'm not stupid." They didn't know James. They didn't understand that what he and she shared was something she couldn't make herself pass up. "You don't understand."

"No, I goddamn well don't. He kidnapped you. Christ only knows what he did to you when you were in his house."

Carrigan turned to glare at him. "Christ has nothing to do with it. *I* know what happened—and, more importantly, what didn't happen—to me. And it's a moot point now anyway."

"No, it's not a fucking moot point." He pointed a finger out the side window. "That guy is the enemy. He might be someone you're attracted to or whatever the fuck was going on back there, but he's a Halloran. He's not for you, and you damn well know it."

Yeah, she did. Not too long ago, that forbidden aspect would have been enough to make James even more attractive to her. *Was that all this is? The lure of the untouchable?* She hunched lower in her seat, every instinct crying against that belief. It was different with James. *He* was different. Maybe she'd originally entertained thoughts of him because he was the one man her father would lose his shit over, but that had quickly morphed into something…genuine.

Aiden gripped her shoulder. "Look at me, Carrigan."

She wanted to dig in her heels and shut her eyes like she had when they were kids and he pissed her off. But they weren't kids anymore. They were adults, and she was facing real-life consequences. So she turned and met his gaze, doing her damnedest not to drop her eyes. Her brother's face seemed to have acquired new lines in the last few hours, and every single one of them was because of her. "Aiden—"

"He is *not* for you. I'll keep this from our father, because we both know what he'd do if he knew."

Nothing good. Seamus's potential reactions ranged from locking her in the attic for the rest of her life to marrying her off right away to the first man he could find that wasn't an enemy of the O'Malleys. Nowhere on the list was him smiling, patting her on the head, and telling her that he just wanted her to be happy. Her happiness was, and always had been, secondary.

On her other side, she could practically feel Cillian seething. He shifted. "You can't seriously be thinking of letting this go, Aiden. He defiled our sister."

"Are you serious right now?" She turned and smacked him. "I'm a grown-ass woman, and no one defiled me."

"Except that time he threw your ass into a trunk and *kidnapped* you. Since when are we so willing to forget *that*? Aiden, you have to tell Father."

"I don't have to do a damn thing—and neither do you." The boy she'd grown up with, the one she'd played countless hours of imaginary games with, was gone, replaced by a cold son of a bitch that Carrigan would think twice before crossing. Apparently Cillian felt the same way, because he jerked back. Aiden looked at her, and then Cillian. "Neither one of you is going to do anything that might jeopardize the peace deals we have going. Not a single fucking thing, do you hear me? That means *you* keep your mouth shut." He jerked his chin at Cillian. "And *you* keep the hell away from Halloran. We can fix this, but you're going to do exactly what I say."

She didn't want to. She wanted to rail and scream and hit in protest. But it wouldn't do a damn bit of good. She was as trapped as she'd always been. *Damn you, James. Why did you have to come to the wedding? Things were going good.*

And he'd been her dirty little secret.

She tried to smother the shame the thought brought. Today had more than proven that James wasn't ever going to be accepted by her family. He wasn't on the list. Hell, he was so far *off* the list, he was probably the last person in the world her father would allow her to marry.

She pressed a hand to her throat. *Oh God, where had that thought come from?* She liked how he made her feel, in bed and out, but that was a long way from considering a serious relationship—*any* relationship—with him.

"Promise me, Carrigan." Aiden's hand tightened on her arm. "Promise me that you'll focus on our father's list and leave Halloran alone."

She didn't have a choice. If she fought him on this, he'd throw her to the wolves. She cleared her throat. "I promise." Even as the words settled in the space between them, she wasn't sure if she was lying or not.

The town car pulled up in front of their home, saving her from this conversation. Cillian was out of the car before it stopped moving, slamming the door behind him and striding down the street. She had a feeling she knew where he was going, but there was nothing she could do about it. Carrigan could actually feel her siblings fracturing around her—from Aiden down to Keira—and she was partly to blame.

She followed Aiden out onto the shaded sidewalk, but

apparently he wasn't through with her. "Which one of the men is the top of your list?"

She wished she could pretend she misunderstood him. "I haven't met them all." When he just stared, she sighed. Really, there was no contest. "Dmitri Romanov." He might be dangerous, but at least he was up-front about it.

"Call him."

She jerked back. "Excuse me?"

"Call him. See him again. Get this fucking thing moving. The faster you're married, the faster we can sweep this whole clusterfuck under the rug."

And the faster the cage door would close behind her. She took a deep breath. "Aiden—"

"You're being deliberately dense. That wasn't a request, Carrigan. It was a fucking order."

Glaring, she fished her cell phone out of her clutch and scrolled through her most recent calls. "This is bullshit."

"You don't get to play righteous fury right now. Stop stalling and call him."

She was stalling, and for what? If it was two weeks or two days, her time had nearly run out. With a sigh, she called Dmitri, hoping he'd let it go to voice mail.

"Hello, Carrigan."

Damn it. She'd had such shitty luck today, and apparently it wasn't going to change now. "Dmitri." She held Aiden's gaze while she spoke, part of her surprised that her voice was so even despite the inner turmoil she could barely breathe past. "I'd like to see you again."

"Excellent. Are you free Tuesday? I had to make a trip back to New York to take care of some business, but I should have returned to Boston by then."

She didn't ask what business he had to take care of personally. She didn't want to know. "That would be wonderful. Dinner this time?"

"Of course. I'll send my driver to pick you up at seven."

High-handed. She gritted her teeth and bit out the next words. "I look forward to seeing you." She hung up and turned to Aiden. "Are you happy now?"

"Not even close. Don't fuck this up, Carrigan. You have no idea what's at stake."

She would if he talked to her instead of stepping up like he was their father and she was his little minion. But that was how Seamus operated, so why would Aiden do anything differently? "You're just like our father." The words came out poisonous and low, and she instantly wanted to take them back.

He just stepped aside with a short nod. "I do what I have to in order to keep our family safe. You'd do well to remember that." He turned on his heel and walked up the stairs and into the town house, leaving her staring after him.

She *was* doing what was best for the family. She hadn't run like she'd considered. She hadn't fought her father's ridiculous list. The only thing she'd taken for herself in all these years was the occasional night of freedom.

And James.

She pushed the thought away. She didn't know what she was going to do about him, but her brother was right—there was no future there. Even if by some miracle he fell in love with her and she...Well, it was impossible. Her family would never give their blessing.

His family wanted her dead. That wasn't the material that happily ever after was made of.

Maybe it really would be best to cut things off now. It seemed like every hour she spent with him attached more strings to her heart. Too many more and he'd rip it out of her chest when he walked away.

CHAPTER EIGHTEEN

Cillian didn't have a destination in mind when he set out. All he wanted to do was escape the monster in his head. Seeing his sister touching a Halloran had sent him back to that dark street, to the sound of gunshots, to Devlin dying on the street. It was a Halloran who gave the order that resulted in their little brother's death, and she was *kissing* one.

He couldn't even stand to look at her right now.

The band around his chest that never quite seemed to go away tightened until black dots danced across his vision. He'd thought Carrigan understood, but how could she? She hadn't been there on that street so strikingly similar to this one, hadn't seen the headlights cut through the darkness—the only warning they got before things went tits up. And she sure as fuck hadn't been there on her knees, helplessly watching Devlin bleed out.

They'd both lost a brother, but he was only now start-

ing to realize that the demons inside him that rose that
night weren't ones easily exorcised.

Lights broke up the relative darkness of the street and
he glanced up, not even a little surprised to find himself outside Jameson's. His feet always seemed to take
him here when he wasn't paying attention, as if he could
somehow change the events of that night if he walked
through it enough times.

He almost turned around and left. There was nothing
for him here and he damn well knew it. But the siren call
of the last happy night he'd shared with his brothers was
too much to resist. Maybe if he went inside, he could
actually manage to draw a full breath again. He pushed
through the door, the heat of the room making him realize just how cold he'd been.

The place was packed tonight, though the crowd
seemed subdued. Or maybe that was just him. He made
his way through the full tables and snagged a seat at
the bar. The normal bartender, Benji, was nowhere to be
found. Hell, no one was behind the polished wood. He
took in the people's drinks on either side of him. Benji
must have run out back for something.

But when the door to the storage room opened, it wasn't
Benji who backed through. Cillian's first glimpse was of
a mane of dark hair, wild and untamed. Then she turned
around and every cell of his being went still. She was the
most striking woman he'd ever seen. Her features were
timeless, and combined with her dusky skin tone, seemed
to indicate Middle Eastern descent. And the body he got
a glimpse of when she hauled the giant box onto the
bar...*Fuck*. More curves than a racetrack, her clothes
seemingly designed to bring that to his attention without

trying at all. The writing across the front of her faded T-shirt was mostly gone, and her holey jeans probably hadn't come that way.

He had to know more about her.

He leaned forward, deciding to start with something simple. "Hey, sweetheart, how about a drink?" A minute passed, and then another. Nothing. She just kept unpacking bottles into the fridge below the bar. Cillian frowned. "Hey, I'm talking to you."

"I heard you, pretty boy." She didn't look up. "And since your eyes don't seem to be working, let me clarify something—I'm not your bar wench."

"I never said—"

"Leave me alone. I'm working."

He sat back on his stool, stunned. He'd thought he was being perfectly polite. Charming, even. He'd never had a woman shut him down so effectively when he didn't actually deserve it—there *had* been plenty of times he deserved it, but tonight wasn't one of them.

The storage door opened again, and this time it was a familiar face who came through. Benji grinned when he saw Cillian. "Back again?"

Like I can stay away. "You knew I would be."

"That I did, that I did." He moved around the woman, a careful swing of his body that left as much space between them as possible, and ambled over. "The usual?"

"Yeah." Even though he told himself not to, his gaze angled toward *her* again. She'd moved further down the bar and was now unloading a second box of beer bottles. "What's the new girl's story?"

"Olivia?" Benji raised furry eyebrows. "I wouldn't."

He couldn't look away from her. Olivia. The name made him think of someone old world…or just plain old—definitely not a fit for the woman in front of him. "Why not?"

"She's not like the other bartenders who come through here." Benji paused. "Don't step on toes."

Easier said than done. He seemed to have offended her just by sitting down at her bar. Cillian had frequented a lot of bars, clubs, and pubs, and the universal rule seemed to be that bartenders were flirty and snarky and good times. They had to be, since tips could make or break them. They sure as hell didn't snarl at a man just trying to get a drink. It couldn't be clearer that there was something about him she blatantly didn't like, and damn if a perverse part of him didn't want to know *why*.

A glass hit his hand, breaking his thought process. Benji crossed his big arms over his chest. "She's not for you. I like the girl, and she's a hard worker. I won't have you running her off because you don't know how to take no for an answer."

Cillian jerked back, stung. *Why the fuck is everyone so goddamn determined to think the worst of me?* "I'm not a creep."

"Then stop staring at her like one."

He immediately dropped his gaze, and then realized what he'd done. Why the hell was he fighting this? He needed a complicated woman in his life like he needed a punch to the face. This Olivia didn't want a damn thing to do with him? Good. He'd have his drink like he normally did, tip well, and then leave. He stared at the apple juice, all too aware of the impulse to look over at her again. To watch her.

Like a fucking creep.

He sighed. "I get your point, Benji."

"Good. Enjoy your drink." The big bartender moved down the bar, refilling drinks and chatting.

Cillian was surrounded by people, but it didn't make a damn bit of difference tonight. It never did. And now there was this prickly woman on the edge of his vision, her presence poking at him like a toothache. *I don't need this shit.* He shotgunned the juice and threw a twenty on the bar. There was no escape for him tonight, and he damn well knew it. He might as well go home, lie on his bed, and face the demons waiting for him when he lost his battle with sleep.

Morning might come, but relief from the nightmares never did.

* * *

Carrigan met Dmitri's car outside, torn between feeling like a sacrificial victim and a call girl. She'd put aside her virginal wear for the date. Dmitri had already proven that he wasn't stupid enough to be fooled by the persona, and she hated wearing it. So she'd picked a jade green dress that hit her at mid-thigh and hugged her body. It wasn't the sexiest thing in her closet, but it was the first time she'd left the house feeling like *her* in longer than she cared to remember. She always wore one mask or another. Tonight she was setting them aside.

Let Dmitri think of that what he would.

Liam stood next to her, disapproval embodied in human form. He'd been like this since she got back the other day, and she deserved it. Carrigan took a deep breath.

"I'm sorry. I shouldn't have disappeared and turned off my phone."

"Not for me to say." He didn't look over. "But if I were going to speak my mind, I'd say that was a dipshit thing to do and we both know it. My job is to keep you safe, and I can't do that if I don't know where you are."

"I know."

But he wasn't through. "In all these years of you dicking around, have I ever reported you?"

He is seriously pissed. She wanted to snap back, but she fought the impulse down. He needed to say this and, after what she'd done, it was the least she could do to listen. It wasn't like he was the first one to lecture her on her shitty life choices. Of the men in her life, Liam was probably the *least* judgmental. He deserved a chance to give his opinion, no matter how little she wanted to hear it. "No."

"Have I ever passed judgment or said shit to make you feel like I'm one of your goddamn brothers, expecting you to act a certain way?"

"No." She hated the guilt worming through her. The last thing she needed was to feel bad for disappointing yet another man in her life. She hadn't even realized she cared about what Liam thought of her. He had the tendency to fade into the background—there when she needed him and invisible when she didn't. They weren't friends. They'd never be close. But she hated that she'd damaged what little respect he seemed to have for her. "I'm sorry, Liam. I screwed up. It won't happen again."

But apparently now that he'd broken his customary bodyguard silence, he wasn't done. "I don't like this any more than you, but we both have a job to do."

"I know."

He nodded, still not looking at her. "This Dmitri guy isn't safe."

"Probably not." One encounter with him and she knew enough to know *safe* didn't make the top twenty list of descriptions for Dmitri Romanov.

"Okay." He rolled his shoulders. "You need me, you text. I don't care if he's the king of England. I'll get you out of there."

He'd be defying her father's wishes to do it. She turned to face him fully, wanting to...hug him? Show him how grateful she was by reaching out? Neither fit in the realm of their roles. So she just stood taller and nodded. "Thank you, Liam."

"Will you be making any excursions afterward?"

She shot him a look. "I was under the impression I'm confined to house arrest."

He snorted. "Since when has that ever stopped you?"

It was a fair point. But hadn't she just reasoned last night that things with James had to be over out of sheer self-preservation? Turning around less than twenty-four hours later and running into his arms wouldn't do a damn thing to put some distance between them. "We'll see."

A black car pulled up to the curb, and a nondescript man got out. "Ms. O'Malley." He hurried around to open the door for her, but Liam beat him to it. The man sputtered. "I was told—"

"You were told wrong." She slid into the backseat and then scooted over to make room for Liam. He was right. He'd been there every step of the way and done his damnedest to keep her safe. She wouldn't ditch him again. Especially since he alone didn't see her time with James as one giant betrayal to the family.

I wonder why that is?

It didn't matter. What mattered was that he was apparently on her side when she desperately needed someone in her corner. The driver seemed to have recovered from his confusion because he was back in the car and pulling away from the curb. She sat back and crossed her legs, trying to relax. She'd dealt with dangerous men before. She could do it again. At least this one was willing to negotiate and give her some freedom in return for her dancing to his tune.

It just didn't seem like the silver lining it might have a few months ago. She'd had a taste of freedom—*real* freedom—with James, and now everything else seemed like a sad substitute by comparison. She was starting to fear that the man might have actually ruined her.

Carrigan stared out the window, not really seeing anything. It seemed like they made the trip between one blink and the next, because the next thing she knew, the car had stopped and the driver was opening her door with a defiant look at Liam. She stared at the sidewalk, suddenly sure she was about to take a step that she couldn't take back. If she said yes to Dmitri, that was it. It was over. *Everything* was over. The man might offer her a measure of freedom, but he wasn't the type to be crossed. The second she stepped out of line, he'd smash her like a bug.

I don't want you, you can't make me, please don't make me get out of this car. It was the voice of a small child afraid of the dark—a child she'd thought she'd put behind her once and for all. *Face your fears. To do any-*

thing else is inexcusable. She steeled herself and took the driver's hand, letting him help her out of the car. Behind her, Liam was already on his feet.

He nodded at the door. "Remember what I said."

One text and he'd get her out of there. She nodded. "Thanks." And then there was nothing left for her to stall with. She squared her shoulders and walked into Slingshot. Like before, it was completely deserted and, like before, she was struck by the wild fear that he'd invited her here to kill her.

Stop being an idiot. You *invited him.* Right. Maybe that would have actually put the power in her court... except he'd taken control of the situation the second the invitation left her lips. She'd arrived in *his* car to a place of *his* choosing at a time *he* picked. So much for leaving herself any bargaining power at all.

She followed the pretty blond hostess back into the depths of the restaurant. There, at the same table with his back to the wall, sat Dmitri. He stood as she approached and moved around to greet her. "Carrigan. You look as lovely as ever." He pressed a kiss to her cheek. "I must admit I prefer you in color."

"Dmitri." She ignored the sideways compliment and took a seat in the chair he'd pulled out for her. "Thank you."

"I was surprised to hear from you so soon."

No, he wasn't. He knew he'd given her the best offer she was going to get. But she smiled all the same. "You play coy so prettily."

He chuckled. "And you're too smart by half. How was your brother's wedding?"

The memory of James at her back, whispering in her ear as he fucked her, swept over Carrigan. She reached for her water, hoping like hell that the low light hid her blush. "It went off without a hitch. Both he and Callie are very happy."

"In addition to their being happy, they've managed to forge an alliance that will protect both their interests. A rare meeting of personal and professional."

"You could say that." She waited for the waiter to fill their wineglasses and melt back into the shadows around them before she continued. "That's what you're looking for with this arrangement, isn't it?"

"An alliance, yes. A love match?" He shrugged and took a drink of his wine. "Such a thing only exists for fools and fairy tales."

A cynical outlook, but she didn't blame him. It was one she shared, after all. Her mind tried to shy away to the thought of James again, but she forced herself to stay focused on the present. James wasn't here. He'd *never* be here, never be the man across the table from her, never be able to offer her what Dmitri was. Even if he *had* . . . she couldn't accept. Not without restarting a war that they'd all been working so hard to put to bed. Carrigan was selfish, but she wasn't *that* selfish.

Not to mention he hasn't asked.

Shut up.

She sipped her wine, trying to get her head on straight. "I don't expect a love match."

"Nor should you. I respect the woman you are, Carrigan. I find you beautiful and I like the passion I can see in your eyes, even though you try to hide it. I think our marriage could evolve into genuine affection."

Somehow, she didn't think so. This man was so cold, she doubted he had *genuine affection* for anything. Except for power. He seemed to like *that* well enough. "And the sex?"

His eyebrows rose, and he laughed. "You do cut right to the chase, don't you?"

"I like to have all the cards on the table before I make a decision."

"Carrigan, you've already made the decision and you know it." He motioned with his wineglass, every inch the waiting predator. "But, by all means, let's discuss the sex. I mentioned last time we spoke that I require an heir and at least one backup."

"I remember." The thought of bringing children into the world solely to serve as political pieces made her nauseous, but it wasn't a surprise. Children were an expected part of her future, no matter what her personal feelings on the matter were.

He smiled, and while it wasn't his shark's smile, there wasn't any real warmth there, either. "It doesn't have to be all bad. I'll leave sex on the table at your discretion once the required children are established. It's not necessary, but I think we would both enjoy it."

He didn't really want her. He might say all the right things about her being beautiful, but he could take her or leave her. There was no passion there. Carrigan hadn't really expected it to be there to be but...the lack still stood out. "I'll consider it."

"Perfect." He sat back. "Now, on to less pleasant things. This affair you're having with James Halloran has to stop. Immediately."

She blinked, her mind taking several seconds to catch up to and process his words. James. He was talking about James. "How could you possibly—?"

"How I know isn't the issue. Your choice in bedmates is. Certain things must be kept up for appearances' sake. I'm not keen on being cuckolded in general, but I've reconsidered since our last conversation. I'm now willing to look the other way as long as you're discreet."

Holy shit, is this guy for real? "How generous of you."

"That being said, your willingness to lie down with the enemy, as it were, puts a less-than-desirable shade on you." He sat back. "And before you claim it's none of my business, I'll remind you that considering marriage to you makes it my business."

Technically, he was right... but still. She set her glass aside. "Are you planning on remaining faithful?"

"It's a moot point. I'll ensure there are no bastard children running around. That's enough." His dark eyes saw too much. "But I won't be sleeping with the enemy, either."

There it was again. Everyone loved to remind her that James was the enemy. What they couldn't explain was why he was the only one who seemed to have her back—the only one who asked nothing of her but her time. It was the ones who claimed to be concerned for her who demanded the most. *Marry this man. Do this thing. Don't touch the one person who actually makes you feel alive.* She met Dmitri's gaze. "And if I don't give him up?"

"You don't have a choice. Your father requires you to marry, and you've already decided on me. Give Halloran up." His gray eyes didn't so much as flicker. "If you don't, I'll have him removed. Permanently."

CHAPTER NINETEEN

James spent all Tuesday in a foul mood. It was his own damn fault and he knew it, but not knowing what was going on with Carrigan—and knowing he'd been the one to put her in that position—drove him nuts. So he did the only thing he could do and put his frustration to good use.

He took Michael and went on rounds. If his time at Tit for Tat was anything to go by, it had been too long since he'd done them. Really, as soon as he realized Ricky was taking advantage, he should have touched base with the managers of his various businesses. Should have, but didn't, because he was too busy chasing Carrigan. Even when he wasn't with her, he was thinking about her, and it threw him off his game at a time when he needed to keep shit from falling through the cracks.

Sure, Ricky had said he'd follow orders like a good little soldier, but James didn't believe him for a second. His brother would do whatever he thought benefited him best—including stabbing James in the back when the opportunity popped up.

So he couldn't give him the opportunity.

To his relief, no one else had any problems beyond the shit that popped up here and there. Tommy had to run off some Sheridan boys last week, but it had been drunk men acting like assholes and not an actual skirmish. Harmless stuff, especially since Tommy had defused the situation before anyone got violent.

He still needed to figure out what he was going to do to keep Ricky busy—and soon. The longer his brother sat idle, the more likely he was to say "to hell with it" and go back to doing exactly what he'd been doing before James was forced to take such extreme measures. *I just have to keep him away from the girls*. He turned to Michael, sitting in the passenger seat of the Chevelle, his hands in his lap, like he was afraid of touching anything. "When's the next shipment coming in to replace what we lost in the Sheridan attack?"

"Got a hundred AKs two days from now."

He thought fast. "Those the ones we owe our friends on the West Coast?"

"Yep."

They didn't transfer goods often, but his father had created a trade with some group back west. Guns for… something. James wasn't sure. He wasn't too keen on sending guns off to people he didn't know, where they'd be used for God knew what, but he had enough enemies. Courting more was stupid, even if they were three thousand miles away. His father had made a deal, and he'd follow through on it. After that… Well, once it was done he'd reevaluate.

But this might be a blessing in disguise. He'd get Ricky out of Boston for a while, and maybe the distance between them would be enough to dim some of his brother's anger. He doubted it, but it couldn't hurt to try.

Plus, then he wouldn't have to be looking over his shoulder for a knife—at least for a week or so. "Put my brother on it. Send him and..." Not Jake. He'd just get Ricky into more trouble. Joe wasn't up to work yet, not after...James moved past what he'd done to the man. "Matthew and Eddie." They were solid, and they'd made that run before so they should be able to keep his brother in line. He might not trust them like he trusted Michael, but they could take orders, and he'd be reasonably sure that they'd obey. Especially after they'd seen Joe's hands.

"Will do, boss."

"Good." He headed for the house, satisfied that he'd made the right decision. A little space would do both him and Ricky good.

He hadn't thought about Carrigan for a whole ten minutes.

What was she doing right now? He wouldn't put it past her father and brother to have shipped her out of town again, well beyond his reach. *My fault. Never should have gone to that stupid wedding.* Normally, he never would have made such a reckless decision, but the woman made him crazy. A little over forty-eight hours since seeing her and he was already twitchy, his temper fraying over every little thing. He wanted her safe in his arms. Ironic, because in his arms was where she was in the most danger. He had no doubt that Aiden meant his threat—it meant war to continue his affair with Carrigan.

The problem was...he wasn't sure it *wasn't* worth it.

No, he had to stop pussyfooting around. Carrigan was worth it. He'd never had a woman make him feel the way she did. He'd happily set the world afire and watch it burn if she asked it of him. She wouldn't, though. He knew her well enough to know that. She'd never been put first in her life before, and the truth was that he was a shitty leader for being willing to do it. He just didn't give a fuck.

He couldn't call her. The stakes were too high. He wouldn't put her in that position unless he knew beyond a shadow of a doubt that she wanted to be there. She had to be the one to reach out to him.

And she hadn't.

The problem was that he didn't know if it was because she didn't want to or if she couldn't. He could understand her being furious with him. He'd screwed up, but it didn't change anything between them—at least not as far as he was concerned—and not knowing where she stood pissed him the hell off.

He parked and they headed into the house. "Brief Eddie and Matthew. Make sure they know how important this shit is—and how disappointed I'll be if something goes wrong." After Michael nodded and disappeared down a side hall, James went in search of his brother. It didn't take long for him to find Ricky. He'd posted up in the giant family room on the leather couch, his boots propped on the coffee table, basketball on the TV.

James stopped and looked around the room. This used to be the place where he and his brothers spent most of their time. Where they'd fought and bonded over whatever sports was in season. Where they'd eventually grown apart, so they were more strangers than family.

He didn't come in here much anymore. "Ricky."

"Yeah?" He didn't look away from the screen.

"I got a job for you."

That got his little brother's attention. He turned around, wariness written all over his face. "What kind of job?"

It was like pulling teeth. "The kind where I give you orders and you obey them. Unless you already forgot how the other day played out?"

"No, no. I was just asking. Jesus, James, I was just fucking with you."

No, he wasn't. He was pushing, testing boundaries, looking for weakness. Was this what parenting was like? James almost laughed at the thought. It might be similar, but he doubted most kids were willing to do actual violence to their parents during their rebellious teenage years. Ricky was. James waited for his brother to drop his gaze before he spoke again. "The shipment that comes in two days from now needs an escort over to Northern California. You'll take two men and make sure it gets there without a problem."

Ricky's mouth tightened, but he gave a jerky nod. "Sure thing."

He didn't believe the obedient act for a second, but there wasn't a damn thing he could do about it. He couldn't punish his brother for having a shitty attitude, or because he suspected Ricky was up to no good. His men would think he was crazier than his old man, and it would only be a matter of time before they put him in the ground. *Getting him out of town for a week or so is exactly what both of us need right now.*

"Have you gone to see him?"

James stopped but he didn't turn to face his brother.

There was no need to ask who Ricky was talking about—
their old man. "No." Not since that first time. He'd
shown up at the jail, needing some sort of reassurance
that he was doing the right thing as he stepped into the
role thrust upon him. Victor had turned James away,
leaving the message that he was a disappointment and
always had been. Bitterness clawed up his throat, as familiar as the back of his hand. He'd never lived up to
his old man's exacting standards, and he'd never stopped
trying, either. Now he was doing things his own way.

And making one hell of a mess of it.

His phone buzzed, saving him from the conversation.
He dug it from his pocket, and his breath whooshed
out at the sight of Carrigan's name. She'd called. He
thumbed it on as he walked out of the room. "It's good
to hear from you."

"James." Her voice was so broken, so unlike her, that
he froze. "James, I need you. Now."

He didn't stop to think or question. He grabbed his
jacket and keys from the rack by the door and hit the
sidewalk at a run. "I'm on my way. Tell me where." This
was different from the last time she'd called him. She'd
been upset then. But this sounded so much worse. "Did
someone hurt you?"

She laughed, a jagged wet sound. "Not how you
mean." She rattled off an address.

He did some quick mental calculations. "I can be
there in fifteen minutes." He'd have to break a few traffic
laws to pull it off, but he'd manage.

"Okay...thank you."

"Hang in there, lovely. I'm coming." He slid into the
driver's seat of a black Beemer that he kept for times

when he didn't want to draw attention to himself, and dropped his phone next to him so if she called again, he wouldn't miss it. Then he floored it.

He made the trip in ten minutes. The address was a little coffee shop in Mission Hill. James pulled up outside, but there was nothing that he could see to raise any red flags. Since Carrigan didn't fly out the door and throw herself into his car, he parked and walked inside. The street was technically O'Malley territory, but since it bordered the southwestern outskirts of where they did business, it didn't get the kind of attention it would if it were on the boundary bumping up again Sheridan or Halloran space. That didn't mean he went in relaxed, though. Something was wrong with Carrigan—*seriously* wrong.

It could be a trap.

Didn't matter. She needed him and so he was here. He'd promised her he would be, and nothing that had happened between them had changed that fact. A quick survey of the place found it empty except for a two-person table in the back corner where Carrigan sat hunched over, her hands cupped around a giant mug. He dropped into the seat across from her, categorizing everything he saw. There were dark circles beneath her eyes and her hands shook on the mug, but she looked okay. He knew better than most that it didn't mean she was *actually* okay, though. "What happened?"

She started, as if she'd been so lost in thought, she hadn't realized he was there. Her green eyes were full of shadows. "Do you know Dmitri Romanov?"

The name wasn't familiar. But all that meant was that James had never worked with the man personally. "No."

"I'm going to marry him."

Every cell in his being rejected the words. "*No.*" He took a deep breath and forced the anger out of his voice. "If this is about the wedding—"

"It's not. I'd already decided before what happened that I'd marry Dmitri. This just expedited things."

She'd already decided on a husband and hadn't told him. It shouldn't surprise him—he knew her father had given her a list, and he knew she was working through it—but knowing she was dating these guys and hearing her say she was going to marry one of them were two completely different things. "Carrigan."

"I don't have a choice. You know that. I know that. Hell, everyone in Boston knows that. It was nice to pretend maybe things could be different, but…"

He didn't like this new side of her. Up to this point, every time he interacted with her, she'd been a spitfire and so full of life she made him feel like maybe they could exist in this reality without being broken. Something had happened in the last forty-eight hours to change that, and his fists clenched with the need to destroy it. "What happened? Is this because of your brother?"

"No. Well, sort of." She huddled the coffee closer. "He said I needed to choose and get it over with, and God knows I can't choose *you.*"

Would she choose him if she could?

Before he could ask, she moved on, "Dmitri was the best choice. The only choice, really. And I should be grateful that he doesn't play games."

She didn't sound grateful. She sounded hopeless. "Who is this guy?"

"He runs some kind of business down in New York. I don't really know, but for him to be on my father's list, he's not a good man." She made a face. "Though I knew that thirty seconds after meeting him. He's a shark."

And she was going to marry him. James tried to keep his voice even, but it was damn near impossible. "Is he the reason you're like this?"

She didn't answer directly. "This thing between us is over, James. It has to be. I just wanted to say good-bye."

* * *

Carrigan watched the emotions play over James's face before they settled into one she was familiar with—rage. He sat back and crossed his arms over his chest. "Explain."

This wasn't going how she'd planned. Hell, she hadn't had much of a plan when she walked out of the restaurant an hour ago. All she'd known was that Dmitri had threatened James, and every instinct she had told her that he was a man who didn't bluff. If she didn't cut things off immediately, he'd kill James. It was worse than the threat of war with her family or anything her brothers could bring to bear against Halloran. It was straight-out assassination.

She'd do whatever it took to keep that from happening.

So she forced her spine straight and her shoulders back. "This has been fun—"

"*Fun.*"

"—but we both knew it could never go anywhere." It wasn't in the cards for them, no matter how much her heart cried out for him.

"You're a goddamn liar." He suddenly leaned forward and wrapped his hands around hers, pinning her between the mug and his skin. "You want this. You want *me*."

Yes! She pressed her lips together. "You're not listening to me."

"Yes, I am. You're saying that things are over, and it sure as fuck sounds like your brother's words coming out of your mouth when you do." He stood, yanking her half out of her seat and nearly spilling her coffee in the process. "Come with me."

It was a mistake. If she went with him now, she'd be putting him in danger. She might be signing his goddamn death warrant. "You don't understand..."

He took the mug out of her hands and set it on the table. "You still want me."

Of course she did. She was starting to suspect she'd want this man for the rest of her life and beyond. "That has nothing to do with anything."

"It has everything to do with everything." He pulled her closer, inch by inch, until there was barely a breath of distance between them. "I can't let you go, lovely. I *won't*. Come away with me tonight. We'll figure things out, and the world will look better tomorrow."

He was wrong. He was so wrong it wasn't even funny. Even if tonight was the most perfect a night could be, nothing would be different tomorrow. It was a lesson Carrigan had learned all too well over the years. But if she had to give him up forever, who would blame her for taking one more night before she had to say goodbye? She looked away. She knew who would. *Dmitri*. He wouldn't be forgiving. "It's too risky."

"It's a risk I'm willing to take. Are you?"

He didn't know what was at stake. But, looking up into his eyes, she realized that maybe she was wrong. James might not know the dirty details about Dmitri and his threats, but he didn't live a life free of danger. Death could come for them any day. It was still a risk, and a stupid one at that, but she found herself nodding all the same. *I can't say no to this man. I don't ever want to.* "Just tonight."

"We'll get this figured out." He kept a hold of her hand as he led her from the coffee shop to where he'd parked a black car she didn't recognize, and then held her door while she climbed in.

She typed out a quick text to Liam. *With James. I promise I'll keep my phone on.* It dinged almost as soon as she'd pushed send.

Where?

Carrigan hesitated. What if Liam told her brothers? But then she remembered how things had played out before— he wouldn't betray her. He just wanted to keep her safe. She glanced at James. "Where are you taking me?"

He eyed the phone in her hand. "The beach house."

York. Blue house on the ocean drive. She set the phone aside. She'd kept her promise—at least one of them. "Okay."

"Anything I should be worried about?"

"No." She hoped. She seemed to be doing a lot of hoping these days. But as James reached over and took her hand, she let her worry go. It would still be there tomorrow. God knew she couldn't escape her problems as easily as she and James could escape Boston's city limits.

She could feel James's questions crowding the space between them, but he kept his silence as they drove north. It left her too much opportunity to go over the last forty-eight hours. So much had changed, and yet nothing at all. Saturday James had still been forbidden, even if her family didn't know about their relationship. She'd been considering marrying Dmitri, though he hadn't gotten into the heavy-handed tactics yet. And she'd still wanted James more than anything else in the world.

She was just as conflicted now as she had been then, with just as few places to turn for help. Add it all up, and Carrigan couldn't shake the truth—no matter which way she turned, she was destined for a life of misery and loss.

CHAPTER TWENTY

James parked in almost the exact same spot he had five days ago, and turned the Beemer off. "We're going to talk about it." He still didn't know what the hell was going on to put the bone-deep fear into Carrigan, but he fully planned on finding out. She said no one had touched her, and he believed it. But he also knew far too well how to hurt someone without ever laying a finger on them.

She'd agreed to come to the beach house. It was a start.

He got out and opened her door for her. A car pulled up behind them, a dark sedan with a man in the driver's seat. She glanced over. "It's Liam. I promised."

As much as he didn't like the idea of O'Malley's man knowing that this place existed—let alone where it was—he nodded. It was the price of getting her here, and he would gladly pay it. "Come on." He guided her across the street with a hand on the small of her back. That little touch grounded him. *She's here. We will figure this out.* He knew better, but he couldn't kill the hope in the back of his mind.

After locking the door and closing the shades, he turned to her. "Lovely, I—"

"Not tonight." She stepped into his arms, and he automatically put them around her. He couldn't get over how *right* this was—how right *Carrigan* was. She made him feel ten feet tall, like he could do whatever it took to make things right—like nothing was impossible.

"I want to know what's got you so worked up."

"And I don't want to talk about it. Please, James." She looked up, her red lips kissably close. "Please just give me tonight. The only time I really feel safe is when I'm with you."

The words were a balm to his soul, chasing away the shadows that he thought had taken up permanent residence. It would be easy, so fucking easy, to give her exactly what she wanted and soak up this feeling. But it was a Band-Aid. He'd gone through the same motions enough times to recognize it for what it was. So he framed her face with his hands and kissed her forehead. There had to be some way to balance this. "We don't have to talk about what spooked you tonight. But we are going to talk."

Tension worked its way into her body, and he resented its presence. She twisted the hem of his shirt between nervous fingers. "Talk about what?"

"Whatever you want." As soon as the words were out of his mouth, he fought against the instinctive urge to take them back. There were things he'd done—things he'd seen—that he never wanted to drag out of the darkness where he'd put them. But he would for Carrigan.

He knew the second her expression went tight where she'd go—straight for the heart. "Your scars."

Fuck. He took a step back, needing some distance between them and a strong fucking drink. "Drink?"

"Sure." She sat on the couch and crossed her long legs, watching him. It struck him that she expected to get what she wanted. She knew damn well that he'd rather walk barefoot over burning coals than bring up these ugly memories, and she was betting on him letting her have her way tonight instead of getting into those memories. *Well, tough shit.*

If it were anyone else, they'd be right. But this wasn't anyone else. This woman made him feel things he'd thought were long dead and gone, and he wasn't going to shy away from an ugly experience if it meant he was hurdling over the last of her barriers. She trusted him. She'd come to him time and again when she was in trouble or upset. He'd told her about his mother—something he talked about even less than he talked about his scars. He could tell her this, too.

James found whiskey in the upper cabinet and poured himself a healthy dose in a cup. Then he grabbed the gin and vermouth from the lower cabinet and put together her martini. Once it was done, there was nothing left to stall with, but he felt as centered as he was going to be for this conversation. He set her drink on the coffee table and took the other side of the couch. "Fine, lovely. I'll bare my soul for you—but these things go both ways."

She tensed. "I don't know." He waited while she took a nervous sip of her drink, and waited some more while she looked everywhere but at him. Carrigan was a direct sort and, sure enough, it didn't take her long to gather up her courage and meet his gaze. "You're on."

"Perfect." He drained half his whiskey and set the glass down, doing his damnedest to ignore the shaking in his hands. "You know my father is a monster. All of Boston does. He's got a reputation for being an artist when it comes to torture."

"I've heard the rumors." She nodded, a small line appearing between her brows. "And I looked into it more after what happened over the summer. People don't like talking about it, but I still managed to learn more than I wanted to know."

Of course she'd looked into it. It was completely natural for her to want to know what would have been in store for her if she and Callista hadn't escaped that night. It made him sick to think about. He pushed to his feet, filled with too much agitation to just sit here and calmly talk about her being tortured and murdered. She might have made her peace with it. He hadn't.

He stalked to the window and twitched back the curtain to stare into the night. "My old man wasn't a good person when my mother was alive. He still did the same unforgivable shit that he's been doing the last fifteen years. He was still at least half as crazy as he is now. But when she was alive, he never touched us. It was like this one last bastion of goodness that he had going for him. He might be a monster and a shitty father, but he wasn't *that* much of a monster. I heard her say that one night while she was praying for his immortal soul." He felt his lips quirk into a smile, but there was no joy behind it. "And then she died and everything changed."

He paused, trying to get control of his breathing. If he dwelled on it too long, he could feel the whip against his back, the tip tearing through flesh. It had been a long time ago, but there weren't enough years to completely banish the memories. His skin tightened, his whole body tense in fear of another blow. *He's gone. It's not happening anymore. It won't happen again.* Cold comfort. "It was like the last glimmer of light in his soul died with her. He took it into his head that we'd been coddled and were pussies, and to my old man, there was only one way to fix it."

She didn't say anything, and he couldn't bring himself to look at her and see pity on her face. He'd survived. He hadn't been broken, not completely. James took a deep breath. "So one day he drags us down to the basement where he interrogates Halloran enemies, and he tells us..." He could still see the mad gleam in Victor's eyes, hear the rasp of his voice. James's skin broke out in goose bumps. "He tells us that any sons of his have to prove that they won't break. And then he took us, one by one, and told us to pick—the whip or the canes. Brendan chose the canes, and he had to be carried out of the room afterward. So I chose the whip."

Her soft gasp reached him, but he still didn't turn around. "It wasn't the last time it happened, but it was the worst. After that, we knew if we stepped out of line, that was the fate that waited for us."

Her tentative touch made him face her. He braced himself for the pity, but that wasn't what he saw when he finally turned. No, there was pure and unadulterated rage. Her green eyes practically glowed with it. She took his hands. "Say the fucking word and I'll see it taken care of."

Shock left his mouth hanging open. "What?"

"Some things aren't done, James. Some lines aren't crossed. Family might be the weight that pulls you under, but they protect their own. These..." She ran a finger over his shirt, directly across one of the deepest scars. "He tortured his own flesh and blood, his *children*. You protect your children at all costs. To hurt them on purpose?" She shook her head, the fire in her eyes only growing. "The punishment is death."

"You'd kill my father for me." He was still trying to catch up with the unexpected reaction. She was so fierce, so furious, so ready to do violence on his behalf. And she wasn't backing down. *She'd do it. She'd find a way to get to my old man in prison and see justice done, and she wouldn't blink or feel bad while she was doing it.* He framed her face with his hands, his entire body shuddering with the strength of his realization. "I love you, Carrigan O'Malley."

He kissed her before she could say anything else. He wouldn't let her kill Victor. She carried enough. He wouldn't be the reason she added to that burden. But that she'd offered and meant every word...it was a priceless gift that he could never repay. No one had ever gone to bat for him. Brendan might have stepped up more often than not to direct their old man's rage away from his younger brothers, but this was different. Carrigan wasn't family. She didn't have a damn thing to gain by this. The only reason she'd be driven to demand Victor's blood was because she felt just as deeply for him as he did for her. It didn't matter if she said the actual words aloud. Her actions made that shit more than clear.

Her arms snaked around her neck, and she drew back enough to say, "This conversation isn't over."

"I know." He kissed her again, delving into her mouth and showing her all the things he'd never have the words to say. How much he appreciated her, that he loved how fierce she was, how much he never wanted to let her go.

He didn't know what the fuck they were going to do about their current situation, but he was determined to find a way around it. He couldn't do anything less for the woman in his arms.

* * *

Carrigan's fury didn't abate as she kissed James. If anything, his words only drove it higher. *He loves me*. She'd known there was a feeling growing inside her, getting stronger every time she saw him, but she'd refused to put a title on it. Love. It was love. And she was putting him in danger right now for even being here with him.

One night. I'll figure everything out tomorrow.

Things would fall into place where they would. Right now there was just her and James and several hours of freedom. She tugged on his shirt, pulling it up and over his head, needing to be skin to skin. Apparently he had the same idea because he had her dress off seconds later. He lifted her, and she quickly wrapped her legs around his waist while he carried her through the house to the same bedroom they'd been in the other night. "I'm never going to get enough of you, lovely. *Never*."

That's what she was afraid of. Because she felt the same way—that this was the end all, be all, and everything after this would be like living in a shadow. She kissed him harder. *There is no tomorrow. There is just right now, in this moment, with this man.* The feeling of a clock counting down in the back of her head intensified. This might be her last chance to have him, to feel his hands on her body, to have him whispering filthy things in her ear.

To tell him how she felt.

She opened her mouth to do just that, but some instinct held her back. If he knew she loved him, too, he'd never let her go. He'd fight to his dying breath for her. Which was the damn problem—his *dying* breath. *I can't let him die for me.*

So she kept silent as he laid her on the bed and kissed her as if he never needed to breathe. His clever fingers did away with her bra and he sat back, pulling her panties with him. He stopped with them around her ankles, her feet resting against his chest. "What do you need from me tonight?"

She pressed her lips together to keep from confessing everything—her fear and her shitty future and all the worries crowding to the forefront of her brain now that they weren't losing themselves in each other. She focused on his blue eyes. How had she ever thought they were cold? They weren't. They were the hottest flame. Really, there was only one answer. "Everything."

He nodded like she'd confessed to more than a single word. Maybe she had. "Everything and more, lovely." He tossed her panties to the side.

She didn't give him a chance to retreat, though. Carrigan unbuttoned his jeans and pulled them down just enough to free his cock. His whole body went tense, and she looked up the long line of his chest, meeting his gaze and waiting to see if he'd stop her. He didn't.

So she took him into her mouth, sucking him down until his curse rang to the ceiling. He fisted his hands in her hair. "I've been thinking about that hot, wet mouth around my cock, lovely. I've come more times than I can count to that fantasy."

She hummed her approval, sucking him deeper, never taking her eyes off his face. He watched her, his jaw tight and his eyes hooded. "The fantasy doesn't even come close. Slip that hand between your legs. Does sucking me off get you wet?"

Yes. She ran her tongue along the underside of his cock as she obeyed him. Though a part of her wanted to finish him like this, to see him lose control completely, she needed to lose herself in him more. "James, I need you."

"And if I tell you to finish me this way?"

His control was better than hers. It had been since they started this dance around each other all those months ago. But she had an ace up her sleeve, and she didn't hesitate to use it now. "Please, James. I want to come around your cock. *Please*."

He cursed long and low. "I couldn't deny you even if I wanted to." He grabbed a condom from the nightstand, put it on, and crawled onto the bed, settling between her legs. He shoved against her, the angle wrong to push inside her, his cock sliding over her clit. "This is what you need, lovely." He hitched her leg up, opening her further.

"Yes!" She grabbed his shoulders, arching up to meet his thrusts, trying to move to eliminate that last tiny distance between them.

But he was having none of it. He nipped her neck. "Not yet."

"Damn it, stop teasing me."

"Never." He slid over her again, the sensation not enough to push her into oblivion. "I love the way you writhe for me, how your body goes soft and tight at the same time, like you'll never get enough." He kept his free hand on her hip, pinning her in place and preventing her from changing the angle. "I love how you'll do damn near anything to get me inside you."

She would, too. She grabbed a fistful of his hair, yanking it a little harder than she would have normally. "And you're a goddamn tease."

"You love it." Another stroke.

"Maybe."

He shifted, his cock notching in her entrance, and pushed just the tip into her. She hissed out a breath, needing so much more, but he seemed content to hold that position. *"James!"*

He sank another inch into her. "This is what you need. What you can't go another second without."

"Yes. Oh my God, yes."

Another inch. And another. Slowly and surely, until he had sunk into her to the hilt. And then he kissed her, his tongue working hers, taking what he already knew was his. She moved against him, only able to shift the slightest bit because of his weight pinning her to the mattress. That barest amount created a delicious friction, though, so she kept doing it. Pleasure built with each breath, low and deep and more profound than anything she'd ever felt before. She clutched his shoulders, her legs sliding over his, sweat slicking her skin. "James, I—"

"I know, lovely." He thrust a little, spiraling her pleasure higher. "I feel it, too."

She was so damn close, but she never wanted it to end. She ran her hands down his back, lightly raking her nails over his skin, to dig into his ass. "Please don't stop."

"I'm never going to stop." He thrust again, and that was all it took. She undulated wildly beneath him, taking him as deep as she could in this position, holding him so close she wasn't sure where she ended and where he began. He moved back, spreading her legs even further and pounding into her. "I've said it before, lovely, and I'll say it again. You're mine and mine alone."

CHAPTER TWENTY-ONE

James traced Carrigan's tattoo and then moved down the center of her stomach. Her muscles twitched beneath his finger, but she just turned her head and looked at him. Tired pleasure radiated from every line of her body. "I needed that."

"I know." He kissed her shoulder. Having her beneath him had been almost cleansing. He felt new and whole and vulnerable in a way he wasn't prepared to deal with. He'd told her he loved her. She hadn't said it back, but she also hadn't run screaming from the room. He knew she cared about him. There was time to build things between them.

He wasn't about to let her go without a fight.

"Do you ever think about just...leaving?" She closed her eyes. "Sometimes I fantasize about getting in a car and driving until I find some tiny little town where no

one's heard of the O'Malleys and where everyone knows
everyone else and things are just *simpler*."

"I've thought about it." But he'd never left for the
same reason she hadn't. *Family*. "I figure those small-
town people have their own problems and secrets and
bullshit. It's the human condition."

"Maybe. Or maybe that's just what we have to tell
ourselves not to take out a gun and put it in our
mouths."

He froze. "What?" No fucking way was she talking
about what he thought she was talking about.

"Not me." She opened her eyes and grabbed his hand.
"I'm not talking about me. I swear. I love life too much
to go down like that. I'll have to be dragged from this
world, kicking and screaming, no matter how shitty
things get. But I worry about my sisters."

He watched the expressions play across her face.
"They're strong."

"That's what I keep telling myself, but I don't know
if I believe it anymore. My brother's death changed a
lot of things. Everyone is so much more brittle now."
She stroked her hand down his arm, starting at his
shoulder and moving over every muscle. "My brothers
are so angry and afraid, even if they try to cover the
latter with the former. I don't think my baby sister has
spent more than a half an hour sober since we were
hustled out of town after all that shit went down. And
Sloan…" Her eyes darkened. "She's a ghost of the
woman she used to be."

He knew all about how the death of someone
beloved could change everything—ruin everything.
But this wasn't about him. It was about saying what

was necessary to comfort Carrigan. "It won't always be like this."

"Oh, no doubt something even more horrible will come along and push our already teetering family off the cliff."

"That's not what I meant." He was seriously worthless as this comforting bullshit, but that wasn't going to stop him from trying. "Your family is strong. Your parents will hold things together and your siblings will find their feet. Life will go on, whether anyone wants it to or not. This tragedy won't break you—any of you." He brushed her hair back. "I don't know if I've said how fucking sorry I am that it happened. I didn't give the order, but it doesn't matter. It was Halloran men who did it." *Ricky* who did it.

"I won't lie and say it's okay." Her eyes shone, but no tears fell. "Devlin was too good for this life. I think any one of us would have stepped in front of that bullet to give him a second chance at life. But...it's not your fault. When you live the lives we do, your family has a nasty tendency not to tell the right hand what the left hand is doing."

Wasn't that the fucking truth. He traced over her cheekbone and down to her bottom lip with his thumb. "I know. But I *am* sorry. I wish—"

"We all do." She sat up, the move knocking his hands away. "There's no use talking about it. It's over and done with. Practically ancient history."

What the fuck? James sat up, too. He didn't realize what she planned until she lurched off the bed and reached for her dress. "What are you doing?"

"I gave you tonight. We're done now."

It took him a full five seconds to hear and process her words. "No fucking way. Get your ass back in my bed."

She shimmied into her dress. "This has been fun—too much fun—but it's over."

He could barely believe she was doing this *now*. It was stone cold. James scrubbed a hand over his face. "It's over when I say it's over. We have a long way to go before that, lovely. I said I love you and I fucking meant it."

She froze, her back to him. "Well, that's just too damn bad. I'm not responsible for how you feel. I didn't ask you to fall for me. *I* know how to keep my emotions in check."

"Liar." He was on his feet before making the decision to move. "You're running scared. Again."

"What I'm doing is going home before my brothers follow through on their threats to start another goddamn war. We lost too much last time. I'm not letting that rest on my head."

It was an excuse, and not even a good one. If she'd wanted to avoid the threat of war, she never would have called him in the first place, let alone come out here with him. "Don't you ever get tired of dancing to whatever tune your family sets?"

"No." She stepped into her heels. "Unlike some people, my family will always come first."

She was going to throw *that* in his face? He crossed his arms over his chest. "Whatever you have to tell yourself to sleep at night." He wanted to grab her, to shake her until some sense popped into that gorgeous head of hers, but he'd never laid a hand on a woman in anger and he sure as fuck wasn't about to start now. Tying her up until she saw reason wasn't an option, either. He was left with nothing but standing there and watching her get ready to walk out of his life.

He couldn't shake the feeling that if she left now, it would be for good.

So he tried to be calm and rational. "Carrigan, sit down and we'll talk this through."

"Talking never did anyone a damn bit of good." She stopped in the doorway, her knuckles white where they fisted the hem of her dress. "Good-bye, James. For good this time." Then she was gone, disappearing as if she'd never been there to begin with.

And he just watched her go.

As soon as he heard the door close behind her, he slowly got dressed. It didn't take a genius to realize what she was doing—making yet another personal sacrifice for her family. She'd said as much. She might even be trying to protect him, too. It didn't matter. All that mattered was that she'd walked out without talking about it, without giving him a chance to find a way out of this mess.

She might care about him, but she didn't trust him. And fuck if that didn't hurt.

He rubbed a hand over his chest, knowing damn well that it wouldn't do anything to combat the dull ache that started there the second she walked out of this room. There would be no more phone calls. She wouldn't come running to him again, no matter how deep into shit she got. No, she was off to marry this Dmitri Romanov and sail away into the sunset.

Fuck.

He walked through the still mostly dark house, letting the memories wash over him. Play fighting with his brothers in the living room. Watching his mother knit in the rocking chair, looking more at peace than he ever saw her in Boston. The loud meals served around the tiny dining room table, while he and Brendan and Ricky all competed for her undivided attention. She'd always managed to make each of them feel like they were the center of her world.

And their old man...James touched the thickest scar running across his upper chest. He could feel the ridge of it through the thin fabric of his T-shirt. His father hadn't dared touch them while she walked this earth. He'd always thought that it was because her death broke the man, but now he wondered. Victor had been batshit crazy for as long as James could remember. Had his mother been the reason he stayed his hand? The shield between her boys and their sadistic fuck of a father?

The more he thought about it, the more it seemed to fit. He'd never seen her in a swimsuit. Whenever he thought about it now, he'd chalked it up to the summers that were never quite warm enough. But what if it wasn't? His hands clenched. Had Victor hurt her as a proxy and then turned his attentions on his boys when she was no longer available?

His stomach lurched, and he had to close his eyes and concentrate on breathing. It was the past. Knowing that didn't magically make the hurt go away, but it helped him focus. Right now he had bigger problems than worrying about if his old man beat his mother fifteen years ago.

He *would* find out, though.

In the meantime...James turned to the front door. He'd give Carrigan some time. Chasing her down now wouldn't do either one of them a damn bit of good. She was freaked out and she had reason to be. As much as it stung that she didn't believe in him enough to give him the chance to fix things, a part of him understood. A very small part. The rest wanted to track her down, but it would only make her run farther and faster from him.

No, he'd find a way around this, and then he'd come for her.

He walked out of the house and locked the door behind him. The first order of business was to get through the exchange tomorrow with those pieces of shit bringing in women. Then he'd deal with the mess with Carrigan.

It wasn't like she'd be married in the next twenty-four hours, after all.

* * *

Sloan drifted up the stairs, moving down the hallway on bare feet, taking silent count. Keira had stumbled home sometime after one and was currently passed out in her bed. But she was safe. Cillian hadn't come back from wherever he'd gone when he left this afternoon, but she suspected he was wherever he'd been spending all this time lately—most likely a bar. Aiden... well, Aiden was the easiest of her siblings to keep track of. He rarely left their father's study anymore, except when business demanded it. More and more he'd taken up the mantle of leadership, and she sometimes wondered if she was the only one who could see how heavily it weighed on him. But he wouldn't accept a shoulder to lean on because it would mean he was *weak*.

She shook her head and walked into the formal living room. It was one of the few public rooms on the front of the house with windows looking down over the sidewalk. Not that she could see much between the trees and darkness, but it didn't stop her from trying.

Carrigan hadn't come home yet. She glanced at her watch, a diamond MICHELE that she'd gotten on her sixteenth birthday from her parents. Most days it felt more like a shackle than a way to tell time. Two a.m. Too late.

She knew something had happened at the wedding, but she didn't know what. Not that she was surprised about her family's unwillingness to talk about it—they never had been free with their information unless forced. All she knew was that it involved Carrigan and had whipped both Cillian and Aiden into a fury that still hadn't abated two days later.

And now her sister had pulled another of her disappearing acts.

Sloan touched the glass, as if that would do something to draw her home and to safety faster. Things were happening too quickly, spiraling out of control. She sighed. Even though it had been banishment for all intents and purposes, she craved the simplicity of their house in Connecticut. When they were there, the drama and worries that populated daily life in Boston seemed worlds away. She could almost believe they were normal people who didn't believe in arranged marriages and who didn't do unmentionable things on the illegal side of their operations.

But it was a childish dream. Just like her hope for one day marrying a man she loved—and who loved her. And her wish to be a schoolteacher. And countless other things that had fallen by the wayside as she turned eighteen and had to face the facts—she was expected to marry a man of her father's choosing, and to devote her life to making him happy and giving him children. There was no room there for a career of her own. And love? Love wasn't even on the radar.

Movement below drew her attention to where Carrigan and Liam appeared from beneath the tree directly in front of the town house and hurried up the steps to the front door. A few seconds later, the sound of it opening and shutting whispered through the near-silent halls. If she hadn't been waiting for it, she wouldn't have known that it'd happened.

Sloan walked back through the hallway to the top of the stairs, reaching it just as her sister did. "Carrigan."

"Holy shit!" Carrigan jerked back, her hand on her chest. "I didn't see you there."

Which was the point. Her mother had already lectured her about how unseemly her nighttime wanderings were. So she made sure that Aileen didn't know about them anymore. The thought of spending the night locked away in her room had panic fluttering in her throat. She was already locked up in every way that counted. She couldn't be locked in physically, too.

She frowned at her older sister. "What's wrong?" She hadn't come home from some nameless club like Sloan had originally suspected. Not wearing that green dress that Carrigan would consider respectable, and certainly not with her makeup done up for the day, rather than nighttime. It was more than that, though. Usually when she rolled home in the small hours of the night, she had an expression like a cat who'd stolen the cream. Not tonight. Tonight her eyes were shining, and there were little tremors working their way through her sister's body that she could see from several feet away. "Carrigan?"

"I..." She wrapped her arms around herself, the shaking getting worse.

If there was one thing Sloan recognized, it was a person on the verge of a complete breakdown. She'd danced along that edge herself too many times to miss the signs. She slipped an arm around her sister's waist and guided her to her room, carefully shutting the door behind them. "It's going to be okay."

"It's not okay." The shining in her eyes overflowed, a tear slipping free. "Nothing's ever going to be okay again."

She froze. Carrigan was *crying*? She could count how many times she'd seen her older sister cry on one hand and still have all five fingers left over. *What in God's name is going on?* "We can talk about it."

"I'm marrying Dmitri Romanov." More tears fell, as if that first one had broken a dam and now they all rushed to fill the new space. She stared into the distance, seeing something that wasn't in this room. "I have to. I don't have a choice."

"Carrigan..." There was nothing she could do. She couldn't tell her sister that she had a choice—she didn't. Their father wouldn't think twice about dragging her bodily down the aisle himself if she tried to protest. She could run, but he would find her. He had all the resources that came with more money than most people could dream of. If Carrigan left the fold, all of that would become focused on finding her and bringing her back.

Since she couldn't speak the lies that would comfort her sister, Sloan wrapped her arms around her sister. "I'm sorry."

"I love him, you know." Another sob, so harsh she thought she misheard until Carrigan said it again. "I love James Halloran."

Shock almost had her dropping her arms. *James Halloran?* She'd suspected her sister was seeing someone, but he was the last person she would have guessed. Sloan pressed her lips together to keep the accusations inside. *How could you? His family is responsible for Devlin! He might as well have pulled the trigger himself! He* kidnapped *you!* All things her sister already knew. And she obviously needed comfort right now more than she needed to be yelled at. So Sloan rubbed soothing circles on her back and let her sister cry herself out.

It took time, the minutes ticking by until the sky beyond Carrigan's bedroom window began to lighten. But she finally lifted her head and wiped at her face. "I'm fine. I'm okay."

No, she wasn't. But Sloan wasn't about to point it out. Instead she took her sister's hands. "I know you care for"—she almost choked on the name—"James, but you have to marry Dmitri. You know that, don't you?" To do anything else courted their father's rage—and he wouldn't be alone. The entire family would unite to make sure Carrigan and James never had a chance to be together. The wounds of the summer were too raw and, even if they weren't, some things were unforgivable.

Devlin bleeding out in the street with a Halloran bullet inside him was one of them.

Her sister exhaled, her shoulder bowing down. "I know. James isn't for me. I'm marrying Dmitri. It's the only option." She sounded like she'd just delivered a death sentence to herself.

CHAPTER TWENTY-TWO

Carrigan woke up the next morning feeling like she'd been run over by a truck. Her life hadn't been picture-perfect to begin with, but it'd sure as hell gone downhill faster than she could have imagined. She touched her face, still feeling puffy and raw from her crying jag last night. She hadn't meant to break down, let alone in front of Sloan, but once she'd started, she hadn't been able to stop. She'd seen the look on her sister's face, though, when she'd finally gotten control of herself. Sloan sided with Aiden and Cillian. She thought Carrigan was a monster for sleeping with James, let alone being stupid enough to fall for him.

I told her I love him.

She shouldn't have let the damning words past her lips, but if there was one person who wouldn't pass it on, it was Sloan. Carrigan rolled over and stared at her ceiling. The temptation to pull the covers over her head and sleep the day away was almost too much to pass up. But then she'd have to admit to hiding in her room to avoid seeing her brother or father or any other member of her family who'd get in her face and call her a traitor at the first available opportunity. Which would mean she was afraid.

No help for it. She had to get out of bed.

She padded to her bathroom and took a leisurely shower, telling herself all the while that she wasn't *actually* stalling. After styling her hair and putting on her war paint, there was nothing left to do but go downstairs and face the firing squad. *Could I be any more melodramatic?*

Probably. Anything to keep from thinking about last night. James told her he loved her. *He really loves me.* She stared at her reflection, the image blurring to replace the tortured look on his face when he'd confessed what his father had done to him. Abuse was too kind a term— and death was too kind a penalty for it. She clenched her hands, her nails digging into her palms as fury washed over her in waves. She'd already believed Victor Halloran deserved to die after this summer. Knowing what she did now? She hoped that he suffered horribly before he went. If there was any way she could arrange for that to happen, she wouldn't hesitate to do it.

James couldn't be her priority anymore—at least not as far as anyone else was concerned. She had to put on an obedient expression and jump through all the hoops set out before her to keep him safe. That was the *only* thing that mattered. As much as she'd wanted to take him up on the offer blazing from his eyes last night and say that their enemies could go fuck themselves, she knew the truth. They might have a few days, maybe even a few months, but the debt would come due at some point and then James would die. She'd be lucky if she went with him, but Carrigan didn't like her chances.

Either way, it was a lose-lose scenario. The only way she was going to get through the next however many years of her life and marriage to Dmitri was knowing that James still walked this earth. She'd suffer untold horrors to make sure that happened.

Taking a fortifying breath, she walked out of her room and down the main staircase. The house was oddly hushed, making the hair on the back of her neck stand on end. She caught sight of Aiden coming out of the library. "I did what you wanted."

He didn't look up from the papers in his hands. "It has nothing to do with what I want and everything to do with what's necessary."

Necessary. She hated that word. It ranked right up there with loyalty and obedience and *family*. "Whatever. Dmitri agreed." She just had to hope that her last desperate night of freedom wasn't enough to drive him over the edge. She never should have taken that chance, but it was too late to worry about it now. Really, she didn't *want* to take back those hours with James, talking with him, losing herself at the feel of what he was doing to her. She just wished she could have fallen asleep listening to the steady sound of his breathing.

Let it go. It will never happen again. You can't let it.

She wouldn't. She'd had a moment of weakness, but it was enough to shore her up for the foreseeable future. It had to be. She fell into step with Aiden down the hall, her stomach rumbling. She'd barely let the idea of breakfast cross her mind, when the door to her father's study slammed open. He marched into the hallway and glared at her. "You."

Aiden tensed next to her. "Father—"

"Not now. You don't know what your sister has done." His gaze flicked over her brother. "Unless you already *do* know, in which case we'll be having a discussion about loyalty in the near future." He pointed at Carrigan. "In my office. Now."

She followed him because there was no other option, and nearly tripped over her feet when she saw who occupied one of the chairs in front of the desk. *Dmitri.* "What are you doing here?"

"Protecting my investment." His face gave nothing away. No anger. No worry. Nothing.

"Sit down."

She sank into the open seat, her heart in her throat. There was only one thing that could bring Dmitri *here* and put that look on her father's face. *He knows.* "Father—"

"I highly suggest you keep your damn mouth shut before you do more damage." He straightened already perfectly straight papers. "Did you or did you not spend the night with Halloran?"

They *did* know. She swallowed hard. "I can explain."

"I don't need your explanation. Answer the question."

She dropped her gaze. "Yes, I did."

The study was so silent, her father's sigh sounded like a bellow. "In that case, I would like to formally apologize, Dmitri. I had no idea the trouble she was getting into. I completely understand if you're no longer interested in the marriage pact on the table, but I'd hope that this won't color our dealings going forward." He paused. "Though I do have two more daughters."

Sloan or Keira married to this shark? *Never*. Carrigan raised her head. "That's not necessary."

"What did I say?" He was so furious that she actually feared he might strike her this time.

"It's perfectly all right, Seamus," Dmitri cut in smoothly. "I fully intend to marry Carrigan, and the night's events haven't changed those plans."

She didn't know whether to be relieved or terrified. Carrigan sat perfectly still, a small, fuzzy animal sensing a predator, knowing an attack was coming but not being able to see what direction it'd be from. She kept silent because what she thought didn't matter to either man in the room.

Her father raised his eyebrows. "If you're sure."

"I am. I find myself quite enamored with your oldest daughter. So much so, I'd like to take her back to New York for the time being until we can finalize wedding arrangements with your wife. I'm sure she'd like the opportunity to plan it at her leisure instead of with a time constraint like the most recent one."

Panic had black spots dancing across her vision. Leave Boston? *Now?* She'd thought she'd have more time. "Father, please."

He ignored her. "That would suit perfectly. Carrigan has proven herself a poor judge of character, and removing her from further temptations is wise."

Like she was a naughty child being sent to timeout. Or, worse, an invalid incapable of thinking for herself. She opened her mouth but couldn't make words come out. The feeling of her life spinning out of control around her only got worse as Dmitri stood and shook her father's hand as if conducting a business deal.

Which is exactly what he was doing.

He turned. "It's time, Carrigan."

It took her entirely too long to understand what the hell he meant. "You want me to come with you *now*?" She shot a panicked look at her father, but he was no help. "But I need to say good-bye to Sloan and Keira and—"

"That's what a phone is for." Her father's expression didn't so much as twitch. "If you're going to be difficult, I'll have Mark come in here and carry you out over his shoulder. Why don't you save us all the indignity of throwing a tantrum and act like an adult?"

He'd just sold her to further his business arrangements, and he wanted her to act like an *adult*. Only the knowledge that he'd follow through on his threat without batting an eye had her finding her spine and shooting to her feet. "Then, by all means, let's not make a scene." Neither man flinched at the venom in her voice.

"Wonderful."

She ignored Dmitri's offered elbow and strode out of the room, nearly hitting Aiden with the door as she came out. "I hope you're happy, big brother."

His green eyes went wide before he schooled his expression. "What's going on?"

"Father's handed me off to Dmitri. So I won't be your problem anymore." She ignored the way he flinched and strode for the front door. She wasn't surprised when Dmitri met her stride for stride without seeming to hurry. She glared. "I expect you to send men over to collect my things before you cart me off to New York."

"I'll see it done."

He was so...unflappable. Stone cold. It made her want to poke at him, but instinct said he'd respond in a way *she* wouldn't like, so she didn't. Instead, she followed him out to his car and into the backseat. He closed the door, sealing her into the silence of the limo. She started to shake and wrapped her arms around herself to cover up the involuntary movements.

Oh God, what am I going to do?

* * *

James couldn't shake the nasty mood that made him want to punch something. It was a bad place to be in because he had important shit going on tonight. Meeting the flesh traders without his head on straight was just asking for trouble. He met Michael in the kitchen. The man leaned against the counter, hunched over a cup of what smelled like coffee. "Morning, boss."

"Everything a go for tonight?"

"As good as it gets. I have men posted at the transfer spot making sure we don't have any surprises when the time comes."

Smart. He poured himself a cup of coffee. "I get through tonight with money in my pocket and without getting shot, and you're getting a bonus."

Michael gave a toothy grin. "Just what I live for." He slurped his coffee. "I'm going to check on the boys. Unless you need something else?"

"Go." He waved the man away. There was nothing to say to Michael that he didn't already know. A good leader delegated when possible, and his second in command had proven he was capable of handling whatever shit arose. Michael had barely been gone thirty seconds when Ricky sauntered through the door.

"Hey, James."

He set the mug down. "Ricky." It'd only been a few days since he let his little brother out of the basement, but there had been no incidents. It was almost too much to hope that that would continue for the next few days until he left for California. He wasn't about to let his guard down—Ricky was rarely up before noon, let alone at this early hour. He wanted something. "What can I do you for?"

"The deal you have going on tonight. I want in." He held up his hands, not that James was rushing to jump in and fill the silence. "Just hear me out. I brokered this deal, and I busted my ass to get the contacts in place so that these two would trust us enough to bring the shipment in. I deserve to be there."

Considering he didn't trust his brother with the women at Tit for Tat who voluntarily worked the darker aspects of their trade, he sure as fuck wasn't going to trust him with a container full of terrified refugees in God only knew what state. That being said, it wasn't like he was going to send Ricky off without someone to watch his back—and make sure he didn't do anything shady. James would be there to ensure things stayed on target, and he wouldn't look the other way if his brother tried something. Maybe this would be the thing that would get them started on a better path.

Or maybe Ricky was just waiting for him to lower his guard so he could slit James's throat.

He took another drink of coffee, watching his brother

over the rim of his mug. "If I say yes—*if*—then you follow orders. I don't care if I tell you to strip down buck-ass naked and run through the street, you do it with no questions asked. Understand?"

Ricky gave a sharp nod. "I get it. You say jump and I ask how high. So can I go or not?"

Fuck, he just wanted to punch the shit out of his brother. The feeling used to be the exception to the rule. Now it was all he ever felt. Whatever friendship they'd had had died with Brendan. Maybe it had never existed in the first place. "Yeah. Talk to Michael about where he wants you." James would be talking to Michael, too. He didn't intend on letting his baby brother out of his sight tonight.

"Will do." Ricky hurried out of the kitchen like he was afraid James was about to change his mind. Good riddance.

He checked the time. Ten hours until the meeting. Too long. He wanted to keep in motion, to keep from thinking about the reality lurking in the back of his mind. Carrigan was gone, and he still didn't have fuck all for a plan of getting her back.

He made his way to the gym and spent the next hour working his body to the breaking point. It didn't matter how many reps he did, he couldn't escape the way his chest hurt with every breath. He felt like the walking wounded, still going through the motions despite missing vital parts of his body. He dropped the dumbbells with a curse. This wasn't working, and every minute that passed pushed him closer to doing something stupid like driving over to the O'Malley house and demanding to see her.

It wasn't what a good leader would do. He'd be putting everything he'd busted his ass for in jeopardy for a woman. *Not just any woman.* It didn't matter. She was one person. He couldn't endanger everyone under his command for a single person—not even when his own happiness was on the line.

There's a way around it. There has to be. He just had to find it.

A shitty plan formed in his mind, but a shitty plan was better than no plan. He put the weight room back into order and then went up to his room to shower and change. Twenty minutes later he was in the Chevelle and dialing his phone.

Teague answered almost immediately. "I didn't expect to hear from you again." Not outside of formal negotiations.

James drummed his fingers on the wheel. "I'm not going to make excuses for what happened before. I should have done something differently—something *more*." They'd seen each other since the night Callista was captive and escaped with Carrigan in tow from his family home, but he and Teague hadn't really talked. He got it that the man hated him. He'd hate anyone who willingly put Carrigan in danger, too. He shook his head. "I fucked up. And I'm sorry for that."

"You did." He sighed. "But there were more than a few fuckups to go around. You could have stopped Callie's escape before it even started and you didn't. That means something."

All he'd done was step aside. It had felt like a risk then, but looking back it was nowhere near enough. He should have escorted them out. "If I could go back—"

"I know. Me, too. We can't go back. We can only go forward." Teague paused, the sound of a woman's voice in the background. "But you didn't call today to apologize and shoot the shit."

"No, I didn't." Now that he was on the line, though, he wasn't sure what to say. Teague might not hate him, but he was a long way off giving his blessing for James to steal Carrigan away. He probably wouldn't respond as violently as his other brothers, but no way would he think James was good enough for her. Hell, he was right. But there was no one else to turn to. He had to man up and broach the subject, and hope that Teague hated the idea of his older sister married to some Russian from New York as much as James did. "You know your old man's making Carrigan marry some stranger."

"I'm aware." And pissed as hell if his tone was anything to go by.

It was now or never. "I'm not going to let that happen."

The silence stretched into one minute, and then two. Finally Teague said, far too calmly, "I might have lost my fucking mind, but you seem to be insinuating that you and my sister have something going on."

Oh yeah. Teague was pissed as hell.

James scrubbed a hand over his face. "It's not what you think."

"Talk fast, James—talk really fucking fast."

He weighed his words. They had to be the right ones. If Teague wasn't in his corner, then he was in this shit alone. But, really, there was only the truth. James had never been all that good at pandering, and he wasn't about to start now. "I love her. It didn't start out that way, but sometimes you have to take these things as they come. I've never met a woman like her, and I could go the rest of my life and that would still be true." His breath caught, and he didn't bother to hide the feeling that welled up. "She's everything, Teague. You get what I'm saying?"

More silence. He let it go, knowing that he couldn't rush the man when it came to this shit. Finally Teague cursed. "Goddamn it, you don't ever take the easy road, do you?"

"You know me better than that."

"Yeah, I do." Another pause. "And Carrigan? What's she got to say about all this?"

She left me. He clenched his teeth together. "She's doing whatever it takes to keep everyone around her safe, even if that means walking away from me."

"Well, hell." Teague cursed again. "I'll help if I can, but you know as well as I do that my father isn't a man to cross. Are you prepared for the consequences?"

War. The very thing they'd all busted their asses to avoid over the summer, and now he was considering running headlong into it. This was different, though. Carrigan was worth it and more. "Yeah, I'm prepared."

"Then sit tight and don't do anything stupid. I'll see what I can find out and get back to you."

He started the Chevelle. "Teague?"

"Yeah?"

"Thanks." He hesitated. "If you want to go get a beer when this is all over, first round's on me."

"I'd like that. Now stay the fuck out of trouble until I call you."

Easier said than done. He wasn't the type of man to be comfortable sitting on his hands, but at least he had other shit to occupy him. James glanced at the clock. A few short hours until it was time for the meet up. He checked on Michael, but it looked like so far so good.

He was too fucking realistic to hope that the rest of the day would go down without a hitch.

CHAPTER TWENTY-THREE

Dmitri's man drove them down to the Mandarin Oriental, and he didn't say a word the entire drive. Not that Carrigan expected him to. What did he have to say? He'd won. He'd gotten everything he'd wanted, and he'd put her father in a position of being grateful to him. It really was brilliant.

Not that she was ever going to say so.

She climbed out of the backseat before the man had a chance to open the door, and looked around the parking garage. "How long will we be here?"

"Tonight. I have some remaining business to take care of in Boston before we return to New York." Dmitri offered his elbow, and she forced herself to take it. She might resent the hell out of him, but she knew when to hedge her bets. She was marrying him, whether she liked it or not. Getting them started on the right foot—as much as possible—might mean more freedom for her down the road.

I hate this. I hate that I can't choose a man for myself. I hate everything.

Her fingers itched for her phone, and the thing she wanted most in the world was to hear James's raspy voice over the line telling her that it was okay and he'd be at her side in no time. It would never happen again. God, that hurt.

Dmitri led them up through a set of elevators to one of the absurdly large suites. Everything about it was opulent and expensive, all with a vaguely Asian theme that didn't quite commit to any specific culture. She made a beeline for the kitchen, finding a bottle of vodka stashed in one of the cabinets. Why wasn't she surprised? She poured a healthy splash into a tumbler and then poured some more. Alcohol wouldn't do anything to change her circumstances, but it'd numb her to some of the sharper aspects of it for tonight, at least. If that was the best she could do, then she was going to happily do it.

If I hadn't gone and fallen for James, would I be so upset about marrying Dmitri?

She didn't know. That was part of the problem. She'd never been on board with this whole marrying-a-stranger plan, but at least she understood the Russian. He was a cold bastard, but she could be cold, too.

Or so she'd thought.

She glanced up as the glass touched her lips to find Dmitri watching her. "What?"

"Nothing at all. Help yourself." It irked her that he had her over a barrel in every way that counted, and all the while he'd never once lost his polish and poise during the whole process. *My fault*. Knowing that didn't help her mood a damn bit, but there it was. She'd made her bed and now it was time to lie in it. It didn't matter if she'd been forced into a corner by circumstances beyond her control.

She tightened her grip on the glass, trying to remind herself why this was all necessary. *To keep James safe*. She'd screwed up last night and let her heart get the better of her head. Dmitri didn't seem like the kind of man to be forgiving, but if he was going to make an exception this time, she had to do whatever it took to make sure that happened. No matter how much she hated the thought of playing subservient wifey to him.

He motioned around the room. "Feel free to make yourself at home. I have a few business calls to make. Afterward, we'll order a meal and have a conversation."

Peachy. She forced a tight smile. "I look forward to it." How much vodka could she drink before he got done with his calls? Enough to muffle the soul-searing pain demanding she go running back into James's arms? Somehow, she doubted it. There wasn't enough alcohol in the world.

But that wouldn't stop her from trying.

Is he going to expect me in his bed tonight? She couldn't play the blushing virgin waiting for her wedding night. He'd already more than proven that he'd done his research when it came to her—not to mention that she'd put this entire thing in jeopardy for one more time with James.

I didn't even get to say good-bye.

She took another healthy gulp of the vodka. Dmitri wasn't ugly or gross, but the mere thought of his hands on her body made her stomach lurch. *I don't know if I can do this*. If she hadn't had a taste of how good things could be with James, she'd probably be able to fake it with Dmitri. Or, more likely, she wouldn't have had to fake it at all. He seemed like the kind of man who knew his way around a woman's body. Before she'd experienced how good it could be when her heart was involved, that would have been enough for her.

She wasn't sure it still was.

"Perfect." Dmitri pulled his phone out of his pocket. "My men won't come into the room, but they are stationed at the doors. I don't have to tell you not to do something ill advised."

It wasn't a question, so she didn't deign to answer it. His threat to James kept her in place, and he damn well knew it. "Don't worry about me. The most damage I'll do while you're busy is to your vodka." Maybe a little distance from him would let her get her game face back into place. She was in the middle of a death spiral, and that was unacceptable. This was a man who would capitalize on any weakness, and she'd more than given him enough ammunition in the last hour. It was time to get back onto the playing field. Carrigan braced herself, smiled, and touched his arm, letting her hand linger there even though she was dangerously close to having the vodka she'd drunk make a reappearance. "I want to thank you."

"Oh?"

"You didn't have to show mercy." She made herself move closer. "I'm very, *very* grateful that you did."

His expression didn't so much as twitch. "Good." He turned and walked away, cutting an imposing figure in his perfectly fitted suit. Though he hadn't technically agreed to anything, he was a smart man, and a smart man would know it was more important to secure her obedience and loyalty early on, rather than exact petty revenge to assuage his pride.

She hoped.

She downed another gulp of the vodka, relishing the burn because of the future oblivion it promised. She looked around the room, taking in the understated elegance. Sitting here in the kitchen like a lush, just waiting for Dmitri to wander back in and pay attention to her...No, thanks.

After topping off her vodka, she wandered around the living room. Everything was top of the line and completely soulless. She would have traded it in a hot second for the faded, lived-in feel of James's beach place. She rubbed her chest. How was it possible to miss someone so much when she'd been with them a day before? Carrigan sipped her vodka, going slower now that she'd started to feel its effects. Getting drunk was a dumb decision. The last thing she needed was to break down in front of Dmitri in an alcohol-infused sob session. He already had too much power over her. She refused to hand him any more weapons.

Needing to combat the fuzziness threatening, she crossed the living room and muscled open one of the large windows overlooking Back Bay. Instantly, she got a face full of icy wind. She closed her eyes and tilted her head back, letting the cold sink into her, driving away her buzz. Better. Much better. She wouldn't be able to stand here too long, but it was exactly what she'd needed.

I need a plan in place to deal with him. I've spent too

much time letting my emotions get the better of me and
giving the advantage to everyone else. It ends now.

It didn't take long for shivers to start racking her body,
but she wrapped her arms around herself, not willing to
close the window just yet.

"Yes, yes, I know."

Carrigan frowned. *What the hell?* She angled to look
out the window, trying to figure out what she was hearing. It didn't take long to recognize Dmitri's voice. Apparently the window in the master bedroom was cracked
open as well. There was no reason his business calls
should interest her, but she needed every piece of information she could get when it came to this man. One
never knew when the opportunity would arise where it
could be used for leverage.

She stepped out of her heels, picked them up, and
padded closer to the window. His voice was partially
muffled, growing louder and quieter. He must be pacing.
She didn't dare peek to confirm.

Inside, he kept speaking. "Are you threatening *me*?"
He muttered something in what sounded like Russian.
"Listen to me, you little *der'mo*. You agreed to this and
you took your payment. That means I own you. Though
I'm starting to think I overpaid."

She grinned despite the cold sinking into her bones.
Apparently the perfectly temperate Dmitri *could* get
frazzled.

"No, things haven't changed. If anything, it's even
more vital now to follow through on this." A pause, and
then his voice dropped until she had to strain to make out
the words. "Don't misunderstand me, Michael. If James
Halloran doesn't die tonight, you will go in his place,

and I will take personal satisfaction in drawing out your last breaths until you're begging for the mercy of the afterlife."

Carrigan clamped her hand over her mouth to stifle her gasp. That murdering backstabbing *bastard*. She reached blindly for the wall, the world turning slow circles around her. All she'd done, all she'd sacrificed, and James was still in Dmitri's crosshairs.

From the sound it of, he had been even before she agreed to marry the Russian.

He kept speaking, oblivious to her world falling apart around her. "And that is if Ricky doesn't get to you first. You know what happens if you fail me. Don't."

She held her breath as he paced and muttered in Russian. Surely he had more phone calls to make? She tensed, ready to slam the window shut to prevent him from realizing she knew. But then his voice rose to normal speaking levels. Another phone call. She listened for a few moments more, long enough to realize she wouldn't be able to glean any information from this particular call since he wasn't speaking English.

It didn't matter. She knew enough to know she couldn't stay here another minute longer.

Carrigan carefully closed the window and slipped on her shoes. They weren't ideal for escaping guards and fleeing into the night, but she'd run in higher. She eyed the door to the master bedroom, half expecting Dmitri to rush out and demand to know what she thought she was doing. He didn't, and the longer she waited, the greater her chances of discovery were.

How the hell was she going to get out of here? This wasn't like the Halloran house, where she could slip out a window and onto the roof and then drop to the ground safely from there. They were at least twelve stories up. The only person who jumped from this balcony would be someone courting death.

She grabbed her purse, digging through it for the one thing that could tip the situation temporarily in her favor—the Taser. For the first time since Aiden had given it to her, she wished it were a goddamn gun. The men outside that door weren't good men, and while a Taser might put them on the floor temporarily, they'd be up and after her before too much time had passed.

I'll just have to be quicker than they are. Or smarter. Or something.

Before she opened the door, she ran her hands through her hair, mussing it, and then smeared her lipstick a little. She held the Taser in one hand, tucked behind her purse, and opened the door. "Help!"

There were two guards. One was less than a foot from the door and the other several steps beyond him. Too far. This had to be quick, before they realized what was happening, or it'd be over before it began. She put some stumble into her step, and lowered her voice to little more than a whisper. "Help."

The guards exchanged a look. The closest one frowned. "Where is Mr. Romanov?"

"He's…" She ducked her head, watching them through the shield of her hair. "He's…" They moved closer, trying to hear her. When they were an arm's distance from her, she raised her voice a little. "On the phone." She tased the furthest one, holding down the trigger to keep shocking him even after his body hit the ground. She hit the other guard's body as he drew his gun, her purse flying from her hand as they slammed into the wall. He dropped his gun, and she dove for it, rolling and coming up to fire wildly. The shot took him in the shoulder, knocking him onto his back, and she wasted no time scrambling to her feet.

Then she ran for the elevator, their groans ringing in her ear. It wouldn't take long for the tased one to recover—less than a minute if Aiden was right—and that hadn't been a killing shot to the other one by any means. She had to be out of here *now*.

The damn elevator would take too long, so she shoved through the doors to the stairs. Her bare feet slapped the cold concrete and she almost went down before she realized that was exactly where they'd expect her to go. Carrigan ran up the stairs; all the while a small voice in the back of her mind pointed out that she was violating the cardinal rule of horror movies—*never run up*.

She made herself slow down as she reached the door two floors up. Her stomach hurt and her breath was coming too fast, but she pressed herself against the wall when she heard the door open below her. Dmitri's men shouldn't be able to see her from their angle, but she couldn't take any chances. She was trapped up here.

Idiot.

They conversed softly in Russian and then the sound of a door opening whispered through the quiet while a second set of feet started down. Carrigan waited ten seconds, and then thirty, and then a full sixty. Only then did she slip through the door into the hallway behind her and press the elevator button.

She almost cried out when the elevator door opened and it was empty. The ride down to the second floor seemed to take forever, but in reality it was less than a minute. She looked both ways as she stepped into the hallway. As tempting as going down to the lobby and running out the front doors was, by now the men had contacted Dmitri, who might have contacted whoever he had guarding the entrance. She'd be better suited to take a less obvious path.

She wound through the hallways toward the back of the hotel. At this time of night, the place was mostly deserted, and she kept glancing over her shoulder, expecting to be found out at any second. A quick trip down the corner stairs to the back door found her at a carefully cultivated courtyard, complete with trees, grass, and walking paths. She put her shoes back on and hurried through it to Ring Road and headed south, away from the bay. It felt unnatural to keep her head down and her stride even, but if Dmitri's men got this far, they'd be looking for a woman in a black dress running from them. She wasn't about to make finding her that easy. She eyed the people around her as she turned the corner on Huntington, this time heading northeast. People were suspicious these days, but she looked like a hot mess, so surely some well-meaning Good Samaritan would help her. She just had to pick the right mark.

A block later, her gaze fell on an older guy trying to flag down a cab with his wife. Perfect. She stopped a foot away from them and made her voice as pathetic as possible. "Excuse me? Sir? Ma'am?"

The man turned, a frown on his face, but it melted away when his wife put her hand on his arm. "What?"

"Do you have a phone I could use?" It wasn't hard to dredge up some tears, though they didn't fall. "My boyfriend and I had a fight and he took his car and abandoned me down here. I..." Her voice caught. "I need help."

"Of course, honey." The wife grabbed the phone from her husband's hand and passed it over.

Carrigan stared at it for half a second. She wanted to call James, to hear his voice and know that he was okay, and warn him of the danger. But she didn't know his damn number—she'd just put it in her phone and used his contact every time she'd called him. *Lazy*. Really, there was only one number she had memorized. She dialed, and then held her breath while it rang. She almost cried all over again when her brother answered. "Teague O'Malley."

"Teague, it's me."

Instantly his voice lost its cold, professional tone. "What's going on? Why are you calling me from a strange number?"

"I'm in trouble." Conscious of the couple's gaze on her, she kept it as brief as possible. "I'm down on Huntington and Dartmouth. Can you pick me up?" As soon as the words left her mouth, she wondered if she'd made a mistake. By now, Teague had to be aware of both her pending marriage to Dmitri and the fact that pretty much their entire family saw her as a traitor for falling for James. *What if he—?*

"Go to the Copley Square Hotel and wait in the lobby. I'll be there in twenty."

"Okay." She hung up and handed the phone back to the wife. "Thank you." *I never should have doubted Teague. He didn't let family get in the way of offering me a way out before. Obviously that hasn't changed.*

"It was no problem." The woman watched her with

concern written across her face. "Do you want us to wait with you?" From the disgusted look her husband sent her, he wasn't happy with the idea.

"No, but thank you for offering. My brother will be here in a few minutes."

"Good, good." She put her hand on Carrigan's arm. "Get rid of that good-for-nothing man of yours."

She managed a smile. "Oh, I plan on it."

* * *

Jameson's was nearly empty, and Cillian was doing his damnedest not to stare at the new bartender. She wore a pair of jeans that were holey enough to be considered indecent, layered over fishnets, with a black tank top. The combination would have been sexy as hell under normal circumstances, but the glimpses of those fishnets killed him. He drank his apple juice, knowing damn well that he was focusing on this woman—Olivia—because he didn't want to deal with the shit storm waiting for him back home.

He'd gotten a text from Aiden this morning telling him that Carrigan had basically been handed off to Dmitri Romanov—who was, as far as he could tell, the same Dmitri who had chatted him up a little over two week ago. He *knew* he hadn't given the bastard anything then, knew that it was ultimately his father who made the decision that treated his sister like a piece of furniture, knew that there wasn't a damn thing he could have done to stop it.

It didn't matter.

Hate the man or not, he'd seen James Halloran's face when Aiden shook Carrigan. The guy loved her, or cared about her so much it was the same damn thing. If Aiden had shaken her again, James would have thrown out their tentative peace without a second thought.

That, more than anything else, had stayed with Cillian over the last few days. No one in their family put personal health and happiness above the needs of the O'Malleys as a whole. It just wasn't how shit went down. Up until Teague's wedding, he would have said the Hallorans were the same way—worse, really.

And he'd have been wrong.

There isn't a damn thing I can do to help her. Just like I couldn't help Devlin.

"You keep looking at the drink like that, it's going to curdle."

He glanced up to find Olivia standing on the other side of the bar, and hell if she wasn't even more striking up close. Her dark eyes were damn near black and held secrets he could only guess at. What was this woman's story? Benji usually hired guys because apparently he'd had enough bad past experiences with female bartenders to make him gun-shy. This woman had to be something special for the big man to have made an exception. "Maybe I like my drinks curdled."

"Sure you do." Her mouth tightened.

"You know, I might not be the most charming guy around, but I've never had a woman decide she despises me at first sight like you apparently have." And if he was going to be coming in here like he normally did, being hated by a bartender that Benji obviously adored was going to be seriously uncomfortable. He put his best smile on. "If you let me know what I did to piss you off, I'll do what I can to avoid it in the future."

If anything, her expression only got more annoyed. "You're right. You're not charming."

He sat back. "That wasn't an answer."

"Maybe I just don't like the look of you." She waved a hand to encompass all of him. "With your fancy haircut, expensive suit, and I'm-a-bad-boy tattoos. You're the kind of man who thinks he owns the world."

Cillian snorted. "Hardly."

"I know your type." She shrugged. "It doesn't matter if you agree with me or not. If it walks like a duck and quacks like a duck, it's most likely a duck. And I'd bet my last dollar that you're a duck."

His phone rang, saving him from coming up with a response to her absurd assumption. *Or is it really that absurd? You're trouble and you know it. If she's smart enough to recognize it on sight and avoid it, who the fuck are you to blame her for it?* He pulled out his phone and frowned when he saw Teague's number. "Hey."

"Where are you?"

"Beacon Hill." He wasn't about to tell Teague he was in the same bar they'd been in the night Devlin died. He wouldn't understand. Worse, maybe he actually would.

"Carrigan's in trouble."

He bit back the instinctive response to throw her whatever-the-fuck-it-was with James Halloran in his brother's face. Hadn't Cillian just been thinking that she didn't deserve to be passed off to the Russian when it seemed like Halloran really had feelings for her? "What kind of trouble?"

"The kind where she's in over her head enough to call for help."

Considering their sister had never hesitated to take

care of her own problems, that meant something bad. He straightened. He might not like the idea of her with Halloran, but she was still his big sister. There was no going back in time and saving Devlin, but if he could help Carrigan, then maybe that would do something to start to balance his karmic debt. "When and where do you need me?"

"My apartment, and as soon as you can get there."

He was already reaching into his pocket for his cash. "Consider it done." He hung up to find the pretty bartender watching him, a frown on her face. "Careful there, you frown like that often enough and your face is going to stick in that expression." He tossed the money on the bar and walked away, the sound of her sputtering behind him making him smile despite the clusterfuck he was most likely walking into.

When life was going to hell around him, sometimes it was all about finding pleasure in the small things.

* * *

"Tell me again."

Carrigan bit back her impatience. "I already told you twice. Dmitri is planning on killing James. You have to call him and warn him."

Teague ran his hands through his hair. "I did. Five times. He's not answering."

She knew that. God, of course she knew that. It didn't stop the panic from hurtling through her, growing stronger with each minute that passed. Where was James now? Had this Michael already done his work, and was the love of her life even now bleeding out in some back alley? She dug her nails into her palm, trying to keep control of herself. "Then we need to find out where he is and go to him."

Her brother shot her a look. "Easier said than done."

"You have connections. *Use* them." She'd never felt so helpless in her life. Not when she was shipped off to Connecticut for supposedly her own good. Not when her father basically sold her into a marriage she didn't want. Not even when Devlin died. James was in trouble and she was stuck here in Teague's apartment, pacing the increasingly small space and throwing shitty ideas at the wall.

She bet Aiden knew where James was. He always seemed to know everything. But he wasn't someone she could call in for help and know without a shadow of a doubt that he'd help her instead of hauling her back to Dmitri. He didn't approve of James, and she couldn't risk him working against her instead of with her.

Callie came out of the back room, the phone to her ear. "Thank you, Micah. You're a lifesaver." She hung up. "The Hallorans have a meet up with a flesh trader tonight down at the docks. I can't confirm that James will be there, but if he's not answering his phone, it's a safe bet."

He'd been serious when he asked her the other day about freeing women from the slave trade. She'd wondered but... *It doesn't matter right now. All that matters is getting to him and making sure he's safe.*

And if she put a bullet into this Michael in the process, she wouldn't cry herself to sleep at night over it.

She started for the door, but Teague blocked her way. "No."

"We know where he is. We have to go now, before it's too late."

"If you think for a second that I'm taking my sister and my wife into a meeting with two enemies, you're out of your mind." His gaze jumped from her face to Callie's and back again. "We're not rushing into anything."

She eyed the door, but even if she got past Teague, what was she going to do? She needed help, no matter how much the delay had her in danger of tearing her hair out in frustration. "You have a plan? Then let's hear it."

"We need backup."

The last thing she wanted to hear. Carrigan threw up her hands. "Who are we going to call? There isn't a single member of our family that would help with this. Every one of them would be willing to let James burn if it meant they wouldn't have a Halloran at their back." Or with her.

"I wouldn't be so sure of that."

As if on cue, the door behind him opened and Cillian walked through, Liam at his side. Her younger brother raised his eyebrows at her shock. "I don't like that bastard, but even I can see that he's head over heels for you. And if the Russian is willing to take out one of the three main players in Boston, there's nothing to stop him from trying the same shit with us whenever he feels like it."

Nothing except Carrigan marrying him. But he'd already proven he wouldn't keep his word if it didn't suit him. He'd had James's death planned from the beginning, regardless of what he'd promised her. She swallowed hard. "I appreciate this. From both of you."

Liam came to stand next to her. "I've been doing

whatever it took to keep you out of trouble for years. I'd be a heartless monster to stop now."

She smiled her thanks and turned her attention back to Teague. "I'm all for backup, but do you really think two people will be enough to turn the tide?"

"No." It was Callie who answered. "That's why Micah and a group of my men will be meeting us there."

She realized what the goal was—to keep as many O'Malley people out of the mess as possible—and nodded. "Then I'm going to need more Taser cartridges." The Sheridans were now more stable than either of the other families in Boston. They couldn't care less if she married a Halloran, since all it would mean was that Boston would become stronger as a whole for the new alliance. If only her family could see things that way.

That was a battle for another day.

Right now all that mattered was making sure James lived to see the dawn.

CHAPTER TWENTY-FOUR

James breathed in the briny air and wished he was anywhere but here. The docks after dark had always set his teeth on edge. There were too many shadows and places to set up an ambush. That was why he'd sent Michael and a few handpicked men in earlier—to make sure things went off without a hitch. It didn't help that it had started to snow a few minutes ago, the flakes quickly creating a curtain that further obscured his vision.

The van sat behind him, ready for its cargo. He kept reminding himself that these women would get a chance at a different life, but it didn't do a damn thing to make him feel better. It was entirely too possible—likely, even—that they'd already seen abuse he could only imagine. That kind of thing left a mark on a person's soul that a Band-Aid couldn't touch.

But he could do his part to put them back on the path

to freedom. It wasn't enough, but he wasn't a fucking superhero.

Ricky wandered around the van, whistling tonelessly. James wanted to tell him to shut the fuck up, but that meant admitting that it bugged him to begin with. His brother was still on his best behavior, which only made his paranoia increase with each passing hour.

He turned and watched the water, searching for the lights of the boat. He should have known better. When it came, it slipped through the snowfall soundlessly without a single beam to announce its presence. Several men jumped to the dock and tied it off, and then one broke away from the rest to approach. "You have the payment."

James gestured to the bag at his feet. "The product?"

The man unzipped the bag and rifled through it before nodding. He whistled and made a sharp motion. The men spoke quietly, and then one of them grabbed a stumbling form and guided her down the dock to the van where Ricky waited. James caught a glimpse of her haggard face, eyes vacant, and had to fight back a shudder. Every single woman who passed him had that same expression on their face. He caught the man's eye and jerked his chin. "Explain."

"Opium." The man shrugged. "They got riled up half-way through, so we did what we had to do. Shouldn't be permanent damage."

Questions pressed him. How long had they been in a forced opium-induced haze? When was the last time they ate? Drank? This man didn't care, and James wouldn't win himself any points for acting too concerned. He'd already decided that this wouldn't be the last batch of women he purchased, and he needed the seller to be willing to work with him again. That meant not rocking the boat. *Yet.* As the last girl—twenty total—walked past him, he nodded. "Pleasure doing business with you."

"Likewise."

He waited for the men to climb aboard the boat and cast off before he made his way back to the van. The women huddled in the back, piled in like sardines. He started to reach for some kind of comforting bullshit to say, but they shrank from him as a single unit when his shadow darkened the door. *Fuck.* There wasn't a damn thing he could say that they'd believe, and trying would only scare the shit out of them. He slammed the door shut. Lisa Marie would know the right way to go about this.

Carrigan would know what to do with them. She's the one who had that idea for the nonprofit. I bet she's got more ideas. He pushed the thought away. There hadn't been time to figure out what the fuck he was going to do when it came to her. Letting her go wasn't an option, not when he knew she cared about him. She wouldn't have acted the way she did before if that wasn't true. *Keep your head in the game, Halloran. Now isn't the time to get distracted.*

He turned, and caught sight of the shiny barrel of the gun his brother held. James froze. *That little motherfucker.* "Ricky."

"Sorry about this." His brother laughed. "Actually, no I'm not. You're a pussy, just like our old man always said you were. So I'm taking the Hallorans."

Jesus Christ. He eyed the gun. His brother had made

sure he was out of easy reach so he'd be able to pull the trigger before James could get to him. Smart. His own gun was in a holster around his ankle, also out of easy reach. Less smart. Damn it, he should have expected this. "Why don't we talk about this?"

"There's nothing to talk about." Ricky's eyes were too wide. "You didn't really think I'd let you lock me up for a fucking week, did you? You're shit, and everyone but you sees it. *I'm* the one who deserves to run the Hallorans." He motioned with the gun. "Get in the back."

Like fuck was he going to get in the van and let his little brother drive him to somewhere more private, or whatever the hell he had in mind. *If I hadn't been obsessing about Carrigan . . .* James shook his head. "Not going to happen."

"What's going on here?"

James didn't take his attention off his little brother as Michael approached. "Just a little familial disagreement." With the other man, they'd be two on one against Ricky. He glanced at his second in command. "Ricky's feeling a little overtired."

"I have a fucking gun! You should be pissing your pants! Not making goddamn motherfucking jokes!" He waved the pistol. He never saw Michael move, slamming his own gun across the back of his head and dropping him.

James sighed. "He's a problem."

"He's not the only one."

He glanced up. It took his mind far too long to process the change in Michael. The man stood straight and held his gun pointed *at James*. He slowly held up his hands, trying to calculate his chances of dropping to the ground and getting his gun from his ankle before Michael shot him. They weren't great. "Think about this."

"I don't have a choice." Michael motioned him away from the van. "If it's any consolation, after the last few weeks, I wouldn't have chosen this."

"Well, shit, Michael. Since you're obviously not going to let sentiment stop you from shooting me in the fucking back, it's not much of a consolation at all." He moved slowly. "I hope they're paying you well, whoever the fuck they are, because you're going to die for them." He wasn't going down without a fight. He had too goddamn much to live for. *Carrigan*. He loved the woman and if he died, she'd end up married to that Russian and fading away as the years passed. James couldn't stand the thought of the wildness that he loved so much in her dying any more than he could stand the thought of another man's ring on her finger.

He watched Michael closely. "Want to tell me who bought you off? I'll have to send them something nice as a thank-you gift."

The man's hand shook, and he brought his second one up to the grip of the gun to steady it. "I tried to change my mind, James. I told that Russian bastard I couldn't do it. But it's you or me now. No one crosses Dmitri Romanov."

Dmitri Romanov. There was that fucking name again. *Where's Carrigan now? Is she with him?* There were no innocents in their lifestyles, but there was also a huge gap between the families in Boston and the kind of shady shit Romanov was pulling right now, turning his best man against him. Carrigan had never been one to color inside the lines—it was only a matter of time before she did something to piss Romanov off. And then...

I've got to live so I can get her out of there.

"I'm not usually down with killing fools, but for you, Michael, I'll make an exception."

"I wouldn't." The apology was gone from Michael's voice. "He sent me to make sure this goes off without a hitch. Even if you take me out, it won't do a damn bit of good."

God*damn* it. James looked around, but all he could see was shadows. "Where?"

"Like I'm telling you that." A pop of gunfire sounded in the distance. Michael half turned. "What the—?"

James *moved*. He tackled the other man, shoving his arms over his head as they went down. He was vaguely aware of more gunfire in the distance, but he was too busy trying not to get shot by the little weasel to worry about it. After he got over his initial surprise at the attack, Michael fought like a man possessed. He let go of the gun and punched James in the side, stealing his breath, and then went for his eyes.

There was no finesse. James grabbed his throat and slammed his head back into the ground, but it only stunned Michael for a second and then he was attacking again, rolling James beneath him and rearing back to get some force into his hits. A sizzling sound broke through, and he suddenly started spasming, his eyes rolling back in his head. He slumped to the side, revealing a woman standing behind him.

Carrigan.

* * *

Carrigan saw the blood on James's face and pulled the trigger on the Taser to deliver another devastating bolt of electricity to the little shit on the ground. She held the button down, wishing it was something more permanent. And then James was there, pulling her away from the man and into his arms. "What are you doing here?"

"Saving your ass." She clung to him, trying to process the fact that they hadn't been too late. He was okay. A little bruised and bloodied, but he was alive. "God, I was so worried about you."

The only warning she got was his arms tightening around her, and then James dragged her to the ground. Gunfire sounded, too close. She twisted around but, pinned between the ground and his body, she couldn't see anything. "What's happening?" She smacked his chest. "Get off me."

"Not yet." He did lift up a little so she could breathe. "You didn't come alone?"

"No. I have Teague and Cillian and some of the Sheridan men with us." *My brothers.* She rolled over, and squirmed to get out from beneath him. "I need to get to my brothers."

James kept her pinned easily, and he'd pulled a gun from somewhere. Their position left their right side shielded by the van, but they were seriously exposed out here. He must have been thinking the same thing because he wrestled his free arm beneath her and started hauling her back toward the vehicle. "We're getting the fuck out of here."

She wanted him safe, but she was still hearing gunshots. "My brothers are out there." And so was Callie. *If something happens to one of them because of me...* She hadn't thought of the cost when she'd argued and bullied them into coming with her. All she'd been thinking of was how desolate her world would be without James in it. She struggled harder. "Let me go." This was a mistake and not a mistake and, oh God, she needed to do *something*.

He climbed to his feet, taking her with him. "Where are they?"

She pointed at the approximate place she'd left her group. They'd been moving slowly, but she'd slipped away, determined to get to James before it was too late. *Stupid, selfish bitch.* "Around that building."

"I'll go." He opened the passenger door and shoved her in before she could protest. When she tried to climb out, he stopped her with a hand on her chest. "Carrigan, there are twenty terrified women in the back of this van. We can't leave them."

We. She stopped fighting him, her breath coming too fast. "I love you."

"I know." He kissed her, quick and brutal. "There's a gun underneath the seat and the keys are in the ignition. If I'm not back in ten minutes, you get the fuck out of here." He slammed the door before she could respond, leaving her with only the sound of her heart pounding and her harsh breathing.

Stay safe while everyone around her put themselves in danger? *No fucking way.* She scrambled over to the driver's seat and cranked on the engine. She couldn't just sit here and hope for the best. She had to *do* something. Carrigan froze when someone wailed in the back portion of the van. *This is about more than me.* She turned and muscled open the window panel looking back into the rest of the vehicle...and promptly stopped breathing. There were so many women back there, she couldn't even start to count them. Several of them were crying. *Oh God.*

If she hauled ass after James, someone could shoot the van. If it was just her, she wouldn't think twice about making that choice. But if she got some of these women killed because she couldn't take orders...Carrigan gritted her teeth. *Ten minutes. I can wait ten minutes.* She tried to make her voice as reassuring as possible. "It's okay. You're safe now." They wouldn't believe her—if she was in their position, *she* wouldn't believe her—but she repeated the words all the same. "You're safe. Just hang in there for a little longer."

Then she turned around and settled down to wait, her gaze on the clock in the dashboard.

* * *

James moved through the snow, his gun cold in his hand. He still couldn't wrap his mind around the fact that Carrigan was *here*, and she'd brought reinforcements. God, he loved the fuck out of that woman.

He followed the sound of gunfire, skirting the edge of a warehouse. The weather made it hard to see more than a few feet in front of him, and he was doubly glad he left Carrigan back at the van. She'd keep the women safe— and herself safe in the process.

A man stumbled out of the darkness and went to his knees. James didn't rush forward immediately, checking the surrounding area to make sure he was alone. It was only when he stalked closer than he saw it was

Carrigan's younger brother—the one with the fancy duds and tattoos. Cillian. He clutched his side, rolling onto his back with a harsh gasp that told James he was hurt, and hurt badly.

He went to his knees next to the man and spoke softly. "Cillian."

"Halloran." He cracked open his eyes. "Karma is a bitch, isn't it?"

James didn't know what the fuck he was talking about, but he patted the man down, constantly scanning the surrounding area. The not-so-distant sound of gunfire hadn't stopped, and it was only a matter of time before someone saw the blood trail Cillian had left behind and came to investigate. He touched the man's shoulder and cursed softly when his hand came away wet. "Kid, I think you're shot."

"That's . . . what I meant about karma."

Fuck. "You're not dying on my watch." There hadn't been a damn thing he could do to stop his men from killing Carrigan's other brother. But he *could* do something about this one. She'd already suffered enough. He shrugged out of his coat and yanked off his shirt, wadding it up and pressing it against Cillian's bleeding shoulder hard enough to make the other man hiss. "Hold this." He put his hands over the shirt and sat back, taking precious seconds to pull his coat back on.

A voice sounded close—too close. "I think he went this way."

"Let's get the little bastard."

If their Russian accents weren't enough to go by, their words would have been. James sent a silent prayer of thanks to the weather gods for the cover the snow offered. If it weren't for that, he'd be a sitting duck right here next to this wall.

Two figures melted out of the gloom. One of them must have seen him because they cursed in what he figured was Russian. That was all he needed to know. He sighted down his gun and fired once, twice, a third time, dropping them both. His finger hovered on the trigger as a third man appeared, but the guy held up his hands. "Not one of Romanov's men."

Teague. James set his gun aside. "Get your ass over here. Your brother's been shot." The man had passed out sometime in the last fifteen seconds, and the light coating of snow on the ground around his shoulder was stained red. *Goddamn it.*

Instantly, Teague was by his side. He probed beneath the shirt, his face a mask of concentration. "I'm not medic, but I think it's a through-and-through."

Which was good on one hand, because it meant the bullet wasn't going to shift and do more damage, but it also didn't take into account the damage *already* done. He put a bit more weight onto Cillian's shoulder. "Call your people in. We need to get him to the hospital."

"My sister?"

"Safe. She's back that way." He jerked his chin in the direction of the van. "The rest of Romanov's men?"

"These were the last of them." He put the phone to his ear. "Callie? Round up the boys. Cillian's been shot. We'll meet you at the entrance of the docks." He hung up.

When he moved to take Cillian, James shook his head. "I got him. You guys were here to help me out. My responsibility."

Teague gave a jerky nod and let James carefully scoop his brother up. It was hard to tell how bad the bleeding was in the darkness, or if it'd slowed at all, but the faster they got moving the better. "Watch my back."

"I will."

James turned and started for the van, willing the man in his arms to live, willing Carrigan to be safe when they got back, willing them to get through this night without yet another loss in the O'Malley family.

They found Carrigan exactly where he'd left her. She jumped out of the van and rushed to his side. "Cillian?"

"He's going to be okay." He hoped like hell he wasn't lying to her. "Get back in the van. We're going to meet your people at the entrance of the docks."

It took mere seconds to get them loaded up, and he put Cillian down across the backseat, his head in his sister's lap. Then James slammed the door and moved around to the driver's side. He looked over the hood at Teague. "I owe you."

"You owe my sister. None of this would have happened without her."

Without her, James might be dead right now.

He climbed behind the wheel and threw the vehicle into gear. Two minutes later, they were off-loading Cillian into a plain black SUV. Carrigan reached for the door and stopped. "James—"

"Go with your brother, lovely. I have a few things I have to take care of." Michael and Ricky were back in the docks, and he wasn't about to leave those two fucks behind. He hooked the back of her neck and drew her in for a quick kiss. "Don't worry. You haven't seen the last of me."

"Good." With that one last word, she climbed into the SUV and was gone.

* * *

The ride to the hospital was a blur, but it was more than enough time for Carrigan to wade through past nightmares. Of standing next to Teague's bedside and wondering if he'd live after he'd been so badly beaten, of wondering if there was something she could have done to save him. To save Devlin. Guilt was a funny thing sometimes. Rationally, she knew there was plenty of blame to go around, but she'd been all too willing to take more than her fair share.

This time, it really *was* her fault.

She was the one who'd thrown a bitchfit and demanded someone—anyone—help James. All she'd been thinking of was that life would never be the same if he wasn't somewhere, breathing and going about his life and *alive*. She could submit to any number of fucked-up things as long as she knew he was okay. She'd willingly put her family in danger. Worse, she wasn't sure she'd do anything differently if given a second go-round. *I am a terrible person. So incredibly selfish.*

They slammed to a stop in the ER entranceway. Someone must have called ahead, because there was a pair of nurses and a stretcher waiting. The men took Cillian from the backseat and strapped him into the stretcher, and then they were gone, rushing through the door and spitting medical jargon back and forth.

"It will be okay."

She glanced at Callie, taking in how pale the other woman was. "I hope so."

This hospital had to hold terrified memories for her sister-in-law, too. She'd been the one to save Teague before. Carrigan followed her though the corridors to the appropriate waiting room. It looked like a thousand other waiting rooms across the US. And probably the world, too. She sank into the faded chair. "This is all my fault."

"Cillian made his own decisions. He knew the risks." Callie sat next to her. "He's going to live."

As much as she craved the words, she couldn't trust them. "He got shot because of me."

"No, he got shot because Dmitri Romanov called for James's death." Callie's smile barely twitched her lips. "I seem to remember having a similar conversation a few months ago."

The one where Carrigan had told Callie that the war escalating would have happened one way or another, even if she hadn't killed Brendan Halloran. She scrubbed her hand over her face. "Guilt is such a sticky emotion."

"Tell me about it." Callie's phone rang again. "Yes? You're sure? Thanks, Micah." She hung up. "Romanov is gone. I'm not sure when, but his hotel room is empty, and he's nowhere to be found."

It was tempting to think he was gone for good, but Carrigan knew better. "He'll be back." Dmitri wasn't the kind of man to take defeat lying down, and he'd lost twice now. Carrigan wasn't marrying him, and James was still alive. She slumped down into her chair. "This isn't over."

"Probably not." Callie's blue eyes were harder than she'd ever seen them. "But now we know he's an enemy. He can't play at being an ally while stabbing us in the back. That's something." Maybe. But it wouldn't be enough. It had taken her all of ten seconds to realize how dangerous Dmitri was, and Carrigan had the feeling that the knowledge was just a drop in an ocean.

He'd be back, and he'd be back for blood.

CHAPTER TWENTY-FIVE

James sat on the snow-covered pavement next to his little brother for a long time. Ricky wouldn't be getting up again. The blow to his head from Michael had killed him. Maybe if they'd been more focused on getting him to a hospital...There were a lot of maybes circling his head right now, and they weren't doing him any favors.

Both brothers, gone.

He was well and truly alone now.

"Mr. Halloran."

He looked up. The Sheridan men stood around him in a staggered formation, half of them turned to face any potential outside threat. The black man speaking looked barely in his mid-twenties, but he seemed more than capable of taking care of business. James just wanted him to go away. He shook his head. That wasn't right. He had to get the fuck out of here. It was a fucking miracle they hadn't brought any cops down upon themselves until now. He reached out and stopped just short of touching Ricky's face. "How long have I been sitting here?"

The man looked away. "We can transport your brother for you. What do you want to do with your man?"

His gaze fell to Michael, trussed up and gagged. He'd tried to make a run for it in the middle of the confusion, but Callista's men had found and retrieved him. "He's not my man anymore. Bring him. He has a lot to answer for." Though he doubted Michael had much in the way of information, he couldn't finish the man off until he knew for sure.

James climbed to his feet, feeling decades older. "Carrigan?"

"She's at the hospital with her brother—it looks like he might be okay."

She was safe—or as safe as anyone could be. He nodded. "Good." He wanted to go to her, to hear her tell him she loved him again, to hold her in his arms and never let go. But there was shit he had to deal with before he could. First order of business was getting these women cared for. He went around to the van and found his phone on the floorboard. A few minutes later, Lisa Marie came on the line. "What do you need, honey?"

"A place for twenty girls. They aren't going to be able to answer questions until they're sure they're safe."

"Are they safe?"

He listened to soft sobbing coming from the back of the van. "As safe as I can make them. They'll have their freedom, one way or another."

"Bring them here. Me and the girls will get it taken care of. I'll let you know the arrangements once I have them in place."

And send me the bill. "Good. I'll be there in twenty."
He hung up and tossed the phone onto the passenger seat.
The Sheridan man was still waiting. "Get that piece of
shit"—he jerked his chin at Michael—"and meet me at
my place. I have one stop to make first and then I'll be
there."

The man nodded. "Got it." Then he was gone, melting
into the darkness with the rest of his people.

James took a harsh breath and got into the van. The
constant crying couldn't be escaped and grated on his
nerves something fierce, but he didn't try to make them
stop. These women had already seen enough trauma to
last them a lifetime—he wasn't going to add to that if he
could help it. He met Lisa Marie at the back of Tit for
Tat, and she surveyed him with a critical eye. "Trouble
tonight."

"You could say that." Betrayal everywhere he turned.
Ricky he'd expected, though the loss was still there,
waiting for him to drop his guard so it could sucker
punch him. But Michael? Michael he'd trusted. He
hadn't seen that coming. *No wonder my old man was
nuttier than a squirrel.* He motioned to the van. "What's
the best way to play this?"

She snubbed out her cigarette. "Stand back and don't
say anything to spook them." Without waiting to see if
he'd done what she asked, she opened the door and spoke
softly to the girls. He couldn't quite catch the words, but
the tone was big on soothing—like something a person
would use with a wild animal or a rabid dog. Lisa Marie
stepped back and, one by one, the girls crawled into the
pale light thrown off by the propped-open back door.
Two of the strippers—Echo and one he couldn't place—

appeared and led them away. It took all of five minutes, but James held his breath damn near the entire time.

"You did good, honey." She shook another cigarette out of its pack and lit up. "Some of them won't survive— it's the nature of the beast—but most of them will."

He crossed his arms over his chest. "And if we start getting regular shipments of this kind in?" He couldn't take for granted that Carrigan would be with him, let alone willing to put the fledgling nonprofit plan she'd talked about in place. That would solve a number of problems, but there would always be women who were more comfortable with the life he could offer them— women who didn't want to go home.

"Regular shipments." She shot him a sharp look. "James Halloran, I never pegged you for a white knight." She continued before he could confirm or deny. "We can make it work. We might need another club, or at least more opportunity on the legal side of things for those who want to stay here, but it can be done. Some of them will want to go back to wherever they came from, so you'll have to figure that shit out."

He hadn't realized how tense he was until her words relaxed something inside him. All the bullshit and evil and monstrous things he'd done...this wouldn't make them right. But it'd be a start. James nodded. "Get me the relevant information from the women and I'll figure it out." He had a few feelers he could put out, though his connections weren't as vast as, say, the Sheridans. *I bet Teague knows a thing or two about tracking down this type of information.* He'd have to ask the other man the first chance he got.

He got back into the van and drove home, and another

interview that he desperately didn't want to have to go through.

What the fuck am I going to do?

He'd never felt so goddamn alone in his life.

* * *

Carrigan marched through the front door of her house, and straight into her father's office. He was there, along with Aiden, just as she'd suspected he would be. Plotting, always plotting. A freaking spider in the middle of his web with no concern for the flies caught in its strands. *It stops now.* She slammed her hands down onto the desk. "In case you're wondering, Cillian's come through surgery and he'll survive."

Seamus didn't look up from the papers in front of him. "He shouldn't have been down at the docks to begin with."

"Are you fucking serious?"

That got him to look up. "Language, Carrigan."

"For fuck's sake, Father, your priorities leave something to be desired." She took two steps back, carefully not looking at Aiden. He hadn't said anything, but he didn't need to. He was here instead of the waiting room, with their father instead of their brother. "It's done. Dmitri is gone, and I'm not marrying him." She rushed on before he could say anything else. "I practically killed myself to be an obedient daughter. I put aside all my ambitions and dreams to do it." At least part of the time. "No more."

He didn't move. "If you're done with this tantrum—"

"God, will you listen to yourself? Look around you.

Devlin is dead. *Dead*. And for what? Because you wanted to make a grab at power. Cillian is in the hospital because he realized that a man who'd break his word without blinking isn't someone we want to ally with."

"What Dmitri does with James Halloran is no concern of mine."

It was like beating her head against a brick wall and expecting it to be reasonable. She wanted to rail and scream and throw things, but it wouldn't get through to him. "I love James Halloran." She turned, feeling so damn defeated.

"Carrigan."

For a second she thought she'd gotten through to him, that something had penetrated the stubborn wall he kept around himself and opened his eyes to what he stood to lose. Then he went and dashed that tiny hope on the rocks of reality. "If you walk out that door, you're dead to me and every person in this family."

It was always like this with him, all or nothing, obedience or threats. She kept going. "Then consider me as dead as Devlin." Closing the study door behind her felt like she'd sucked all the air out of the hallway. Despite everything he'd put her through, she wanted to curl into a ball and sob at the injustice of it all. Damn it, she loved her father despite all his faults. And he'd just effectively banished her.

That got her moving. She had less than ten minutes before he sent someone to make sure she was gone, and there were things she refused to leave behind. Carrigan rushed up the stairs and to her room, ignoring Sloan when she poked her head out of her door. She tore through her dresser, breathing a tiny sigh of relief when she came up with James's album. After dumping it into a small overnight bag, she grabbed a few sets of clothing and a picture of her with all her siblings, grinning at the camera like fools. It was a few years old, but it had always been one of her favorites.

"Carrigan? What's going on?"

She didn't glance at her sister. Her makeup went into the bag. "Tell Keira that I love her." She slipped a few pieces of her favorite jewelry into her pocket. They'd all been gifts on milestone birthdays from her mother, and she didn't want to walk out the door without them. She turned and nearly ran over Sloan. "I love you, too. I don't want to leave you like this, but if I stay he's going to make me marry someone else. I can't do it."

Sloan's normally pale skin was ghastly white. "He'll kill you."

"He already did. He just pronounced me dead to the family." She hugged her sister, holding her tight for a long moment before she released her. "Take care of yourself. No one else is going to do it." Another quick hug. "I've got to go." As much as she didn't want to leave her little sisters in this house, there wasn't a damn thing she could do about it. Her father might be willing to let her walk out of here with only a symbolic death, but he wouldn't let them all go. "I'm so sorry."

Voices sounded at the bottom of the stairs, and Sloan shoved her down the hall. "Take the back stairs. I'll stall for you."

"I love you."

"I love you, too. Now *go*."

She went. The back stairs were deserted and she made it out of the town house without seeing anyone else. As soon as she hit the street, doubts assailed her. She'd been so busy trying to get out, she hadn't stopped to consider what she'd do next. Carrigan stopped on the corner, the sheer weight of the decision she'd just made nearly sending her to her knees. Free. She was *free*. It was almost too good to be true...until she started thinking about what she'd sacrificed for the chance. Her siblings. Her parents. Her entire life. She could go anywhere, do anything, be any kind of person she wanted to, and no one would appear to drag her back into the fold.

I can actually get a job—use my degree in communications and journalism for something I'm passionate about. I can have a real life.

Really, there was only one destination for her.

She walked down to the corner, her heels crunching over the newly fallen snow, and hailed a cab. She rattled off the address to the one place she'd sworn up and down that she'd never go back to. The Halloran house. *James.* Her nerves kicked into high gear as the cab entered Southie and finally pulled to a stop in front of the place where she almost spent her last day on earth. There was something ironic about coming here on the day her family declared her dead to them. She paid the cabbie and started for the front door.

What if he doesn't want you anymore now that you're not an O'Malley?

Her stride hitched, but she readjusted her grip on her bag and kept going. If he didn't want her, then she'd find something else. Yes, the Hallorans were just as perfectly suited for the plan she'd always dreamed of as the O'Malleys were, but if he turned her away, she could just as easily offer that to the Sheridans. Teague would see the value of going as legit as possible and earning more power *that* way. She hoped.

She ignored the potential of James trampling all over her broken heart if he rejected her. The temptation to turn around and run was almost overwhelming, but she made it to the front door and rang the bell.

James himself answered, freezing at the sight of her. She froze, too, not sure what to say. *Hi, I'm now homeless and broke and so desperately in love with you that if you turn me away, I think it might shatter something in me irreparably.*

"Lovely?" He still didn't move.

"I'm so sorry. For everything. I finally told my family where to shove their ambitions." As she babbled, she unzipped her bag and dug out the album. "They've declared me as dead as my little brother." A hysterical laugh bubbled up. "Here's the album, so I guess there's no reason for you to keep stalking me...except that I love you. God, James, I love you so much it makes my head spin. But if you don't want me—"

That's as far as she got before he swept the offered album aside and dragged her into his arms. "Stop talking." He kissed her. "If you think for a second I'm going to let you walk out of my life, you're fucking crazy. You're mine, Carrigan. Mine and mine alone."

"Oh."

James laughed. "Oh? That's the best you've got?"

"I'm not rich anymore. Or an O'Malley." For some reason, it was vitally important he understand that had changed.

"As if I give two shits about either of those things. I want *you*—the woman." He pushed the hair back from her face. "I was coming for you, lovely. I wasn't going to let Dmitri take you, and I sure as fuck wasn't going to let your father ship you off with someone else."

Her heartbeat picked up. "I walked out on my own."

"And that's just another reason I love you. You're strong and you don't need a man to lean on." He cupped her face. "But that doesn't mean you can't lean on me. It has nothing to do with need and everything to do with me wanting to be the man who's by your side every step of the way. *Your* man, Carrigan O'Malley."

He kissed her, taking her mouth as if he already knew her answer. Carrigan fisted her hands in the front of his shirt, pulling him closer yet. Things with James might have started off in the strangest way possible, but he'd been solid every step of the way. He was the only person in her life who put *her* first for the woman she was, rather than the assets she could bring to the negotiating table.

That's why she was here, in his arms, loving him like crazy.

He pulled back enough to say, "And I fully intend on making an honest woman of you the first chance I get so the entire world knows we belong to each other."

Belonged to each other. She liked that. She liked that a lot. "Good God, was that a proposal?"

He grinned and pulled her into the house, never letting go of her. "Not yet. Just making my intentions clear. When I propose you're going to damn well know it."

I love this man so much it hurts.

But there were still things they needed to talk about. She squeezed his hands as she took a tiny step back. "Dmitri's gone. It won't be for good."

"Let him come. We've faced down threats before, and

we will again." He stopped. "Your father might not be willing to believe he got into bed with the enemy, but your brothers aren't stupid. They won't take this sitting down any more than I will."

She wasn't so sure, but she also wasn't willing to argue about it. There was time for plotting and scheming in the future. Right now she had the man she loved and the freedom she'd spent her entire life craving. But first... "Your brother?"

"Gone." There was no mistaking the way he meant. Gone the same way Devlin was gone.

"Oh, James." She stepped back into his arms and hugged him tight. "I'm sorry. I know he was an evil little bastard, but I'm still sorry."

"Me too. I wish things could have been different, but they weren't. I'm just glad...I'm just glad I wasn't the one to kill him."

That would have broken something in him beyond repair. She hugged him tighter. "And the girls?"

"Safe." He stroked a hand down her back. "What would you say if I told you I was serious about that nonprofit we talked about? I can't save them all, but I can save some of them, and you could help with that. Hell, I don't know if I can do it without you. These women deserve their freedom."

She framed his face with her hands. "I'd say yes." *I'm going to have it all—the man, the dream, the life I was always too scared to let myself want*. She smiled, her mind already whirling with plans. The Hallorans didn't have the same reputation in the elite circles of Boston that the O'Malleys did, but that wouldn't make a difference in the long run. James could be charming when he wanted to, and *she* knew how to navigate that part of society. Once she got the foundation set up for the non-profit, they'd have those people eating out of the palms of their hands.

Even better, they'd be doing some serious good in the world while they built their power base.

A year ago, if someone had asked her where she'd end up if she ever got her freedom, she never would have said in Halloran territory, a stone's throw from the part of Boston she'd fought so hard to escape. But it wasn't the same thing at all. She was choosing this life—choosing James and everything that came with him. It made all the difference in the world. "You, James Halloran, are a good man. I love the shit out of you, and I'd happily share the rest of my life." She grinned. "You know, when you get around to proposing."

"Lovely, the world isn't going to know what hit it."

The sizzling saga of
the O'Malleys continues...

Greed. Ambition. Violence. Those are
the "values" Olivia learned from her
Russian mob family—and the values
she must leave behind for the sake of
her daughter. When she meets Cillian
O'Malley, she recognizes the red flag of
his family name...yet she still can't
stop herself from falling for the
smoldering, tortured man.

Please see the next page
for a preview of

AN INDECENT
PROPOSAL

To say that Cillian O'Malley had had a shitty year was like commenting that the sky was blue. The entire field of his life had changed, and not for the better. He picked up the glass in front of him—apple juice, since he hadn't had a drop of anything harder in nearly a year. Not since the night Devlin died. They'd been in this very bar the night it happened, so by all rights, he should never want to set foot in the fucking place again. Instead, this was where his feet seemed to bring him whenever he wasn't paying attention.

Or at least, it *had* been his destination of choice.

He grimaced and touched his shoulder where a bullet had hit him six months ago. It had shattered his collarbone and hurt like a bitch, but the lockdown he'd endured as a result had been even worse than the injury itself. Tonight was the first time since he'd gotten out of the hospital that he'd been able to leave the house without an army at his back.

He took a long drink of his apple juice, his gaze going back to the woman behind the bar. *Olivia.* He'd only met her in passing, but she was as prickly as a cactus and even less friendly. Exactly the kind of complication he didn't need now that he'd officially taken on accounting for the family. It wasn't much to ask. He liked numbers. They were the only part of the world he could rely on not to change. Funny how life could go topsy-turvy at the blink of an eye.

"Hey, Cillian."

He started and then cursed when his older sister melted out of the crowd and slid onto the barstool next to him. "What are you doing here?" he asked.

Carrigan had been declared dead to the family six months ago and banished as a result. He had seriously mixed feelings about the whole damn thing. On one hand, she was his sister and had been a remarkable constant in his life. He wanted the best for her, and marrying some Russian piece of shit in New York wasn't what was best for her. Even he could see that it would have killed her in the end.

But that didn't mean he liked that she was shacked up with a Halloran, even James Halloran. The man might not have been the one who ordered the hit on their youngest brother, but he was part of the family that had. Sins of the father, and all that shit. *Family is everything.* It was the one lesson of his father's that he'd internalized, which made Seamus O'Malley's decision regarding Carrigan that much harder to swallow. He touched his shoulder.

Her green eyes followed the movement. "Still hurt?"

"Only when it rains." The doctor said it was something he'd have to get used to, and sometimes that sort of thing happened when a bone was broken. Cillian didn't really care. It was a reminder that people outside the family couldn't be trusted. According to their father, that now included Carrigan. The problem was that he couldn't separate the beloved sister and the so-called traitor. "It's not safe for you here."

"I'm not alone."

He followed her hand motion to the big blond man standing a few feet away, his back to the wall and his arms crossed over his chest. *James Halloran.* Cillian shook his head. "It's doubly dangerous to bring *him* here." Onto O'Malley territory. They hadn't quite devolved into the war his father kept threatening, but they weren't exactly at peace, either.

"You aren't returning my calls. No one is."

"That's what happens when you're dead to the family." He instantly regretted his words when hurt flashed across her face. "Carrigan, I'm sorry. To tell the fucking truth, I haven't been answering anyone's calls. I've been on lockdown in Father's study, going over the last two years of records with Bartholomew." He'd read the old man's spider script writing until his eyes crossed and his head ached—and then he read some more. The records were meticulous, and he'd have to be just as good—if not better—now that he was running things. Both his father and older brother Aiden relied on it. But transferring everything into spreadsheets and finally getting their systems automated was incredibly tedious.

"Don't be sorry. It's nothing more than the truth." She caught Benji's eye. "Martini. Dirty." Then she turned in her seat to face him. She looked a thousand times better than she had the last time he saw her. She'd lost the circles beneath her eyes, and she was...well, hell, glowing. He didn't know a better word for it. Carrigan leaned against the bar.

She reached past him, quick as a snake, and snatched his glass up. She frowned when she sniffed it. "Apple juice? Cillian—"

"I don't want to talk about it."

For a second, he thought she'd leave it alone. He should have known better. Carrigan grabbed his wrist. "Maybe you need to talk about it. When Devlin died—"

He yanked himself free. "It was nice seeing you, Carrigan, but if you want to play shrink, you should do it with someone else." He started to stand, but she beat him to her feet.

"You're going to have to talk about it at some point, Cillian. That kind of thing doesn't just magically go away if you ignore it long enough. It festers and turns you into someone you were never meant to be."

It was like she'd reached across the distance between them and slapped him. He knew he was different than he'd been a year ago. That guy was fun loving and lived life to the fullest. Now he mostly went through the motions. *Damn it*. "Back off."

"Sure. Fine." She held up her hands. "But if you change your mind, you know how to get a hold of me."

"I won't." She was wrong—digging into the past wouldn't make him feel better. All it would do was shine the light on just how thoroughly he'd fucked up. He already knew that. He had the goddamn nightmares to prove it.

Cillian sank back into his seat, watching his sister exchange a few words with James and then walk out the door. Things would have been easier if she could just drink and dance and do all the crazy shit she used to. Since she'd gone off to be with Halloran, she'd developed a nurturing streak—as nurturing as an angry mama bear—and she seemed determined to focus all that energy on giving Cillian what she thought he needed. Unfortunately, it wasn't the kind of help he wanted.

Fuck, he didn't want help at all.

"Need another drink?" The words were clear despite the general ruckus of the bar, the voice like whiskey on the rocks. If he put a little imagination into it—not hard since he thought about alcohol about as much as he *wasn't* drinking it, which was all the damn time—he could almost taste her tone.

He looked up, straight into night-dark eyes that made him think reckless thoughts about leaning across this bar and kissing the hell out of her. It was something the old Cillian would have done, and if the look on her face was any indication, he would have gotten the shit kicked out of him for the effort. It was almost enough to make him smile. "Hey, gorgeous."

* * *

Olivia jerked back, annoyed at herself for coming over to this side of the bar in the first place. She knew better. But this O'Malley had looked so damn lost after that chick walked away that it had called to a part of her she'd never been able to resist. Broken things and children—both were weaknesses of hers, and she'd bet her next paycheck that he was the former. With the wide shoulders, that jawline, and tattoos covering his neck, wrists, and the back of his hands, he sure as hell wasn't the latter. Crap, now she was staring. She propped her hands on her hips and glared. "Do you want another drink or not?"

"Sure. Apple juice."

She paused in the middle of reaching for the whiskey, half-sure he was joking. "Apple juice."

The look on his face told her he knew how ridiculous the order was. "I don't drink."

"I didn't ask." But her stupid curiosity perked up at the information. She ducked down to grab a bottle of the apple juice and a new glass. Filling it with ice gave her something to look at besides the tattoo creeping up the side of his neck like a wild thing trying to escape from his insanely expensive suit. That single outfit would pay her rent for three months. Such an insane waste of resources. If she was smart, she'd finish pouring his drink, take the money that he was obviously so willing to throw away, and move on with her night. Already there were two groups of men eyeballing her, both with handfuls of cash ready.

But her damn mouth got away from her. "Why don't you drink? Alcoholic?" As soon as the words were out, she wanted to call them back. It was none of her business—asking was out of line, and violating all sorts of internal bartender laws.

Surprisingly enough, he didn't tell her to fuck off. "It didn't bring me anything but trouble, so I don't mess with it anymore." He said it like it wasn't a big deal to set something like that aside. Maybe for him it wasn't. Not everyone drank like fish, and pointing out that he was Irish would just make her look like an asshole... probably because she'd *be* an asshole.

"Oh." She finished pouring the apple juice and slid it over to him. "Here you go." *Maybe I should apologize?*

"Thanks." He passed over a giant wad of money. He must have seen the way she gritted her teeth, because he grinned. It was like looking at a different man, one that hadn't been touched by the tragedies of the world. "Take the money, sweetheart. For your trouble."

It was too much. If she took a—she did some mental calculations—5,000 percent tip, it was like she'd owe him. Olivia went out of her way to make sure she didn't owe anyone a damn thing. She wasn't about to start now. The urge to apologize went up in smoke. "I can't." She started to shove the money back across the bar, but he was already on his feet. "Hey!"

"See you around." And then he was gone, melting into the crowd.

Goddamn it. She stared at the money in her hand and, for a long second, actually considered keeping it. But then reality reared up and kicked her in the teeth. She couldn't keep it. *But...*

No. She wasn't the type of woman who could be bought, and she wasn't going to give him the wrong idea that she was. He might not have asked for anything in return, but being in his debt was bad no matter which way she looked at it. "Benji, I'll be right back."

"Sure thing," he called.

She slid around the bar and headed for the door. Several guys tried to approach, but the glares she sent their

way stopped them in their tracks. The last thing she
needed was *another* man being a pain in the ass. Olivia
burst through the front door and looked both ways down
the street. For one breath, she thought he must have
caught a cab, but then she saw him moving south,
strolling down the sidewalk like he didn't have a care in
the world. "Hey!"

He didn't turn around, and she cursed him in both
Russian and English. Growing up the way she did, she
had a lot of creative cursing saved up between the two
languages. "Hey, stop!" She ran after him, thankful she'd
put on her badass studded boots instead of the pair of
heels she'd been jonesing after. An eight-hour shift on
her feet would have her hating herself if she'd gone with
the pretty shoes—and they would have made it impossible to catch up with the O'Malley. She grabbed his arm
and froze at the feel of his muscles flexing in her grip.
Holy wow. "You can't just leave a wad of cash on the bar
and walk off in the middle of a conversation."

"I can and I did." He finally turned to face her and
it struck her that, without the bar between them, he was
so much larger than she was. Not large like Sergei—this
man was built lean instead of for brute strength—but he
still dwarfed her. And he . . . smelled good, like some kind
of spicy men's cologne.

She realized she was still clutching his arm and
made herself let go so she could offer back the money.
"Take it."

"Are you for real?" He shook his head. "It's called a
tip, sweetheart. Deal with it."

"I don't want it." Even as she said it, she wondered
why she was being so damn stubborn about this. He

hadn't asked anything of her. All he'd done was throw too much money at a bartender, which was something plenty of drunks did from time to time. Except he wasn't drunk and he wasn't a normal person. She should be elated—instead, there was a growing anger in her chest. "Just take it, okay?"

"No." He moved closer, giving her another whiff of that cologne that made her whole body break out in goose bumps. Or maybe it was the man himself, the streetlights creating a skeleton's mask of his face, turning his eyes into dark pits of shadows. "Why do you care so much?"

"Oh my God, just take it back." She should drop the cash and go back to Jameson's. Or, hell, at least take a few steps back so that she wasn't in danger of brushing against him if she took a deep breath.

But she couldn't force her hand to unclench or her feet to create any distance between them. She cleared her throat, trying to get her thoughts back on track. "I didn't ask for your charity."

"Yeah, I got it. You win. I'm a dick." His gaze seemed to narrow on her, and he murmured, "If the shoe fits..."

And then the bastard gripped her jaw and kissed her.

She was so surprised that she opened for him—or at least that was what she told herself when his tongue slipped into her mouth and stroked hers. He didn't touch her anywhere else, and somehow that only made their point of contact that much more erotic. Cillian nipped her bottom lip and leaned back. "I'll be seeing you again, sweetheart."

Do you love historical fiction?

Want the chance to hear news about your favourite
authors (and the chance to win free books)?

Mary Balogh

Charlotte Betts

Jessica Blair

Frances Brody

Gaelen Foley

Elizabeth Hoyt

Eloisa James

Lisa Kleypas

Stephanie Laurens

Claire Lorrimer

Sarah MacLean

Amanda Quick

Julia Quinn

Then visit the Piatkus website and blog
www.piatkus.co.uk | www.piatkusbooks.net

And follow us on Facebook and Twitter
www.facebook.com/piatkusfiction | www.twitter.com/piatkusbooks

piatkus

Do you love fiction with a supernatural twist?

Want the chance to hear news about your favourite
authors (and the chance to win free books)?

Keri Arthur
Kristen Callihan
P.C. Cast
Christine Feehan
Jacquelyn Frank
Larissa Ione
Darynda Jones
Sherrilyn Kenyon
Jayne Ann Krentz and Jayne Castle
Lucy March
Martin Millar
Tim O'Rourke
Lindsey Piper
Christopher Rice
J.R. Ward
Laura Wright

Then visit the Piatkus website and blog
www.piatkus.co.uk | www.piatkusbooks.net

And follow us on Facebook and Twitter
www.facebook.com/piatkusfiction | www.twitter.com/piatkusbooks

piatkus